A PASSAGE FROM HOME

First Published in Great Britain 2023 by Mirador Publishing

Copyright © 2023 by Anne Cassidy Waters

First edition: 2023

ISBN: 978-1-915953-48-3

Mirador Publishing
10 Greenbrook Terrace
Taunton
Somerset
UK
TA1 1UT

A Passage from Home

By

Anne Cassidy Waters

Also by the Author

The Ebony Cross

Acknowledgements

A special thank you to all my family and friends for your continual encouragement and support

M ary entered the hotel foyer anxiety furrowing her forehead, her lips tightly puckered, tension emanating in waves. Despite her neat dress and obvious middle-class demeanour, she still felt awkward entering such an exclusive venue. Nervously, she patted her well-lacquered hair. As unobtrusively as her heels allowed, she walked across the marble floor and peered into the dining room, hoping she would not be, as usual, the first to arrive. A flicker of apprehension set her pulse racing, only easing slightly when she spied her two long-ago friends chatting comfortably in a far corner.

Both women had aged of course, but there was no mistaking Elsbeth, or Beth as she was known. The passing years had done little to reduce her distinctive looks. The flame-red hair had not dimmed, if anything it was more vibrant than Mary recalled, the idea of assistance from a bottle not entering Mary's head. Beside her sat Eileen. The girl Mary remembered, bore little relation to the woman now chatting serenely to Beth. She exuded a quiet confidence, her ample frame restrained in a check costume, a ridiculous name Mary thought for a matching skirt and jacket. Silky black hair, now streaked with grey and white, and neatly tied in a beehive, complemented her tranquil features. As Mary approached the table the two women rose and all perfunctorily hugged one another, a slight uneasiness, a characteristic of all three. Eileen was the first to speak, gently breaking the ice with her informality.

'Well, Mary, what do you think of this place? Tis lucky I am, I have been saving for Christmas or a glass of water is all I would be able to afford.'

Beth was quick to respond. 'We could go somewhere else if you prefer? I just thought this hotel would suit us all as it is so central...'

Mary sat down, and replied, 'It is fine, Beth. A good choice and an experience for us all. Where is Anna, by the way?' This last remark addressed to Beth.

'She did indicate she would be here, but she is not the most reliable. I had some difficulty contacting her as we lost touch some time ago. In the end, I had to send a letter to her family, and she replied briefly saying she would try and come. However, I suggest we go ahead and order lunch.'

Mary and Eileen exchanged questioning looks before turning their attention towards the menu.

'By the way, I want you to know it is my treat today,' said Mary.

She waved away the protestations from Eileen and Beth.

'No, I insist. After all, I need something from both of you.

A quick study of the menu and Mary and Eileen chose the same, most economically priced sandwich, with a pot of tea.

'I travelled from Wexford this morning, so I am absolutely famished. I hope no one minds if I order the dish of the day?' queried Beth.

Eileen looked surprised, her lips pursed slightly, not so much in disapproval but conscious of the fact that Mary was footing the bill. Mary glanced at Eileen before turning to Beth,

'No, in fact, I am quite hungry myself. Why don't we all order something more substantial? And Beth, order a bottle of wine as well. We can all have a glass.'

'Why not?' responded Beth. 'I like a glass of wine with my meal, and I think our meeting today deserves a toast. It is quite acceptable in this day and age for modern women like us. Is that not so, Eileen?'

Beth smiled at Eileen who paused momentarily before whimsically replying,

'Do you know, I imagine it is. After all, it is 1963, thirty years since all four of us arrived in Mayo from the islands to learn English. So yes, if it is all right with Mary, I am happy to join you in a glass of wine.'

All three women turned their heads in unison as the tapping from across the polished floor announced the arrival of Anna.

There was a brittleness to Anna that could not be disguised. Throwing her coat carelessly across the back of a chair, she took a seat between Eileen and Beth. Her hair and make-up were immaculate, the silk of her dress a luxuriant deep blue. Yet, the manner in which she crossed and uncrossed her legs indicated a tension within. Immediately, she lit up a cigarette, agreed wine was in order, and without any preamble turned to Mary.

'So, Mary, what is this about a book? I do remember you were always scribbling away.'

'Well, I thought you knew,' muttered Mary, surprised.

Beth interrupted before Mary could speak further.

'Mary, Anna has been away. Beyond notifying her of our meeting and letting her know you have written about our time in Mayo, I haven't had a chance to explain anything else to her.'

'Well, Anna,' began Mary. 'As you said, I was always jotting something down in my diary. It is a habit I continue with to this day. Last year, we decided to clear the attic, and in one of the boxes I discovered most of my old journals. So many memories came flooding back. Remember the first time we arrived in Mayo?' Both Beth and Eileen nodded vigorously but, beyond a slight grimace, Anna didn't respond so Mary continued.

'Anyway, through the letters I received from Eileen and Beth, I followed all of your lives, yours too Anna.'

Anna paused and looked at Beth. 'You wrote to Mary about me? I hope you did me justice.'

Anna's harsh laugh and caustic tone gave a vague hint that she was less than pleased.

'Anna,' interposed Mary, 'the reason I asked everyone to meet here was to be sure you are all happy with the story I have written.'

Pausing only slightly to catch her breath, Mary continued.

'Of course, it is only loosely based on our experiences, and I have used a lot of my own imagination. Nevertheless, there are some personal details gleaned from letters over the years, so I have a copy of the manuscript for everyone. Eimear has already read it and she has no qualms at all. I must tell you I already have a publisher so I hope all three of you will read it and let me know if you want anything changed. Needless to say, I will not be using your actual names. In fact, when you have finished reading, and provided you have no issues with how you are depicted, you can choose how you would like to be known in the story.'

'Eimear,' mused Eileen. 'I had forgotten all about Eimear.'

'She wasn't one of us,' interposed Anna. 'Bit stand-offish I always thought, but then, I suppose we weren't in her class.'

Deliberately ignoring Anna, Mary replied, 'I kept in touch with Eimear over the years, but the story is mainly about us four. Do you remember the day we arrived in Blacksod Bay? How all our lives have changed since that time. I think there is a tale there worth telling. Young people today have no idea how we struggled. The necessity to learn English in order to obtain a job and how so many of us had to emigrate. It is our personal story but also a chronicle of the times that shouldn't be forgotten.'

All three nodded at Mary as memories assailed each and every one.

'Mary, I will read this, although please don't rush me. Reading is not my strong point. Also, I may want some changes if my story is written only from Beth's viewpoint. Now, how about some more wine?'

Anna lifted the bottle and poured a liberal glass for herself.

Mary gazed thoughtfully after Anna as she stalked across the room. She had abruptly stood after quickly quaffing a second glass of wine. The jarring sound of her chair scraping against the wooden floor, thunderous in the quiet dining room, caused eyes to turn and stare. Mary was filled with foreboding. Despite Anna's apparent nonchalance, she was not confident Anna would permit her story to be published. In fact, she was not confident Anna would even read the manuscript.

It was a tired and dishevelled Mary who rose the following morning. A sleepless night left her agitated and snappy. Gerard snapped back.

'What's the matter with you? You met the three women and gave them the manuscript. You should be relaxed, happy. Everything is moving forward.'

Mary shook her head, bewildered as to how he could not understand.

'They might not like the book, Gerry, not everyone wants to remember and have some of their innermost secrets exposed.'

Exasperated, Mary grasped her cup of tea. She wandered out into the back garden, burning her mouth as she gulped the hot drink too quickly. Absently, she deadheaded her roses, unable to concentrate on what she needed to do that day, all too aware her friends might now be turning the first page.

Chapter 1

Eileen lay the manuscript on the table, lost in memories of the girl she once was, a girl who still lingered inside her, nipping at her confidence every so often. She had not remained in Dublin after lunch but travelled in her new Ford Anglia directly back to her home. The manuscript had sat on the seat beside her beckoning her to review an adolescence that held nothing but pain. The following morning, similar to Mary, she had also arisen early, her sleep disturbed by flashes of her time in Mayo. There was no eagerness to begin reading, in fact, the opposite was the case, but curiosity as to how she was portrayed overcame her reluctance. She felt the woman she had become was vastly different from the young shy girl who had arrived in Blacksod Bay in 1933 but echoes continued to haunt. She had kept in touch with Mary, writing every few months and describing the changing fortunes in her life but had she revealed too much? Eileen had no wish to relive that time or be in receipt of the pity of others. Reluctantly she began to read.

The boat butted and bumped against the pier, and amid the shouts from fishermen to secure the ropes, the passengers slowly started to disembark. The four young girls huddled silently together not sure what to do, a forlorn group isolated in their shyness and apprehension, gradually becoming more sodden as the rain intensified. The other passengers moved slowly away but in the distance a black figure hurried towards them frantically trying to control an umbrella with a mind of its own.

'I am Sister Assumpta,' she called fruitlessly, as her words, in competition with the blustering wind, drifted away unheard.

'I am Sister Assumpta,' she repeated, and her round apple face creased in a welcoming smile.

An answering chorus of, 'Dia dhuit, Sister,' produced a mild reprimand.

'Girls, girls, i mBéarla, please. You are here to learn English. Let us start as we mean to go on. I am taking you to the teachers' house and when school is finished Sr Cornelius will greet you there and decide on your placements. Now follow me.'

The little group tramped up the hill, the girls each carrying a similar small case containing meagre possessions. They passed open fields and small cottages before the little town of Kilford, not much more than a village, came into view.

'Tá tuirseach orm,' said Eileen.

'Agus mise freisin,' responded Mary.

'Now, now, what did I say? English, please. I know you are tired but it's not much further.'

Sister Assumpta veered to the left towards a small row of large distinctive houses. She paused outside a yellow brick house, easily the most impressive, and led the girls through the side entrance to the kitchen area. Her knock was answered by a young girl with a sunny smile and enveloped in a blue floral apron. She indicated with a wave of her hand, a wave that initiated a sprinkling of flour that bathed those nearest in a white flurry, that they should follow her into a small sitting room.

'Sit down, you must be tired after that journey. The cook, Mrs Donegan, said to bring you tea and scones. I have just this minute put them in the oven, so I will be back shortly.'

The girls looked around in wonder. The room was comfortably furnished, much more so than their own homes on the islands off the coast of Mayo. Yet, it was a sitting room for servants only and it was there they were to stay for the present.

'Well, girls, tell me your names?' requested Sr Assumpta. 'In English please.'

'I am Mary.'

'Eileen.'

'Anna.'

And finally,

'I am Elsbeth.'

'What kind of a name is that?' was the surprised, if not unkindly, response.

'My mother just liked it,' said Elsbeth with a worried frown.

'Well now, I don't know of any saint called Elsbeth. When you meet Sr Cornelius you might be wiser to call yourself Elizabeth, cousin of Mary the mother of our Lord and Saviour, Beth for short. Now, it will be another two hours before school is over. Wait here and be patient until then.'

Tea and scones arrived as Sister Assumpta rose to leave.

'Stay and have some tea, Sister,' urged the young girl, introducing herself at the same time to the four young women. 'I am Meg by the way.'

Sr Assumpta looked at the appetising tray and patted her generous girth.

'Too tempting by far, but I promised myself that today I will do penance for my usual greed and abstain from all things sweet. So, I had better go now before I fail. Girls, I will see you all again soon.'

Sr Assumpta, with a final wistful look at the tray, sailed away accompanied by a swish of her rosary beads.

All four girls chattered in a mixture of Gaelic and English, as they dived into the tea and scones. They hailed from the smattering of islands off the Mayo coast. Although aware of each other due to the proximity of the islands, only Elsbeth and Anna were close friends. Gaelic was their native language also known as 'an teanga bocht' or 'poor tongue'. Although beautiful and poetic, it was only spoken in pockets around the country, and English was the language needed for employment. The purpose of their trip to Mayo was to become proficient in spoken English, the better to obtain work either in Dublin, but more likely in England or the United States. Eileen recalled sitting in that room and her fascination with Elsbeth and, to a lesser extent, Anna. Elsbeth was the most striking of them all. Long red hair swirled around an intelligent face with flashing green eyes. Unlike most redheads there was hardly a freckle to be seen, instead, she was the lucky possessor of pale creamy skin with a soft apricot hue. Her close friend Anna had dark curly hair surrounding a very pretty face. The opposite of Elsbeth, who was tall and slim and exuded calm, Anna was small and petite, restless, almost agitated at times. Yet they were close friends having known each other since they were babies.

'Oh, what's that smell?' gurgled Anna, spluttering as she tried to suppress a giggle with her hand.

'Did someone stand in something and trail it into the teacher's house?'

A faint whiff, barely discernible, made Eileen glance at her shoes and immediately look away again.

She focused on her hands and sighed, now conscious of her bitten nails. Slightly shifting position, she cringed inwardly at the squelching noise echoing in the room when her weight compressed the leather cushion. Anna giggled and pointed at Eileen's feet. On the verge of shrinking further into the chair, Eileen caught Mary's eye, and a comforting glance of understanding passed between them. Eileen could never articulate or understand why, but from the moment she met Anna, she felt uncomfortable and instinctively withdrew into herself in Anna's presence. The opposite was the case with Mary.

Mary smiled at Eileen as her gaze shifted around the table. Her candid expression exuded a trust that indicated a confidence she did not feel. Mary's face was surrounded by a halo of short silky fair hair and her pale blue eyes assessed the others, never quick to bestow allegiance. They were girls she had seen now and again at festivities where all the islanders joined in. Her busy home life had prevented her from making any close friends her own age, especially as meeting them inevitably required a boat journey. She watched, slightly amused, as she could see Eileen eying the one remaining scone, hesitating for some seconds, before stretching her hand out to retrieve it. Oozing with butter and jam she swallowed the scone too speedily for enjoyment. The sparkle from the glisten of tears that welled and threatened to fall could just be discerned in her doleful eyes. Long black hair reaching almost to her waist, masked a well-rounded face and ample body, and Mary felt a kinship with a girl she could readily see felt out of place. Mary smiled at her, liking her instantly, sensing she was nervous and probably already missing home.

Eileen was thinking of her mother and father and the small cottage she had left behind. In her heart, she knew there was no option but to leave but that did not make the parting any easier. The youngest of six, her parents were now aging and glad to take things a little easier. Her eldest brother had taken over the small-holding and moved with his wife and their three children into the family home. The cramped conditions had prompted the decision to leave but now she was in Mayo, homesickness threatened to overwhelm her. Except for one older sister who had married locally, the emigrant trail had been the route for all the others. She glanced up feeling Mary's gaze upon her and for a moment a spark of understanding intruded to dissipate her loneliness.

The time stretched on comfortably enough, the tea and scones and general surroundings making them all wish they could stay in the teacher's house. The girls' chatter was interrupted by the arrival of Meg who directed them to the main living room. They trooped inside and stood as indicated in a line in front of a nun, they presumed, was Sister Cornelius. Starched and stern she regarded the girls one by one before addressing them.

'Name please?'

'Mary, Sister.'

'Good, a lovely name, you can stay here. Next?'

'Anna, sister,'

'Mmm, you can go to the presbytery. You?'

'Beth, Sister.'

'I presume you mean Elizabeth and that is how you will be known. And your name?' This last addressed to Eileen.

'Eileen, Sister.'

'You look big and strong and able for hard work. You and Elizabeth can come with me to the convent.'

Eileen reddened at the comment on her size but was glad she would not be alone in the convent. Conversely, she wished she could stay with Mary, but although she could not explain it, was glad she was at least with Beth and not Anna.

Mary's relief when she heard she was to stay in the teacher's house was short-lived because she was unsure what to do when they all left. *At least they are together*, she thought. Nerves made her restless and she paced the sitting room continuously until Meg returned and took her under her wing. 'Come along with me downstairs and Mrs Donegan will tell you what your duties are.'

A face, flushed from the kitchen heat, smiled warmly as Mary entered.

'Well, Mary, welcome to the McCarthy house. As you know you are here to learn English so English must be spoken at all times. I am sure you know generally what will happen. You work here for about four months and then you are given a ticket for the Dublin train. Don't look so worried. You will be met at the station in Dublin and spend the night in a nearby convent. As soon as is possible the convent will organise a ticket for the boat to Liverpool or Holyhead. Again, you will be met, and a suitable position will be found for you by the nuns over there. It is important you learn English as it is the only way to obtain a decent job. I manage the household with Meg's help, but a young girl called Maggie comes in every day to help with the children and you will mainly assist her. Now, Meg, show Mary upstairs to her room.'

Mary dutifully followed Meg.

The house was the largest Mary had ever been in, but she was still astonished to find she had a room to herself.

'Well, it is a big house, but Mrs Donegan is the only help who sleeps here. She has her own room down the corridor. I live down the road and so does Maggie and we go home each evening,' explained Meg.

'Tell me about the teacher's family, Meg.'

'Well, both the mother and father are teachers.'

'But the mother doesn't work, surely?' responded Mary.

'She does. She got a special dispensation. There are so few teachers around here, she is allowed to continue even though she is married.'

Mary was unable to hide her surprise as Meg explained further.

'There are six children. The eldest girl, Eimear, is attending Teacher

Training College but she is home now for the summer holidays. The three boys are at boarding school but only one, Eoin, is home as the other two are sitting exams. They will arrive home in another week. The two youngest girls go to school locally. They are on holiday now of course and you will mainly help with the girls. Come down to the kitchen at 5.30 for tea.'

Meg then left Mary to her own devices. She examined every crevice in the room before sitting in the window seat with her journal. For a few minutes, she gazed at the mountains towering in the distance, shrouded in mist. Her eyes lingered on the distant shore, but the lowering sky obscured any sight of the islands.

Too far away, anyway, she thought, as memories of home encroached, unsettling her. Then, with a deliberate shake, she opened her journal to enter the events of the day so far. Her journal was her constant companion, the repository of her thoughts, hopes and dreams. She paused for a moment wondering how the other three girls were faring, particularly Eileen.

Chapter 2

B*eth returned to her cosy terraced house after lunch. A glass of wine at midday was a rare event and needed to be followed by a leisurely afternoon nap, but today, that was not to be. Meeting Anna had churned up too many memories to allow her to stretch out, switch off and relax. Instead, she hung up her coat and made a cup of strong coffee. After first reading about the arrival of all four in 1933, she became anxious to read on and discover how she had described her own journey, but more importantly, how she had portrayed Anna.*

Sister Cornelius set off from the teachers' house at a healthy pace towards the far side of the small town, her lengthy stride making short work of the journey, her majestic bearing daring the clouds to burst. The three girls marched behind her, struggling to keep up. Their destination was the presbytery and, before long, a large imposing, house loomed ahead. Situated within the church grounds, the grey, granite exterior exuded gloom and although the garden was well preserved, it was overshadowed by tall oak trees that kept it constantly in shade. It was not as welcoming as the teachers' house and the housekeeper's demeanour did not help. Mrs Walshe was elderly, and her thin lips pressed tightly together only added to her forbidding manner. She announced without any preamble, her tone brooking no response,

'You are not to bother the priest under any circumstances. He does not like to be disturbed and I will not have you upsetting him. He is a man of God, and the chatter of young girls interrupts his communion with the Almighty. At all times stay in the kitchen. I, alone, serve him his meals.'

These chilly instructions were issued without any emotion, and with what appeared to Anna, a distaste for herself, although why, was a mystery. She was taken aback but shrugged her shoulders in response to the list of pointless rules, and gazed out the window as Beth and Eileen faded into the distance.

So what? She had no intention of talking to any priest. She would just learn English and in a few short months, she would be free.

Sister Cornelius continued her healthy stride, never checking to ensure the two girls could keep up. Eventually, she paused for breath outside the convent, a Victorian edifice, ruined by the addition of a squat modern girls' school painted a garish blue. Elsbeth stood beside her whilst Eileen panted in exhaustion a few feet away.

'Come quickly inside, girls,' she ordered brusquely. 'And I will ask Sister Boniface to show you to your quarters and give you your instructions so your stay will run smoothly.'

Elsbeth and Eileen trudged inside to a silent and dark hallway. Sister Boniface appeared out of the gloom and indicated by a nod of her head that they should follow. She glided ahead and not a word was uttered. When they reached the third floor, she opened a door into a small room lit only by the light from a narrow window. It contained two beds and some shelving, the walls decorated with numerous religious depictions, and a graphic crucifix.

Eileen instantly walked across the room and peered out the window, before turning to Elsbeth,

'Look here, Beth, you can see the sea.'

Sister Boniface directed her gaze towards Eileen.

'Talking without some valid purpose is frowned upon,' she admonished.

'But we are here to learn English,' interrupted Beth.

With a finger pointing to her lips, Sr Boniface continued,

'Hush, now. You will have ample time during the day's work and, if it is God's will, you will learn English. In the evenings, within this convent, we put our trust in the Lord and silence allows us to contemplate him, his mother, and our purpose on this earth. Now goodnight to you both, we will see you in the church for morning prayers at 6 am and there will be breakfast in the refectory at 7.30. Details of your duties will be issued afterwards.'

Timidly, confessing afterwards she never knew from where the courage came, Eileen muttered, 'Excuse me, Sister but we have had no dinner today, just some tea and scones at lunchtime. Will there be any meal this evening?'

'Our evening repast is over. It will do both of you no harm to fast in preparation for difficulties ahead, especially you, my dear. You are already too well-fed for my liking.'

Quietly closing the door, Sr Boniface departed, leaving Beth and Eileen with numerous questions but no answers. Eileen turned away to hide her red face and watery eyes from Beth. There was to be no food that evening, and Eileen's only consolation was that Beth's stomach growled in concert with her own.

Eileen got into bed deliberately ignoring her now gnawing hunger. She twisted and turned on the rigid mattress whilst the roughly woven blanket scratched and itched. Sleep was elusive so she contemplated the day's events. She had been glad to have company as they marched to the convent, but she would have preferred if her companion had been Mary and not, in her mind, the exotic Beth. Beth represented all Eileen felt she could never be. Striking good looks with more than a hint of an ancient Gaelic ancestry, perhaps Gráinne O'Malley or Gráinne Mhaol, as she was also known, the ancient Irish pirate queen. Beth had an innate confidence Eileen knew she could never muster. At the same time, she knew Beth was kind unlike, she guessed, Anna. The remark on her size from the formidable Sr Cornelius had made her ashamed in front of the others. That shame had been compounded by the austere Sr Boniface. Her size had never been an issue at home, but twice now, comments had been uttered that diminished her. Her pillow, now slightly sodden, muffled her sobs until sleep eventually overcame her. The gong boomed at 6 am with such a clatter both girls were out of bed and standing on the cold floor, in shock, before they realised the reason why. It may have been June, but it was cool, and they hurriedly dressed, unsure whether to run in their nightclothes to the bathroom in order to first wash. Eileen was starving but it was Beth who first voiced how hungry she felt.

'I think we have prayers first, Eileen, but I am so hungry I don't know if I can last that long without food.'

Eileen nodded her agreement, the cold temperature and cement floor underfoot, inducing uncontrollable shivering.

'I know, Beth, I feel the same, but I don't think we have any choice,' she moaned, and opening their door, the girls were ushered towards the chapel and morning prayers by a train of black-clad women moving along the corridor.

Sr Boniface greeted them at the church door and guided them into a pew. Surrounded by an ebony sea of bowed heads, Beth lowered her own head, glad of the mantilla to hide her crimson locks. As the prayers droned around her, her thoughts turned, of course, to home. Her father had hugged her gruffly before swiftly striding away lest she sees his watering eyes. Her mother had gripped her hands muttering gently that she was always welcome home and to take care of Anna.

'She will need you, Beth, she is not so strong and needs a guiding hand.'

One final kiss and Beth was relinquished into the arms of her eldest brother, the other three waiting patiently to hug her in turn. Despite her inner strength, Beth knew she would miss her family dearly and she wished Anna were kneeling beside her. She had no issue with Eileen, but Anna was like a sister. Their many years of stalwart friendship had created a bond that should help them both get through the next few months, but it would have been nice to be together. Also, there was no denying Anna needed her steadying influence.

Unaware of the churning thoughts of home that swirled inside Beth's bowed head, Eileen knelt beside her with a scarf wrapped tightly around her black mane. She gazed at the mantilla gracing Beth's red tresses and felt a moment of envy at owning something so pretty. She intoned her prayers in the soft cadence of her Gaelic tongue and prayed she might eventually be able to return home. If she could only learn enough English, perhaps she could earn some money back on the island teaching young children the language. Yet as quickly as these thoughts were formulated, so too came the knowledge that they were just a pipe dream. No one had much money to spare. Her only way to stay home was to marry and already the thoughtless words of both nuns had begun to affect her.

Who would want the likes of me? she murmured to herself. *Fat and ungainly. Anyway, her mother and father needed whatever help she could spare once she found herself a job.*

Deliberately shrugging her self-pitying thoughts aside, Eileen determined that their sacrifice to send her to learn English would not be wasted, a small repayment for the cocoon of love that had swaddled her since her birth.

Beth and Eileen were quickly put to work. A number of other young women from the parish joined them at nine o'clock and together they were instructed to clean the entire school, now disbanded, for the summer holidays.

'You will also be required to assist in our home for the sick and elderly but for now, help with cleaning the school,' instructed Sr Boniface.

Camaraderie and banter developed and quite quickly over the coming days, between lots of gaffes and laughter, both girls gained a rudimentary grasp of English. The regular call to prayers ensured their entreaties to God would be certainly fluent in both tongues. The summer evenings were bright and long and soon they were able to meet Mary for a walk along the seashore. Mary's English was also improving and together the three of them tried to converse as little as possible in Irish. Mary, of course, interrogated them on how they felt, their thoughts on home, and their opinions of both the nuns and the convent. Beth and Eileen answered her quite happily, pleased to have their ideas recorded for posterity. They had to battle with the shriek of gulls as fishermen landed their catch or, more usually, the pounding of the waves as they crashed onto the rocks at the furthest section of the beach. Yet, they grinned and laughed as they screeched to be heard, smiling when the odd passer-by commented.

'Tis grand it is to see you enjoying your time here,' remarked one of the fishermen. 'The nuns must be doing something right after all.'

The three girls grinned conspiratorially, the idea that Sr Cornelius or Sr

Boniface could do anything right a totally alien idea. Yet, Eileen privately felt that for all Beth's kindness, there was a barrier between them that could not be breached. When alone with Mary she tentatively broached how she felt.

'Mary, I really like Beth, and Anna too, of course, but they make me feel, how can I say this, awkward, I suppose. They are both so pretty and confident, especially Beth, but she is very nice, different to Anna, in many ways.'

Eileen's voice trailed away, afraid she had been too outspoken, but Mary concurred.

'I know, Eileen, I know how you feel. Beth is just lovely, but she does make me feel a little inadequate. Anna seems so self-assured and maybe not quite so agreeable.'

Mary shrugged her shoulders and both girls grinned comfortably together.

A strong bond was silently forged between them, a recognition perhaps, of similar goals and wishes but most of all inadequacies.

Anna was a constant source of conversation. From time to time, they spied her in the town, and sometimes Mary saw her at Sunday Mass, but she rarely met them for walks. Mrs Walshe kept Anna on a tight leash and although all the girls could sense her loneliness, only Beth really missed her. She alone could discern a developing rebelliousness creeping into her eyes. On the occasions when they did meet Anna, conversation in English was always limited, and it was obvious Anna's grasp of the language had been barely enhanced since her arrival on the mainland.

Chapter 3

Anna could feel eyes burning her back as she left the hotel. The others had not finished lunch, but she didn't care how rude she appeared. It was many years since she had that sensation of being excluded from an inner circle, one that judged and found her wanting. She returned to the small, but tasteful, lodging house. Yet agitated and unsettled, she paced the room continually, puffing on a cigarette. Finally, she opened the bottle of gin in her suitcase and poured a liberal amount into a glass. She had no tonic or ice but that didn't matter. After a couple of long swallows, she calmed sufficiently to sit on the edge of the bed. How had Beth described that turbulent period to Mary and, more importantly, what had Mary written? At the lunch table, Mary had prompted Anna, as she had Beth and Eileen, to discuss her memories of that period in Mayo and how her life had subsequently transpired.*

'Some chance,' thought Anna. 'Why would she describe her inner thoughts to Mary, almost a stranger?'

It was no business of Mary's how she had stood impatiently on the pier that long-ago day, accompanied by her mother, anxious to board the boat and depart. It was certainly no business of Mary's how her life had evolved. Yet, Beth had the temerity to describe to Mary the personal details of her life in

Mayo and afterward, ignoring the woman she now was. Anna began to read.

Initially, she was surprised at Beth's perceptiveness, how she understood Anna's impatience to leave, but also that Anna realised Beth and her family needed time for goodbye. How had she guessed that the closeness within Beth's family sometimes generated a surge of envy inside Anna that displayed itself in a recklessness, that Anna herself, could barely understand? Maybe Beth had perceived more than Anna allowed her credit and as she read, despite herself, memories flooded back.

Anna's family had waved her off without a backward glance, her father already well drunk at eleven in the morning. That didn't matter. She just wanted to get on the boat and was irritated at the delay the various hugs and kisses, that Beth's family considered necessary, were causing. She could see Eileen and Mary already seated, girls she knew by sight but with whom she felt she had little in common. She guessed they were both on the same journey as herself and Anna hoped she wouldn't be stuck with either of them.

Anna was the eldest of four daughters, but unlike many of the girls who left the islands, there was no pressure on her to leave, quite the opposite. Her mother needed her assistance with the younger three girls and her father demanded her help on the farm.

'No sons yet, so yer needed here to help with the plantin' an' the milkin'.'

When Beth, her closest friend, confided that she was hoping to go and live with her aunt and grandmother in England, but first needed to improve her English, Anna was determined to join her. After a month of pleading, her parents finally gave in. On the surface, it seemed they wanted assurance that Anna could also live with Beth's family, but Anna knew it was just for show. In the end, she had worn down her mother with her pestering. Somehow her mother had persuaded her father they could manage. Anna liked to think that perhaps her mother hoped Anna might be spared the drudgery of her own life, but guessed she was just fed up with Anna and her continual pleading.

Anna watched from the presbytery as Sr Cornelius led Beth off in a different direction with Eileen in tow and wished she had also been chosen for the convent. Instead, she had been delivered to the back door of a plain granite house, within the grounds of the church, and met by a sour-faced housekeeper. Mrs Walshe provided an evening meal of stew accompanied by a constant stream of instructions.

'You are not to be bothering Fr Matthew. He is too busy to be interrupted by the likes of you frittering around. You do what I say, when I say it, as quickly as possible. You eat in the kitchen, and in the evening after all jobs are completed, you go straight to your room.'

The litany washed over Anna and, as she stifled a yawn, Mrs Walshe insisted that Anna retire to bed immediately.

'Now? It is too early. It is still bright outside.'

'What did I just tell you?' sighed Mrs Walshe. 'We will get along fine if you do what I say. I can see you're tired. You have had a long day and you need to be up early. Run along now.'

The evening sun still shone brightly as Anna trudged up the creaking stairs to the attic. The room was comfortable, if sparsely furnished, and the bed was soft and welcoming. After ten minutes of investigation, Anna knew every corner of the room and stretched out on the bed. She felt nervous about the long night ahead with no one around. It was the first time she had ever slept alone and the first time she felt a slight pang for her younger sisters. This soon vanished as the peace and space crept around her and, all of a sudden, Anna smiled to herself.

Perhaps it is not so bad to be alone, and before long, I will be in England with Beth.

With that pleasant thought and now enfolded in the warm bed, sleep took possession, and Anna drifted away quite contentedly.

The following morning the strict instructions to steer clear of Fr Matthew were reiterated plus a long list of tasks to be undertaken. Anna's first errand was shopping in the small town, and as the morning was bright and clear, she began to feel she might enjoy her first trip out. It certainly helped with her English practice as she chattered with the grocer and butcher. She did not expect to see Beth, or even Mary or Eileen, but nevertheless kept an eye out just in case. After she returned, she cleaned the kitchen and helped prepare a range of meals for some of the less fortunate members of the community.

'We do this once a month just to help out. In general, it is undertaken by the convent,' said Mrs Walshe. 'You will bring the dishes over there for distribution once they are cooled. I know you have friends there but don't delay, Sr Cornelius does not approve of loitering.'

Anna happily complied and managed to pass a hastily written letter to Beth. The following days, however, were not so enjoyable as Mrs Walshe had a long list of chores to be undertaken within the house and refused permission for her to meet her friends in the evening. Disgruntled, Anna complied but resentment began to simmer.

It was a full week before she heard Fr Matthew in the house, although she knew he had to be there every evening. Mrs Walshe's frosty manner had melted somewhat, but she was still adamant she avoid any interaction with the priest, and to that end, demanded she go to her room after dinner each evening. This night, however, the sweet tones of a piano drifted up to the attic and Anna crept down a few steps just to hear more. Fr Matthew had left his study door slightly ajar, and she could see him bent over the instrument, lost in another world. Anna loved to sing, a love that was fostered and encouraged by her teacher Bean Uí Chonaill.

'You have an ear for music, Anna. Treasure it. Music is food for the soul. It has the power to lift you from the harshest reality of life and transport you to places you can but dream of.'

Anna shrugged. *There had not been much to sing about the last few years*, she thought.

The memory of a mother who used to twirl her about the kitchen, singing, and dancing, had all but faded, replaced by a timorous and downtrodden drudge. Her mother's stories of her own happy childhood and how her family had a variety of instruments, a whistle, a bodhrán, a fiddle, a 'bosca ceoil', how all were produced on any occasion that demanded music, were no longer uttered. Hatred for a father who had killed that gay, carefree woman surged within her and the piano music was drowned by her mother's cries of terror.

A fortnight passed and she had still not met the priest but regularly she left her own door slightly ajar, on the off chance, he sat and played. She did not recognise any of the tunes, but she could tell he had magical fingers and she quietly hummed along, careful not to be overheard. One evening as she was heading for bed as instructed, she noticed the study door was open. She had not seen Beth, never mind the other two girls, in over two weeks, and boredom and loneliness nagged at her continually. The monotony of the days with such early nights had become tedious making her restless. Curiosity aroused, she entered the room, drawn like a magnet to the piano. She lifted the lid and her discordant attempt to play alerted Mrs Walshe.

'Get out of here at once. What have I told you? I am so disappointed, I thought for once there was a girl here who obeyed orders.'

Anna acquiesced, but as she left, she noticed that Mrs Walshe was not checking the piano but a large box, not unlike the one in which her father kept all their family certificates, and the meagre few spare pence he garnered from time to time.

'Go to bed now and don't come in here again,' growled Mrs Walshe over her shoulder.

Anna entered the kitchen the following morning, still smarting slightly over Mrs Walshe's sharp words. She was met with a plea from a reddened face with streaming eyes.

'Anna, I need your help more than ever today. I will instruct you, but you must prepare the meals. I can then take them into Father.'

The housekeeper had developed a cold and not just an ordinary bout of sniffles. Her head ached and her cheeks were flushed with fever.

'Oh, Mrs Walshe, he cannot be that bad that he will object to me serving his dinner,' laughed Anna. Mrs Walshe frowned, and a more observant girl might have noticed the cloud that temporarily suffused her features.

'No, I can manage. Go to bed as usual after you have eaten this evening. I am going to rest now but will get up later on.'

Frustrated, Anna did as she was bid. Fr Matthew was nowhere to be seen anyway, and she spent the day alone, pottering about, attending to the myriad list of instructions dictated in a croak from Mrs Walshe's bedroom. Eventually, the housekeeper reappeared, evidently weak and pale, but insisting Anna head upstairs.

It was late June and the bright evenings made sleep impossible. She knew the other three girls often met and walked along the beach or down to the harbour. She couldn't understand why she was prevented from joining them and determined to do so as soon as possible. Frustration at the confinement made her irritable and bubbling resentment made it difficult to sleep until the early hours. The following morning Anna rose late but Mrs Walshe was even slower to appear. Anna had the breakfast all but ready by the time she hobbled into the kitchen. She looked drained with watery eyes sunken within scarlet cheeks. There was no doubt she was obviously quite ill.

'Go back to bed, Mrs Walshe, I can manage.'

'You don't understand, Anna, I need to pro…'

The words were never finished as Mrs Walshe slowly slid to the ground. Anna moved swiftly to her side as she murmured, 'Water, Anna, get me some water please.'

Mrs Walshe knew she had no option but to go back to bed and for the next week she wallowed in a fever with no sign of it abating. Anna followed the doctor's instructions interspersed with orders from Mrs Walshe. She was directed to just prepare meats and salad for the priest's evening meal and to avoid any contact with him which was, of course, impossible but Anna tried to humour a stressed Mrs Walshe. The priest was polite but distant, and she concluded the deference displayed by Mrs Walshe was unnecessary, and her efforts to keep him undisturbed by the household help was just foolishness.

Chapter 4

Gerard glanced at Mary as she re-entered the kitchen, but even though he forbore to make any comment, his glance was questioning. Mary deliberately ignored him and walked straight past him into the dining room. The manuscript sat on the table. To ease her agitation Mary decided to read it once more and attempt to view it from the standpoint of Eileen, Beth, and Anna. Eimear had already given her blessing.

Writing was a catharsis for Mary, but sometimes, reading back over what she had written was difficult. Whereas writing was a release, reading her written words often transported her to a time and place that brought hidden tensions to the fore. Temporizing, Mary walked over to the mirror hanging above the mantlepiece. Grey hair framed a face mapped with lines that bore evidence of sorrow and worry but also of joy. The blue of her eyes had not dimmed, in fact, the colour had deepened, and sparkled with intelligence. Family and home had always been the bedrock of her life but now she was unsettled. She plumped the cushions before sitting in an armchair but, unable to relax, she once more paced the floor, stopping at intervals to straighten a photo. Eventually, reluctantly, she could no longer ignore the manuscript beckoning from the centre of the table. Slowly, Mary began reading about the young girl she could barely remember.

'Where did I go?' she wondered as she was transported easily into the routine in the teachers' house in County Mayo 1933. The first days were a learning curve, an adventure, at times tinged with homesickness but overall exciting.

Meg was a great help, advising on what was expected and whom and what to avoid. The apprehension she had felt when the other three girls departed dissipated quickly and she felt lucky to have been the one to remain. She met Beth and Eileen every few days at 4 pm for a walk along the beach or pier. She liked them both but felt more comfortable with Eileen. Beth exuded a natural confidence, the antithesis of Eileen who, from the start, seemed to shrink when spoken to but now seemed at ease in Mary's company. Mary understood that Beth was in no way unsympathetic but had an innate faith in herself and her abilities. Their different personalities intrigued her. Why did people with relatively similar backgrounds develop in such a diverse manner? Fortunately, her intrusive questions did not annoy either girl and were, perhaps, more of a diversion on their regular walks.

Despite their best efforts it was a rare event to see Anna. Mary glimpsed her at Mass on Sundays, but Beth and Eileen usually attended Mass in the convent. Twice, Mary managed to slip her a note from Beth, but they rarely spoke for long.

'We have Mass, every day,' groaned Beth to Mary and Eileen. 'It is so boring.'

'Oh, don't say that, Beth,' gasped a horrified Eileen who quickly blessed herself at such a sacrilegious comment.

'Meg told me that Mrs Walshe, the priest's housekeeper, keeps a tight rein on any girls who stay in the priest's house,' said Mary.

'Poor Anna,' replied Beth, missing the interaction of raised eyes between Mary and Eileen.

'It is such a pity she cannot meet us even for a walk in the evening. That housekeeper must be a right auld biddy.'

Neither Mary nor Eileen made any comment. It was not that they actively disliked Anna but they both felt slightly self-conscious in front of her. She seemed both critical and assessing, and on the odd occasion all four girls had been together Anna changed the dynamic, becoming a disruptive force in the group.

Plainly, the absence of Anna was upsetting for Beth, but the girls were powerless to alter the arrangements, and Mary and Eileen could only nod in vague sympathy with Beth, adding by way of solace,

'Sure, all four of us will be leaving Kilford by September. You will be with Anna again before you know it.'

As the weeks passed, Mary's curiosity gave her an insight into both girls. She began to understand how facets within personalities create relationships that are negotiated, varied, but equally strong. Beth and Anna had a bond forged from childhood. They understood each other possessing a loyalty that they assumed was unbreakable. Throughout the walks, Mary and Eileen formed their own particular bond, founded on empathy and rapport. It was to last through the years, despite the differing paths their lives would take and the few opportunities to meet.

The majority of Mary's day was spent organising the younger children, ensuring they ate their meals, attended their music lessons, and in general, keeping a watch over them. All the children were now home from school. The youngest boys ignored her and spent most of their time outside playing football. The same could not be said for Eoin. He was eighteen and provided his exam results were sufficient, intended to go to Galway University the following September. In the meantime, he was at home and bored. Mary was a pleasant distraction for him, but he made her uncomfortable. Tall and athletic, he was not unattractive himself, but he stood too close to her, insinuating himself into her space trying to engage her in conversation. Meg told her not to worry, that it was just his usual teasing manner, but Eoin made Mary uneasy and aware of herself in a manner not encountered before. She had no excess weight, but she was big-boned and had always felt awkward beside girls her own age who possessed slighter frames. Her clothes were made by her mother, usually reconditioned from older garments, but for this trip, her mother had purchased material for two new dresses. Despite her enthusiasm, Mary's mother would never make a seamstress, and Mary was all too aware of her lack of dressmaking skill, as she pulled and twisted the dresses into a semblance of neatness. The realisation that awareness of her appearance was a response to Eoin and what he might think of her, made her even more irritable and conscious of herself in his company.

The necessity to be in the house for the youngsters' bedtime was one of the few restrictions on Mary's time in the evenings. Otherwise, she was relatively free and enjoyed the walks with the other girls along the seashore, or alone, if they were unavailable. Lately, Eimear, the eldest of the McCarthy children, had begun to accompany her especially if she saw Mary was on her own. Twice Eimear had joined all three girls and even met Anna once. Eimear's life had followed quite a different path to the four island girls. Well-educated, with a good marriage the obvious next step, she nevertheless never generated any awkwardness or appeared in any way aware of their social difference. Mary felt at ease with Eimear, sensing loneliness within her, that her comfortable lifestyle was unable to dissipate.

No matter how exhausted she might be, Mary always wrote in her journal before she settled to sleep. Sometimes, all she scribbled were a mundane few lines, other times, life in Mayo provided some unusual colour. The teachers' house was always busy as Mr McCarthy acted as an advisor to many of the locals. His importance in the town was highlighted by the presence of Fr Matthew on many evenings to discuss church, school, and other local matters. The more Mary saw of Fr Matthew, the more relieved she was, not to be in his house. If Eoin made her feel uncomfortable, it was simply a growing awareness of herself as a young woman. Fr Matthew produced a self-consciousness that she could not discern. It was as though he was minutely examining her, with eyes that remained cold and indifferent, before dismissing her. Where possible she kept out of his way.

She understood from Meg that Fr Matthew had a regimen that had to be meticulously followed each Sunday and the teacher and his family were central to its smooth running. The teacher's role was to lead the way to the altar rails for communion during Mass. The other parishioners then followed. Anyone who violated the strict rule that communicants must walk up the central aisle and return to their seat via the side aisles could expect to be called out from the pulpit, and publicly embarrassed. The offender had to apologise to the congregation for the disturbance. The amount each family must contribute for Christmas and Easter dues was also dictated by Fr Matthew. The McCarthys were both teachers and so there were two salaries entering the house each month. Of course, Mrs McCarthy, as a woman, and despite being comparably qualified, earned less than her husband. A substantial donation was therefore demanded but Mr McCarthy ensured the correct figure was always remitted. If the offering produced from any family was less than that demanded, names were called from the pulpit and reputations disgraced. The clergy in Mary's home were not as demanding, understanding the poverty on the islands. She was loath to criticise another priest openly, so kept her thoughts to herself while expressing them freely in her journal. Yet, that too was difficult. Committing with pen and paper such disloyal criticism of the Church produced profound guilt that only time and space abated. That Fr Matthew's actions were simply a display of power from an unpleasant man took time to understand. All Mary's rearing had generated a profound adherence to the Church and its rules and an acceptance they could do no wrong.

Thoughts churned and swirled without any format as Mary sauntered along, content from her chat with Beth and Eileen. She gauged her background was akin to Eileen's, and perhaps Anna's, but Beth appeared to be more comfortable. Mary's family had very little and had struggled to fund her placement in Mayo. The cost to the family of providing the fare and some additional clothing for the journey was not enormous but considering their circumstances, almost prohibitive. Her labour on the small farm would also be missed. Summer was busy, but autumn was when Mary would usually gather seaweed from the shore to utilise as fertilizer when planting began.

When she reached the house, she was surprised to see a group of men at the front gate gathered around Mr McCarthy in an animated discussion. Mr McCarthy nodded to her as she passed.

'Evening, Mary, lovely night for a walk.'

'Yes, Mr McCarthy, it was beautiful by the shore.'

Mary went around the side of the house and into the kitchen.

'Is that crowd still out there?' queried Meg. Her hands were wrist-deep in a bowl as she furiously kneaded dough. Flour crowned her hair in shades of grey and white lines streaked her brow.

'Yes, who are they?'

'Oh, they are probably here to borrow McCarthy's coat?'

'His coat?' responded a puzzled Mary.

'Well, yes. Have you not heard of the coat? It is famous in these parts for healing sick animals. Mr McCarthy lets the locals borrow it, but they must be very careful with it and return it as soon as possible. The farmers swear that any sick animal who sleeps surrounded by the coat will be well again in a matter of days.'

'Does it really work?' grinned a sceptical Mary.

'Yes, it does. Me own da borrowed it last year when one of the cows was awful sickly. She was better the next day. Don't you have cures where you come from?'

'I suppose so, but a coat... If it was herbs for a potion or something, but a coat seems well, a bit daft.'

'Get away with you,' laughed Meg, and waved a cloud of flour in Mary's direction, whose head was now spinning as she avidly stored details of the coat for her journal. She climbed the stairs to her bedroom pondering Meg's story. Grabbing her diary, she quickly related the mysterious powers of the coat as best she could before she forgot them, marvelling at such a strange belief. She knew she couldn't dismiss it as foolishness. On her own island, there were many who believed in fairies or had other quirky notions, but even so, the coat seemed such a far-fetched idea. Her father had always told her that poverty and the fear of losing an animal or crops bred strange notions and not to dismiss the power of faith. At the same time, her little knowledge of Mr McCarthy made her doubt if he had a belief in its powers.

Mary set aside her journal and lay on her bed. Her eyes glazed over, hypnotised by the dust motes dancing and floating in the rays of the evening sun as they streaked their way across the room. She thought of Eoin. Meg was the source of all knowledge in the household and Mary hoped she was right about Eoin. She had noticed him in the distance when she was walking with

Beth and Eileen and had hurried back to the house after saying goodbye, nervous in case he caught up with her. At sixteen her experience of boys her own age was limited, but had she been astute enough, she would have realised Eoin's knowledge of the opposite sex was just as lacking. He had been at boarding school for six years and the only females he encountered were his mother, sisters, and servants. Although Mary ranked in the latter category, she was nearly his own age, and more importantly, despite Mary's low opinion of herself, she was quite pretty. Eoin had also spied Mary in the distance, but he was beginning to recognise he made her nervous and had deliberately delayed his own evening stroll so as not to upset her further. That did not stop him from thinking about her at all hours of the day and night. He wanted to touch her skin and feel its softness, and from the moment he first stood close to her and inhaled her scent, a subtle muskiness, not quite masked by her soap, he craved to savour that fragrance again. Yet, he was intelligent enough to know his position in the household might make her feel intimidated.

He now avoided his father's eye as he entered the house, dodging the business in the yard. All his instincts told him no mere coat could work such miracles, but he was under orders to hide his disdain. He was well aware his father had no faith in the coat either, but pandered to the locals, enjoying the notoriety, and if an animal appeared to get well, who was he to discount the coat's power? He had seen a light appear in Mary's room and the younger three siblings were all preparing for bed, so fed up and restless, he went in search of his older sister, Eimear. She was nowhere to be found which, these days, was not unusual. Bored, Eoin headed out once more towards the town.

Once Mary heard Eoin leave, she went downstairs to the children's playroom. The brightness of the long summer evenings made sleep impossible, and the children needed attention until exhaustion overcame them. Although Mary enjoyed them, after such a long hot day she would have liked some time to herself but the younger girls, in particular, continued to demand games played and stories read, accompanied by numerous snacks until bed could no longer be ignored.

Later, curled up in her own bed, Mary read Maureen's latest letter. Maureen, her cousin from nearby Clare Island, was in America with her older brother John, and her letters told of a land of excitement and golden opportunity. Once her English was sufficiently fluent, Mary's long-term plan was not to stay in England but to travel further afield to the States. She intended to work and save all her money until she was in a comfortable position to join Maureen. The letter was full of news. John had a new job. He was now working down at the docks and Maureen had just acquired a position in a boarding house. Despite herself, Mary grimaced at the thought of a boarding house but knew all immigrants had to take what was offered until they found their feet. Her reverie was interrupted by a disturbance downstairs and the loud voice of Joe McCarthy reverberated through the house.

'Get to bed, Eimear, I will talk to you in the morning, and you are not to leave this house until I give you permission.'

Mary opened her door and peered out. Two floors below she could see the teacher, red-faced and glowering, his stance exuding a power she had not seen before. Eimear stared back rebelliously for some seconds, before turning and rushing up the stairs. Puzzled, Mary closed the door gently. In the short time she had known Eimear, she had never seen her display such defiance to her father. She was curious to discover what had occurred, perhaps be of help, if Eimear needed a friend.

Chapter 5

A *nna knew her experiences in Mayo had shaped her future. Maturity had given her an insight into the actions of that naïve and damaged young girl and a knowledge that she had hurt, not just herself, but Beth and many others. Reading about her life and what had occurred was not easy and she felt demeaned as she came to life on the page. The layers that she had grown to protect herself from her past, cracked and splintered as she read on.*

Anna was very tired, that hot, early summer evening, and was glad to escape to the attic. Yet, sleep was elusive as the attic retained the heat of the day and the only breeze came through the partially opened doorway. Mrs Walshe was slowly recovering but was very weak, and according to Dr McMahon, it would be some weeks before she would be fit to leave her bed.

'At her age, it will take time to get her energy back. She needs to stay in bed resting. Lots of fluid and warm soup,' he instructed. 'I will call again next week but contact me if you are worried.'

As the evening waned Anna brought up some soup to Mrs Walshe as directed by the doctor. She checked on her a short while later and was pleased to see an empty bowl and that Mrs Walshe appeared to be in a deep, comfortable sleep. Restless, she wandered back to the kitchen, but nothing was amiss. Reluctantly, she climbed the narrow stairs to the attic room. Lying on her bed she dozed in the heat of the evening, but soon the dulcet tones of the piano seeped up the stairs, and she crept onto the tiny landing to hear more. The music flowed through her, and she closed her eyes, all her emotions stirred by the enchantment wrought by his gifted fingers. As another tune commenced, a lively one this time, she sang to herself whispering nonsense words as the melody took hold. A voice penetrated her private celebration, and she heard Fr Matthew call,

'Who is that singing? Such a lovely voice.'

'Sorry, Father, so sorry. I didn't mean to interrupt you.'

'No, no come down, I love accompaniment.'

Slowly Anna descended the stairs, reluctance apparent in every step, Mrs Walshe's warnings ringing in her ears. She did not want to be sent back home. She needed to learn English and obtain her ticket to England and the future.

'Come, come, don't be shy. Let me play something and you sing along.'

Anna sidled slowly into the room and stood by the piano as Fr Matthew took his seat. His hands danced along the keys and Anna watched in fascination as he played first one melody, before seamlessly segueing into another.

'Now, hum to this one, sing if you can.'

Unsure, Anna began, but with his encouragement, she became more confident, and together they spent a happy hour enjoying each other's talent. She did not see him the following evening or the next but on Sunday, he asked her to sit with him after dinner. Mrs Walshe was still unable to rise from her bed and Anna was pleased at the thought of some company to while away a Sunday evening.

Once dinner was over and the table cleared, Anna braced herself and knocked on the study door, before peering cautiously around. Fr Matthew nodded, indicating she should enter. Slowly Anna walked across the room, slightly nervous, aware Mrs Walshe would not approve. Nevertheless, she sat on the chair next to Fr Matthew and while he played, she sang along as best she could. On the surface, the evening was as pleasant as before, but Anna recounted later to Beth, that although she could not describe it, she thought he seemed a little different.

'His face was more flushed, and I thought he might be getting the flu like Mrs Walshe. It was only later, Beth, when I was in bed, that I remembered the empty brandy bottle on the dining sideboard and his ruddy complexion made me pause, made me think. I was reminded of me da and how he would look when he came back from the pub. And then there was the sherry, Beth. I wasn't sure what to do.'

'Anna, this is wonderful,' enthused Fr. Matthew. 'I think we should celebrate this newfound delight for both of us. Yes, a sherry, my dear. We will both have a sherry.'

'Oh, no, Father, I don't drink alcohol. Me mother would kill me if I did.'

'Nonsense, dear, a little sherry will help you sleep.'

Unable to protest further Anna accepted the drink wincing at first at the taste, but gradually relaxing, and quite enjoying it. A little tingle of adventure flickered at something so daring but it was speedily quenched. She was slightly taken aback when she noticed how Fr Matthew had a somewhat larger glass, which was finished quite quickly, and then further replenished.

'Thank you, Father, that was nice. Goodnight now, I do need to be up early in the morning.'

Anna rose and scurried upstairs, relieved he didn't insist she stayed longer.

The comfortable bed welcomed a now tired and slightly fuzzy-headed Anna. She sank gratefully into its warmth. The extra work while Mrs Walshe recovered, combined with the evening with Fr Matthew, not to mention the sherry, allowed sleep to envelop her in seconds. She awoke with a jump; the darkness was so intense it was impossible to ascertain what startled her. Then she heard it again, a creak on the stairs, footsteps slowly ascending. She was rigid in the bed, her imagination running riot, unable to fathom who or what would come through the door. The looming silhouette revealed Fr Matthew, slightly unsteady on his feet.

'Fr, Fr, what are you doing here?' was the shocked whisper from Anna.

'Why, Anna, I need to talk to you.'

'Talk to me now, at night?'

'Why yes, my dear. The night shadows can make discussion easier. Thoughts and actions we cannot contemplate in daylight are made possible when the sun sets on another day. Within the dim light, there is no awkwardness and no blushes.'

An innocent Anna, her dark curls tumbling around her head, her every fibre and instinct screaming, *this is wrong*, but years of training insisting a priest does no evil, stammered a reply.

'Ye... ye... yes, Fr, eh, Fr, what do you want to ask me?'

Fr Matthew sat on the edge of the bed and enfolded one small hand in his own.

'Are we working you too hard, Anna? Your hands should be soft, not calloused from housework. Tell me, dear, do you really want to go away to England or even further afield? Would you not prefer to stay here and settle down, maybe have children? Perhaps marry a local farmer or even a shopkeeper?'

'No, Father, I want to go away with my friend Beth.'

'Why, Anna, you will meet all manner of men. They will be unkind to you in many ways. The local teacher can find you a husband here and I can help you understand your duties.'

Anna had no idea what he was talking about, but she was aware that his hand was now under the blanket and caressing her foot. Even as she recognised this fact, his fingers began to trace a pattern further up her leg.

She jumped up and hissed, 'Stop, stop, Father. Don't do that. Go, please go now.'

Mrs Walshe thought she heard Anna call out but was unsure. She had heard and dreamt so many strange things as her temperature soared and waned. Too weak to leave her bed, she cowered under the covers, praying that if Anna were in trouble her guardian angel would take care of her. Her unquestioned belief in the existence of such figures brought some measure of comfort. Fuddled dreams meandered through her fevered brain, eventually settling on Patricia, the first girl who came to the presbytery ten years ago. Mrs Walshe was new in the position. Her husband had died two years previously and both her daughters were living in Dublin. Always devout, she had offered her services once she heard Fr Matthew had been left alone after the sudden departure of his housekeeper. Patricia had been small and slight, rather nervous, and skittish. Mrs Walshe was never sure if Fr Matthew had interfered with her. He had certainly paid her a lot of attention, insisting he could help improve her English and, in hindsight, perhaps a little too tactile. Patricia's brother had knocked on the door early one morning, and after a heated exchange, had insisted Patricia gather her belongings and return home with him.

It was the arrival of Joanne that confirmed to Mrs Walshe that Fr Matthew was not all he should be. She shivered when she remembered Joanne that fateful morning. Blood streamed down her leg as she sobbed hysterically. Mrs Walshe tended to her as well as she was able, unsure whom to turn to for help. Who would believe any accusation she made? Fr Matthew was highly regarded in the town and there would be disbelief that he would succumb to any temptation. He was regularly seen on his knees and kept his interest in young girls well hidden. The refrain from the town gossips was an insistence that some of the girls, 'were no better than they should be.' Any aspersions or insinuations were treated with disdain. Mrs Walshe resolved that no other girl would be violated under her watch, even if they never learned English. What she hadn't considered was her age and that at 70, how even a minor illness, let alone the severe infection she had contracted, would leave her weak and unable to help. There was no sound now from the attic, not even the soft pad of footsteps. Murmuring a litany of prayers for guidance, a restless sleep finally overcame her, and it was morning before she spoke to Anna.

Anna was late preparing breakfast and relieved Fr Matthew had left the house before she descended the stairs. Dazed and shocked, to such an extent she perfunctorily performed her duties as though nothing was amiss. The tray she prepared for Mrs Walshe betrayed her inner turmoil, as both the teacup and milk were missing, and her distraught features could not hide her agitation. Mrs Walshe held out feeble arms and Anna gratefully sank into them.

'Hush, don't cry, don't speak. I think I know what he did or tried to do. In your own time tell me about it and I will know how best to help you.'

Anna could no longer hold back and cried convulsively for some minutes before settling into a sobbing that tore at Mrs Walshe's heart.

'He came to my room. He, he, was rubbing my foot and my, my leg. He kept telling me I should stay here and marry someone. I have no idea really what he was talking about. I was just so scared and uncomfortable. Then his hand moved further up onto my thigh and then and then…'

Mrs Walshe interrupted Anna, gasping quickly,

'Did he hurt you, Anna, force himself on you?'

'No, no, he just rubbed my leg and kept muttering. I was so scared though, it made me so embarrassed and so uneasy.'

Mrs Walshe took Anna's hand in her own.

'You understand now, lass, why I wanted you to stay in the kitchen. Now, Anna, remember you have done no wrong and I promise to keep you safe. I will help you to leave but it will take some organising. You must keep out of his way until then. There is no lock on your bedroom door but take up a chair from the dining room, anything that will make a lot of noise.'

As Anna convulsed and sobbed in turn, Mrs Walshe felt a swell of righteous anger surge through her. Despite being intensely devout with a profound faith in her Church's teaching, she was an intelligent woman and was able to separate this man's actions from the basic tenets of her belief.

'Anna, do you know where he has gone?'

'No, I was late getting up and he left before I came downstairs.'

'Good, help me get dressed, I have plans to make.'

'No, Mrs Walshe, you're not well enough yet,' protested Anna.

'I am well enough for this. My God will give me strength. Get me my clothes,' and glancing at the tea tray, 'then go fetch a cup for my tea. I need a cup before I do anything else.'

Anna put down the manuscript more than a little surprised at how emotional she felt. Mrs Walshe had been her sanctuary and a veil of loneliness descended upon her.

'How had she fared after I left the presbytery?' she wondered. 'She gave me more consideration than my own mother. Oh, Beth, it was not your story to

relate, especially to Mary.' A tear welled, threatening to trickle down Anna's cheek. Brushing it away before it made headway, Anna switched out the light, a firm resolution taking hold. 'There is no way Mary is publishing my private story.'

Chapter 6

Anna was drifting towards oblivion when old memories surged, and her heart started to pound. The intervening years disappeared, and she was back in 1933. Was it possible Beth had disclosed confidences she believed would always be private? The realisation dawned that if Beth had revealed her personal intimate details, that despite refusing publication, many others would still read the manuscript. Mary, of course, possibly her husband and family, Eileen and Eimear, maybe their friends and families would all be privy to her innermost secrets, and her life would be on display through Beth's eyes. She blushed with a humiliation that before long was usurped by anger, quickly followed by shame. Although her friendship with Beth was long severed, Anna still felt guilty imagining Beth capable of such a betrayal of confidence. To be swamped by such a mixture of emotions left Anna totally drained.

Anna ran down to the cottage. She was still distraught inside but the comfort from Mrs Walshe was like a blanket enfolding her, a shield from the horror that threatened to overwhelm her.

Both Bríd and Bill McDonald were in the garden tending to a pristine lawn emblazoned with flowering trees and bushes. They ushered Anna inside and served her tea while Bríd read the letter, from time-to-time, raising her eyes to look at Anna.

'Right, young Anna, I need to chat to Bill here and then write a reply to Lily, Mrs Walshe. Will you please go into the garden and wait for a little while, I will be with you shortly?'

Anna wandered outside but was unable to relax. She paced back and forth, pausing every so often to examine and smell the variety of blooms. She was surrounded by wildflowers at home, but cultivated roses and violets, climbing clematis, and bowls of petunia, were rarely seen. Gardens such as this did not exist. The land surrounding the cottages was for growing potatoes or carrots but never flowers grown just for their beauty alone. The breeze carried their scent but also the hiss of heated discussion from within the cottage. Eventually, Mr McDonald strode outside, threw a pointed grimace in her direction, and stormed off towards the beach.

'Come here, Anna,' beckoned Bríd McDonald, her voice gentle but authoritative.

'I am going up to the presbytery myself, so stay here until I get back.'

'I thought I was to bring a reply to Mrs Walshe?' responded Anna.

'Well, I know she said that, but it is best if I go. I won't be long.'

Anna watched Mrs McDonald as she puffed her way up the hill, her excess weight keenly felt on the steep ascent. At a loss, she continued to roam around the garden, but the fascination of the floral displays waned as she pondered on what was going to happen, worried at the prospect of seeing Fr Matthew again. She found a hidden nook and sat on a rock to wait. In the distance, she could see a solitary figure she assumed was Mr McDonald, pacing along the beach, head bent against the stiffening wind.

Mrs McDonald was in a quandary as she puffed along. Her instinct was to help Anna and provide a place of succour for her until a new position could be sorted, but that wish presented difficulties. She herself had no time for many of the clergy but especially, Fr Matthew. She had heard enough in confidence from her friend Lily Walshe to have scant respect for him. Of course, in a small town, she obeyed all the social rules and obligations and was seen at weekly Mass and other religious events, but that was just for show. Her husband, Bill, however, was much more devout. He would hear no word spoken against Fr Matthew, dismissing all as unfounded rumours to denigrate a good man. If Anna were to stay with her for any length of time, there would be tension in the house and Bill was difficult to live with at the best of times. Already, he had stormed off so a chat with Lily was needed.

Mrs Walshe was sitting in the kitchen sipping tea when Bríd arrived. Lily's grey pallor and sunken cheeks gave Bríd pause for just a moment before she continued.

'A right to-do this is,' panted Bríd, as she hefted her large body onto a chair noisily dragged from under the table. 'Pour me a cup before we get down to the nitty-gritty.'

Lily obliged. She was not surprised to see Bríd as she knew her request would present difficulties for her. In Lily Walshe's opinion, Bill was morose and stubborn. How Bríd managed to apparently live with him in a semblance of contentment was a mystery. Lily suspected Bill's all too obvious piety was just for show, and his refusal to believe in any negative aspect pertaining to Fr Matthew enabled him to avoid questioning his own faith and belief.

'Lily, I want to help,' began Bríd, 'but you know what Bill is like. God knows he is difficult enough to live with, without another disagreement creating a further rift between us. He thinks these girls either concoct stories to be sensational or are the ones at fault. He refuses to have Anna in the house. I told him she had to stay for two days but I can't do more than that.'

Lily nodded thoughtfully. 'If you can do that, Bríd, I should have something sorted by then. So now, today is Thursday, isn't that, right? I am just all at sea with the days since I was sick. Anyway, by Saturday I am sure I will have something worked out. Sit here while I get a few bits and pieces together for her. She doesn't have much stuff anyway.'

Lily slowly climbed the stairs, leaning heavily on the banisters, her energy drained from her illness, sadness at the turn of events evident in the slump of her shoulders.

Anna was still sitting on the rock when Bríd returned. Her face was flushed from her exertion and her all too ample bosom heaved and wobbled with every stertorous breath.

'You are going to stay here for two days, Anna. Come inside now and I will show you where you will sleep.'

The cottage was small and warm from the glowing fire. Anna was shown to a little bedroom, more of a cupboard really, off the main room. There was no window, but a dim lamp penetrated the gloom outlining a small bed tucked against the far wall.

'You can sleep here. Lily, Mrs Walshe, will come to see you tomorrow or Saturday and let you know what plans have been made.'

Anna sank gratefully onto the bed; thankful she would not have to meet Fr Matthew that evening.

'I will make you something to eat now. Best if you have an early night before Mr McDonald returns.'

Anna ate quickly and retired to the bedroom as Mrs McDonald suggested. She dozed fitfully, as murmured voices from the main room, easily penetrating the thin walls, disrupted her slumber. The saccharine tones of Fr Matthew slid into her subconscious jerking her fully awake. She lay, barely breathing, the conversation from the other room clearly discernible.

'Bill, you know I did not lay a finger on that girl, or any girl for that matter.'

'Sure, I know that well, Father. I agree she took fright at the thought of the matchmaker.'

'Yes, and if she cannot agree to a match, it is best she returns with me and perfects her English. Mrs Walshe is very unwell again today; I worry about her. She should never have left her bed yesterday and the effort she made has cost her dearly. Really, that young girl is quite thoughtless, and I hope her actions will not set Mrs Walshe back.'

'What is going on here, Bill?' demanded Bríd McDonald, entering the living room. 'You woke me up with your mutterings.'

'Hush, woman, hush,' responded Bill. 'I had a word with Fr Matthew. It was all a misunderstanding. He returned here with me and will bring the young one back to the presbytery. She can look after Lily, who is extremely unwell again, no doubt due to worry. The girl can take care of her and learn English, as originally agreed.'

'No, no I won't have it,' was Bríd's angry response.

'Oh, my dear, Bríd, it is not your decision. You do well instead to remember your marriage vows and obey your husband. He is the one in charge.'

Fr Matthew's cloying interruption did not deter Bríd.

'She stays here.'

Bill rose from his chair. 'I don't often put my foot down, Bríd, but this time I insist. The girl returns with Fr Matthew, and I hope at the earliest opportunity you will see fit to go to confession. Shame on you to harbour such scandalous thoughts about Father.'

Anna listened to the exchange with dread, feeling a little like a leaf blowing in a breeze. Decisions were being made about her, orders that she had to follow, with no input from herself. She crossed her fingers and wordlessly beseeched Bríd to defy the demands of the two men and insist she stays. After some minutes, she eased out of bed and dressed quietly, accepting that she had no choice but to return to the priest's house. She opened the door into a room oozing with tension. The smile on Fr Matthew's face did not reach his eyes. His unctuous tones did not hide how they glinted with a rage that made her inwardly quake.

'Well, Anna, what a fuss you are causing and with poor Mrs Walshe so unwell. Such anxiety will not help her recover.'

Fr Matthew reached a hand towards Anna, as Bill snapped,

'You're to return with Fr Matthew.'

Resigned to the inevitable, but refusing to be totally cowed, Bríd moved across the room and put an arm around Anna.

'I will walk down tomorrow morning to see how you are, and Lily too.'

'That won't be necessary,' spat Fr Matthew, and almost in unison, Bill issued a rare order,

'You are to stay here, Bríd.'

From experience, Bríd knew that Bill was not to be trifled with when he was overcome by belligerence. His obsequiousness in front of Fr Matthew was disturbing and the resultant glare from Bríd, had no impact. Any implication that he was not in charge of his own house, especially in front of the priest, reinforced his determination to ensure Bríd follow his diktats.

Anna walked sedately behind Fr Matthew and silently prayed Mrs Walshe had not relapsed as he maintained. Unfortunately, Lily Walshe was extremely ill and for the next few days Anna nursed her as though she were her own mother. Pneumonia had taken a firm hold on Lily and for the following five days, Anna worked tirelessly, often through the night, as Lily battled for her life. At times, Mrs Walshe was agitated, grasping Anna's hand and muttering incoherently. Anna's soft lullabies soothed her as she dampened her brow to ease her temperature. Sometimes as Anna dozed, her mother's face replaced that of Mrs Walshe, and she had to physically shake the image away. The care that exuded from Lily was the antithesis of the indifference she had sensed from her own mother. First Beth's mother and now Lily, made her feel she had value, but against her will, she sometimes longed for her own mother's smile, the one she distantly remembered before despair took hold and quenched the light in her eyes.

Anna rarely saw Fr Matthew. When she did, he did not bother her, yet his speculative look put her on edge. The chair she placed at her bedroom door remained undisturbed but a couple of times she was sure she heard footsteps on the stairs. On the few occasions they bumped into each other, he studiously ignored her, beyond a curt enquiry as to the health of Mrs Walshe.

Anna was not so foolish that she relaxed her guard, but the tiredness from the disturbed nights and long days nursing Lily Walshe made her less vigilant.

Chapter 7

As Eileen read she gained an insight into the friendship between Mary and Eimear. She had never been close to Eimear herself but knew Mary had formed a strong bond with her despite their different circumstances.

Mary hoped she didn't seem too inquisitive, but she was curious to know the cause of the argument between Eimear and her father. Eimear had remained closeted in her room, but Mary's questioning of Meg as to the cause left her none the wiser.

'Sorry, Mary, I know no more than you about Eimear's argument with her father. I think it has to do with some lad she was seeing. Her father doesn't approve but that is all I know. Mary, do you mind but I don't feel too well. Would you sort the children's tea this evening so I can go home a bit early?'

'Of course, Meg. You go home now. I can handle everything here.'

Mary busied herself in the kitchen, not too disappointed her own plans were altered. The usual walk that evening in the July sun with Eileen and Beth would have been nice but there was always another day. Maybe, she could pop down for a quick stroll later if the children were settled. She assumed that Anna, as usual, would not be there. She pondered why she felt relieved when it was just the three of them. She knew Eileen felt the same although they were both reluctant to be too critical. Anna introduced a discordant note. If she weren't grumbling about Mrs Walshe, she was complaining about the food, the weather, her confinement. Regularly she linked arms with Beth as if to isolate her from the group. Mary knew she was probably being a little too fanciful, but Anna had the effect of unsettling her. However, there was still a number of things to finish in the kitchen so it was increasingly likely there would be no walk tonight. Sighing audibly, Mary concentrated on preparing an omelette for the two younger children.

Eimear McCarthy, from the vantage point in her bedroom, watched Mary as she played hide-and-seek in the garden with her younger siblings. She was the teachers' eldest child and yet she was closeted in her bedroom like a ten-year-old. She had barely stirred since the argument with her father the previous evening. The door was tightly closed, and she huddled in the chair by the window. She had no wish to argue with her parents, especially her father, but his demands that she adhere to his will could not be countenanced. She had no idea how long she sat at the window, dusk, stealing the light as the sun began to go down went unnoticed. Only the deepening gloom and the silence from the garden below, made her realise it must have been some hours. Hunger forced Eimear to leave her bedroom and step quietly down the stairs and into the kitchen. Mary was tidying up after the children's tea.

'Hello, Mary. Strange to see you in here,' murmured Eimear politely.

'I said I would help out. Meg was unwell and had to go home early.'

'Were you not expecting to go for a walk with some of the other girls?'

A polite enquiry from Eimear. An attempt at conversation although her mind was on other things.

'Yes, but that doesn't matter. If it is not too late when I am finished here, I might wander down to the beach. Otherwise, I will see them tomorrow.'

'Do you always walk along the beach?'

'Yes, probably we do. The beach is quite stunning and so refreshing in the evening but sometimes we stroll along the pier. For a change, we might saunter up a boreen.'

Eimear looked thoughtfully at Mary for a few moments before asking her to join her upstairs.

'Upstairs, in your room?' queried Mary.

'Yes, please. I want to ask you something.'

Surprised, Eimear led the way with Mary following. Their conversation up to now had been comfortable. A tentative friendship but not intimate. Eimear appeared to have a busy social life. She went out most evenings and slept late in the morning. Although she was always very friendly, Mary felt they were worlds apart.

'Please sit down,' said Eimear, indicating the chair at the dressing table. Eimear sat once more in the window seat. As her story unfolded Mary knew that whatever faint hopes she had harboured, she would not be leaving the house that night. Eimear, usually so sure and confident, hesitantly told Mary of her predicament.

'Mary. I, eh, I don't want to put you in an, erm, awkward position but I have no one else to ask.' Mary gazed expectantly as Eimear wrestled with her next words.

'Will you deliver a letter for me, please? You will need to do it on your own, you cannot tell anyone. That is important, no one must know, especially my parents.'

Eimear paused, eyes down, fingers uneasily twitching the folds in her dress.

Mary, believing she had no choice, nodded reluctantly, nerves already starting to tingle at the thought of the chore ahead.

'I'll accompany you when you take the younger ones out for a walk tomorrow morning. You can then slip away for a few minutes.'

Mary nodded again, anxiety creasing her brow, worried Eimear's parents would discover what she was doing.

After confiding in Mary, Eimear slowly undressed for bed, brushing her long dark locks in the ritual taught from when she was a child. As she lay down to sleep, she fought a rising panic.

Had she been foolish to include Mary? She barely knew her, and she was here to work for her mother and father. Yet, what other option was there? Confiding in Mary was her only choice, but could she trust her?

Her snap decision now made, aware there was no other alternative, Eimear tried and failed to go to sleep. She lay with eyes closed but sleep was elusive as she wrestled with her decision. Disclosing her problem to Mary was a risk, but she had no one else. Over the past few weeks, she had sensed a connection to Mary and a growing friendship. Their circumstances were very different, but she could tell there was a steadfastness to Mary not unlike that within Tommy. Eimear felt she could trust her despite the risk she was making her take. No longer able to dwell on her current predicament, with a supreme effort, she purposely switched her thoughts. She focused on her youth and was transported to the noisy grimy streets of Liverpool.

She had been born and reared for much of her childhood in that busy town, but her Irish ancestry was not forgotten. Her paternal grandfather had done well in that inhospitable land for the Irish, becoming owner and landlord of a substantial number of properties. Yet he was not the proud landlord of neatly kept suburban residences, but the keeper of dwellings for the desperate, the refuge of the sad flotsam that landed daily on the shores of Britain in search of a better life. He regularly attended the courts as an intermediary and interpreter on behalf of the unending stream of Irish men arrested for drunkenness and other petty crimes. He would mitigate dispassionately on their behalf, aware, that but for life's fortune, he could be in their shoes, illiterate, poverty-stricken, and unable to communicate because English had yet to be learned. Eimear's grandmother, Margaret, was third-generation Irish and her connection to the land of her grandparents was sketchy. Her father was a solicitor and, as such, encountered Eimear's grandfather. He was certainly not an automatic choice of husband for Margaret. Despite his now obvious wealth, his accent and manners hinted at poorer roots and the circles within which he moved were a reminder of his own struggle from disadvantage. Margaret was fascinated by him from their first encounter. His tales of Ireland, a land she had never visited but felt she knew, kept her enthralled. Whereas most of her father's acquaintances were boring and often condescending, Eimear's grandfather entertained her with his deep, but often quirky insight into the rich and varied but desperate lives of the Irish, who resided in his many properties. It was with many misgivings from her father and horror from her mother that Margaret's marriage finally took place.

The family grew in both stature and wealth and all the children were well-educated. Eimear's father was sent to Ireland and qualified as a teacher. He returned to Liverpool and married, but the yen to live in Ireland, the country of his forebears, never left him. When Eimear was nine the family relocated to Mayo. A large house was purchased quite some distance from the nearest town. Eimear's mother Jean found she could not abide the silence and longed for the bustle of city life. Consequently, they moved again to the local village, Kilford, so she could be 'near the flags.' It was a sensible choice as both her parents had now procured positions as primary school teachers in the town. Jean was extremely fortunate to be allowed to work as the new Irish State blocked women from working in the public service once they married. However, the lack of teachers in the west of Ireland enabled her to procure special permission to teach, even with her quite basic grasp of the Irish language. Of course, she earned less than a man, despite being more experienced than many, but that was Ireland in the 1920s.

Eimear's destiny was to marry well, but whilst waiting for a suitable match, she too trained as a primary school teacher at Galway University. In the meantime, her father set his sights on Willie, the son of the local publican, who was himself a schoolteacher, but would doubtless also inherit the public house. Parents can decide their children's future but the children themselves often upset the pattern and so it was with Eimear.

So, Eimear confided in Mary and that is how they became so close. Interesting, thought Eileen, how that bond endured and sustained through the years.

Chapter 8

Beth was restless and it took a supreme effort to begin to read. Despite her best intentions, her concentration waned as her thoughts returned to lunch the previous day. She could not control the swell of resentment that suffused her again as she recalled Anna blithely walking across the hotel floor to their table. To further confuse her, that resentment was quickly followed by a deep sense of sorrow at a friendship now lost. That sadness had lingered as she wandered home. Her tea grew cold as she attempted to recall the details, she had given Mary.

'Had she given Mary too much information? Had her anger at Anna coloured her perceptions?'

These thoughts tumbled through Beth's mind, and savagely swiping at her wet eyes, she began to read, determined to be fair and objective in her assessment.

Beth sat in the convent garden, restless and irritated. She liked Eileen well enough, but she seemed to be constantly moaning and pining for home. Beth also missed her mother and father, but common sense dictated she was not leaving home forever. She was anxious to develop a proficiency in English and embrace a new world full of opportunity, away from the stultifying atmosphere of the islands. She was aware her family circumstances were slightly better than the other three girls. Besides having a small farm, her father was the owner of a local shop that catered for the needs of the surrounding families. It sold everything from butter to nails and from boots to pints. Yet it was the culture within her family that was the most important aspect of her upbringing. Her mother, in particular, read avidly and encouraged Beth and her siblings to do the same. Family meals were often hotbeds of discussion, and the fertile ground was laid for Beth to spread her wings. When she returned home it would be with confidence and with knowledge of her place in the world.

The exasperation Beth felt from Eileen's regular blubbering bouts was intensified by the attention she received from Sr Cornelius. Whereas Sr Cornelius could not express a civil word to Eileen and appeared to target her for her obvious loneliness, exacerbated by her morose appearance, she constantly engaged Beth in conversation.

'Beth, your knowledge of English has really improved in the short time you have been here. You are the kind of girl we need in the convent. Have you ever thought of entering the religious life yourself? The life of a nun can be extremely rewarding. You know, we would educate you to a high standard. You could be a teacher here in our school and be able to see your parents and family regularly. There is many a worse life for a girl. I truly believe you would be a good example to our students. You could show them they have choices in life and not just settle for any job until they marry.'

Beth replied as graciously as she could but the continual pressure from Sr Cornelius to consider a life in the convent was straining her effort at politeness.

It was a mid-July evening and the heat of the day still lingered. Beth expected Mary would arrive shortly for their walk. She hoped Anna might turn up as well. Sometimes she felt like a cog at the centre of a wheel trying to manage the other three girls. Jostling Eileen out of her constant misery began at first light. Easing Mary's anxiety in case the eldest lad in the teacher's house spoke to her was an added exasperation. Yet, for the life of her, Beth could not see what the problem was. Added to those irritations was the worry about

Anna. She rarely saw her and knew she was dissatisfied with her allocation to the presbytery. Her English was not improving as it should, and the chance to chat privately was almost impossible as Eileen, and often Mary, usually joined them.

Beth and Anna had been close friends from the moment they first sat beside each other in school. As they grew older Beth came to understand how unalike were their homes. She wished she could speak to her dad about her concerns, but it was not until she was much older that she could articulate her worries. Her uneasiness centred around the pub situated at the rear of their shop. How could she explain, when she barely understood it herself, that her family's comfort was based, in part, on the misery that existed in other homes, where the little money they had was swallowed almost nightly in the pub.

Beth was in and out of the shop all the time and that is where she regularly encountered Anna's father, Peadar. He usually sauntered in around 8 o'clock each evening, once the veil of dusk began to settle. Sometimes, if his pockets were full, he could be there from mid-afternoon. Beth knew his ritual and that is what disturbed her. The stool in the corner by the turf fire was considered Peadar's. One glare was enough to shift anyone foolish enough to occupy it. Peadar's first action was to nod to Beth's dad, a signal to commence pulling his pint. Once seated, he would place his cap on the table and produce his pipe. Tamping down the tobacco with gnarled fingers, crowned with orange-tipped fingernails, he waited patiently until his pint appeared. His patched and well-worn Aran sweater gave testament to long days working the fields in all kinds of weather. His brown boots of scarred and crinkled leather scattered mud across the floor. The first pint was lowered almost in one swallow and the second disappeared almost as quickly. Depending on his mood he tapped along to the local fiddle player. Invariably he was one of the last to leave, and with pockets empty, he would join the stragglers as they weaved their way along the rocky road home, shoulders hunched for warmth against the cold night air. The jingle of the till played the final music note of the night.

Beth was protective of Anna, aware of the tension in her home and the demands of her father. Anna scurried around him afraid of his wrath. She did his bidding, but defiance flashed in her eyes. Her mother was cowed, unable to stand up to his bullying, appeasement, in every movement. Anna's experience as a child moulded and nurtured a disdain for her mother who did not protect her from her father's often violent, rage. Beth's family, but especially Beth's mother, gave Anna comfort and allowed her a glimpse of how families should be. Yet Beth was constantly puzzled by her mother's refrain when she spoke of Anna's father.

'Poor oul Peadar. Beth, look after Anna because God knows, no one in that house knows how to.'

'What do you mean, Mam?'

'Never you mind. Just remember things are not always clear. Life can be hard for many of us. Now, take these with you when you call over to Anna later.'

Reluctantly Beth carried her mother's offering of scones over to Anna's cottage. Sometimes it was a piece of ham but more usually a dozen eggs. She dreaded the chore. The fleeting flash of contempt in Anna's eyes or the submissive 'thanks' from Anna's mother made her cringe. She could never decide what was worse, and why she was swamped with shame, as though she shouldered some of the blame.

When Anna spoke of her own mother, Beth sensed she resented and despised her. Contempt and bitterness at her circumstances gained a sure footing as Anna grew older. It was only with maturity and experience, in later years, that Beth realised few women had a choice and Anna's mother was too cowed and numbed from life's hardships. With hindsight, Beth was able to articulate the place many women occupied when poverty and drudgery was the norm. Dependent on their husbands, and dominated by a Church that subordinated them, they subjugated their own lives in the hope their families could thrive. Inured by years of abuse they became shadows of who they were or could have been. Beth was unaware whether Anna ever came to such an understanding but certainly, Anna, at a young age, could not have comprehended that.

Beth spied Anna now as she slowly traversed the hill to the convent. Her head was bent, and her shoulders slumped. Depression shrouded her like a heavyweight. Where was the Anna who could never stand still, who swayed along to her own rhythm keeping time to a tune that only she could hear? As Anna approached, Beth turned towards Eileen.

'Eileen, I need to speak to Anna alone today.'

'But what, what about our walk?'

Beth was astonished to see Eileen's lips tremble with a silent rebuke. Shrugging off any feeling of discomfort she firmly responded.

'Today I need to speak to Anna alone. We can have a walk later if you want but I am sure Mary will be along shortly.'

Anna reached the two waiting girls. Her eyes were swollen and her cheeks blotchy. Without a backward glance, Beth took her hand and turned towards the beach walk.

'Oh, Anna, I am so glad to see you but what is going on? Is the presbytery so awful? That Mrs Walshe looks like a right auld biddy.'

Anna made no reply as she slumped down on a rock. Her expression was glazed as though she was looking deep inside herself. She seemed not to have heard Beth's words and to be unaware of Beth, now kneeling beside her, beseeching an answer. In a monotone she muttered,

'It's not Mrs Walshe, Beth. It's the priest. I know that now. Mrs Walshe was only trying to protect me by keeping me out of his way. He came to my room, Beth. He was rubbing my foot and…'

Anna shivered and exclaimed.

'Oh, Beth, I didn't know what to do.' Anna's voice now became so low Beth strained to hear her.

'He is a priest. What do I do? Mrs Walshe tried to get me a safe place to stay but he made the man in the house change his mind.'

Anna's tone was muffled as though a scarf covered her mouth, her words staccato, almost unrelated, and Beth strained to connect her words to make coherent sense.

'Mrs Walshe warned me, that is why she barely let him see me, but once she got sick, I had to be around.'

The flow of words quietened, and Beth took her hand.

'But what exactly happened, Anna? I mean, he didn't, did he…?'

Ignoring the interruption, Anna continued,

'I could sense from Mrs Walshe's reaction that there is a lot she is not telling me. But she is sick now and I have had to scurry around to try and avoid him while I also look after her, but he came back early yesterday. The way he looks at me, Beth...' her words trailed away, and it was some minutes before Anna mumbled once more.

'I just hate it here. I want to leave now.'

Beth felt helpless, unable to grasp the enormity of what Anna had said and implied. Eventually she stuttered,

'The priest, Anna? Fr Matthew?' Beth shivered, as a vacant gaze from eyes devoid of expression turned towards her. Beth felt as though Anna was surrounded by fog, impossible to penetrate, her words making only partial sense. Anna seemed to realise Beth could barely follow her and in a slow, colourless tone resumed her story.

'I told Mrs Walshe the next morning about how Fr Matthew had come to my room. She was worried but also still sick. I brought her some tea and that revitalised her a bit. She looked so pale and tired but yet was extremely alert. She spoke rapidly as she handed me an envelope.

'Anna, do you know the white-washed cottage on the edge of the town,' she said, 'the one facing the sea? It is the McDonalds' home now. They moved there once their son took over the farm.'

Beth nodded at the description. She had noticed the cottage herself on the few times she had been out and about.

'You mean the one with the red front door and the flowerpots? Huge pots spilling over with flowers?'

'That's the one,' said Anna. 'Anyway, Mrs Walshe said her friend Bríd McGrath was married to a man called Bill McDonald. Mrs Walshe and Bríd have known each other since they were in school, a long time ago now.'

Anna paused for a moment, shoulders hunched, pensive for seconds before continuing,

'Beth, Mrs Walshe told me to deliver a letter to her and to wait for a reply.'

Anna hesitated once more, and with great difficulty, Beth refrained from urging her to continue, realising that Anna needed to sort out her thoughts.

'Mrs Walshe told me to hurry. *We need to sort this matter out before he gets back,* she said, so I ran almost the full way to the McDonalds' house. Bríd was lovely but Bill was a different matter.'

Anna gazed out to sea, lost in thought. Beth watched, shaken by Anna's calm, but unable to fully understand why, until Anna began to speak once more.

Beth walked back to the convent after her chat with Anna, agitated and perplexed, analysing all she had just heard. The realisation that those she had been taught to revere and place on a pedestal were, after all, just mortal men, combined with Anna's distress, was almost too much to absorb. Sr Benedict saw Beth return, but before she could allocate any chore, Beth announced she was unwell and going to bed. Her features still registered the shock of Anna's news and Sr Benedict agreed without question that she could retire early. When Eileen entered the room sometime later, Beth was already curled up between the sheets. She feigned sleep, ignoring Eileen's clatter as she prepared for bed with her usual thunderous noise.

Chapter 9

*E*ileen sighed. *'This is a difficult read,'* she mumbled to herself. *'I know I was that girl. I remember that pain and loneliness but was I really such a weepy shambles, clinging to everyone?'*

She could feel her cheeks flame but pacified herself that perhaps Mary had exaggerated her character. 'She did say she would embellish the story, after all,' mumbled Eileen. Despite that consoling thought, it was with great difficulty Eileen began to read once more.

Eileen was quite sure Beth was awake and deliberately ignoring her presence. Either way, she made no attempt to be quiet. Disgruntled and out of sorts, she eventually climbed into bed and pondered the day's events. Once 6 o'clock tea was finished, the evening had stretched long and boring until bedtime. She had wallowed in self-pity as she watched Beth and Anna walk towards the beach. Despite the discomfort she felt in their company, she could not help feeling envious of their friendship. They did not appear to be their usual jaunty selves but there was still an aura around them that excluded others. Also, they had an elegance together. Beth's flaming hair and Anna's black locks intermingled as heads bent, they strode along in unison. Alone, Eileen wished Mary would appear. She had debated whether to walk towards the teachers' house but that seemed such a pointless effort. If Mary had been able to get away, she would have arrived by now. The slight cramp at the pit of her stomach heralded the arrival of her monthly period, something she hated. It did not make her feel womanly as other girls indicated but, instead, she dreaded the possibility of stained sheets and the embarrassment of requesting a change.

Nuns were women so they must also experience this monthly inconvenience, thought Eileen, but instinctively she knew Sr Aideen, who managed the laundry, would frown disapprovingly at the reason for Eileen's request.

Eileen wandered into the convent grounds. They were not extensive but there was a nice, wooded area where she could sit and stay hidden from any nuns floating around. As usual, Eileen deliberately walked with shoulders slightly hunched and her hair draped over her face in a mistaken bid to be as unobtrusive as possible. However, there was no one in sight and she reached the small wooden bench in the wood with a sigh of relief. From her vantage point, she was able to watch the road on the off-chance Mary appeared.

Eileen sat quietly as she waited in vain for her friend. Daylight faded and a slight breeze whispered among the trees. She felt dejected and was glad of the privacy away from Beth's impatient gaze. Beth's obvious irritation embarrassed her. Eileen understood she seemed weak in her eyes, but inside she knew her own inner strength and did not feel belittled by her more than obvious emotions. The sacrifice her parents were making to enable her to learn English was an impetus to do her best. This knowledge did not prevent her from missing them and indulging in the odd mopey moment helped her cope. The love that had encircled her all through her early years sustained her. Anyway, like countless girls before her, there was no option. Farms were so small that it was a struggle to sustain more than one family and often elderly parents. Unless she married herself, her best chance was a good knowledge of English, so she had choices in either Dublin or abroad. Eileen believed she had a practicality that enabled her to accept that at times she was too sentimental, but despite outward appearances, she was also the possessor of an inner resolution and determination that would see her through. Yet, few seemed to recognise that fact. It disturbed her to think that missing home labelled her as weak, that an inability to hide her loneliness cast her as feeble and vulnerable. She was astute enough to realise she did not have the sparkle that wove effortlessly around Anna or the beauty that encircled Beth. Mary's steadiness and common sense made her comfortable, but she knew she could not compete with Mary's pretty face. The realisation that others saw her as plain and ungainly, reinforced almost daily by the nuns, initiated a further welling in her eyes which she viciously staunched by biting her nails. Eileen continued to sit as darkness closed in, shivering slightly but unable to move despite the chill, lost in her own isolated world.

It was dark when Eileen finally accepted that Mary was not going to show up and she slowly motivated herself to leave her wooded seclusion and make her way to bed. Sr Benedict stood like a sentry in the hallway and did not display the same pleasant manner she had shown Beth sometime earlier.

'If you have nothing to do, some time spent in the chapel would be beneficial. Pray for guidance, Eileen, so you can glean some idea of God's plan for you. Consider spending some time fasting as that always strengthens the mind.'

The sharp criticism stung Eileen, already in a state of early hormonal depression. The sight of Beth, apparently asleep, depressed her further.

Could she not have looked for me once Anna was gone? thought Eileen as she noisily prepared for bed.

Eileen's melancholy did not improve the following morning. She sauntered slowly to the laundry room before early Mass to ask Sr Aideen to provide clean sheets. Her cheeks glowed as she made her request and the cramps in her stomach did not ease as Sr Aideen insisted,

'Eileen, offer up any discomfort as penance for your sins. Also, try and be more aware of when such a function is due, so you can prepare in advance, and save the linen,' she admonished.

The gentle pat on Eileen's back and her offer of a hot cup of tea with a biscuit, belied Sr Aideen's stern words, and the usual prickling behind Eileen's eyes had to be rapidly quenched. The day slid by much the same as any other except for one thing, Beth was quiet, almost introspective, since her walk with Anna the previous night. Her refusal to discuss Anna and whatever was troubling her added to Eileen's feelings of isolation. She felt very much on the periphery as if everybody knew what was happening but her.

Even Mary had failed to show yesterday evening, she thought morosely.

Mary did not appear the following evening either. It was a warm balmy evening with just a hint of a breeze as Eileen and Beth wandered down to the seashore. They wandered aimlessly along the stony beach. At Beth's suggestion, they climbed up onto the dunes and followed the cliff path. As they awkwardly clambered, hampered by their voluminous skirts and unsuitable footwear, the gentle breeze grew stronger, whipping their hair into tangles and weaving the capacious dress material around their bare legs. Waves that had meandered gently to shore now crashed against the rocks far below, and spume churned and swirled, whipping the sea into a roiling foam. Conversation was impossible. Words tumbled away, caught on the wind, and carried out to sea.

'I wonder where Mary is?' attempted Beth.

Seeing Eileen's blank expression, she tried again.

'Mary? Eileen, do you know why Mary hasn't shown up? Did you see her last night?'

'No, she didn't appear last night, either,' shouted Eileen, 'I think sometimes she gets delayed if the young children have some activity on.'

'They are lucky children. From what Mary says they have music lessons and tennis, even show jumping. Things you and I could only dream of,' roared Beth.

Eileen looked blank for a moment, before nodding in understanding.

'They live in a different world, Beth. I think that is why Mary feels a bit awkward sometimes when Eoin talks to her.'

'Yes,' responded Beth with ease, but at the same time wondering why.

'He is only a boy, Eileen. I think it is nice he is so pleasant to her.'

Seagulls screeched as though in agreement with Beth, and Eileen could only nod, as the cacophony reached a crescendo.

Eileen felt she understood Mary's awkwardness but equally Beth's self-possession. There was no way she could articulate it, especially with such competition from the seagulls, so she just shrugged.

The burning question for Eileen was the problem with Anna. What had upset her the previous night? She assumed Beth would not enlighten her but nevertheless, she tried her best.

'What did Anna have to say last night? She looked upset.'

'Sorry, Eileen, I cannot hear you. Did you say you feel upset?'

'No, not me, Anna.'

'Sorry, it is the wind. I don't know what you are saying. Time to turn back, I think,' roared Beth.

Eileen bowed her head hoping her face was inscrutable and did not betray her inner resentment.

I can hear you all right, Beth, and you heard everything else before I asked you about Anna. Never mind. I really don't care. Keep your secrets.

'But, of course, I did care,' murmured Eileen aloud, *'but it doesn't matter now. Not now after all those years.'*

Chapter 10

Gerard herded the children into the car and headed to the park. Mary was in such a foul mood he thought it best to leave her alone with the manuscript. He could not fathom what the problem was. He read the manuscript and thought it was terrific and a realistic anecdotal account of Ireland in the 1930s. She intended to change the names and alter the narrative here and there, so there was nothing for anyone to worry about. Shouting a quick 'Goodbye, we will see you later,' Gerard shut the front door.

Mary was glad to be alone. She knew she was being unreasonably grouchy with Gerard, but she couldn't help it. She dreaded the news that one of the three, and in her heart she knew it would be Anna, would refuse permission for the story to be published.

'I cannot really blame her. I don't think I would like my private trauma recounted for all to read, especially if it was told by someone I thought of as a friend. Are they still friends I wonder? There was certainly a strain at the lunch table and Eileen appeared the same as ever. Strange too, how I alone always felt a closer bond with Eimear despite our different social circumstances,' mused Mary.

As was usual Eimear had returned home from college the previous Christmas.

The time was spent renewing friendships, meeting for endless cups of tea, and taking long, leisurely walks when the weather permitted, possibly romanticising about her future. The church hall was a favourite venue for many young people to meet, especially over Christmas and the usual bleak January. Social circles have many rings. There are those who are more acceptable than others and within the centre of one such circle was Eimear, but on the very outside, was a young man called Tommy. A coughing fit alerted her to the tall, athletic, man distressed as much as embarrassed, by his hacking bout. He was tanned from labouring out of doors, and he cut a striking figure. Eimear guessed his interests lay in the political arena, as the circles he seemed to favour were active locally and vocal in their demands for a United Ireland. His opinions seemed to carry weight judging by the attention they garnered. He appeared to be constantly in Eimear's eye line and on the periphery of her vision whenever she voiced an opinion. Yet they had not been introduced or had the chance to converse.

'He may be well able to articulate his point of view, but I have opinions too,' thought Eimear. *'Although the subjects might not be quite so political,'* she mused to herself.

Eimear wrestled with sleep as the sequence of the events after Christmas tumbled through her mind. She recalled how Tommy always had half a smile tugging at his lip and a glint in his eye that shielded his thoughts. He had made her feel self-conscious, aware of herself in a manner not felt before. She remembered wondering if she was speaking too loudly or were the opinions she expressed, too foolish. She recalled feeling warmth from his gaze, pondering what were his thoughts, as his unwavering eyes steadily focused on her when she expounded on a topic. Eimear knew she had begun to dress more carefully in case he appeared at whatever event she attended, and if he wasn't there, she raged at herself for being disappointed.

I suppose I was flirting with him, a man I had never been introduced to, let alone spoken to. She whispered to herself, tossing and turning once more, *but he made me feel I had something worthwhile to say and in his presence I felt like a woman, beautiful and desirable.*

Eimear clutched the pillow to smother her giggles when she remembered what Tommy had said later,

'*Do you know I never really heard a word you uttered? Your words were just background noise, all I wanted to do was look at you, devour you with my eyes.*'

Eimear, despite her innocence, recognised the current that rushed between them, a tangible force that was almost physical.

Tommy told her he was bewitched from the moment he saw her, a pull or connection that refused to be ignored. He murmured how it was not her face or the way she dressed, certainly not the argument she was expounding. It was infinitesimal, such as the turn of her shoulders, the haughtiness of her glance, perhaps the pout of her lips or the radiance of her smile, maybe, his desire for the unattainable. Inherently though, he understood that their paths traversed different tracks and he warned her of trouble to come.

And so, the eternal love story of Eimear and Tommy unfolded. An early morning walk, a chance meeting by the river. It was on that day that Eimear knew her life would never be the same. Tommy spied her from a distance and purposely made his way towards her. They walked side by side in the early morning mist, disturbed only by Tommy's inevitable wheeze, and they talked and argued. They spoke, listened, and laughed. Senses were heightened but they barely touched, agreeing only to meet again the following morning. It must have been obvious to all who knew Eimear that someone special had entered her life. She shimmered with excitement each morning, and such was her internal glow that, always pretty, she now sparkled with inner beauty. They wrote endless letters to each other when Eimear returned to college. Reluctant before to undertake the tedious journey home at weekends, Eimear now barely tolerated the weeks at college, impatient to get away on Friday evenings. She sensed of course that trouble was brewing, and tranquillity was harshly broken one beautiful early June dawn when she saw the figure of her father striding towards her. Gesturing with his blackthorn stick that she hasten to his side, his face, always flushed, seethed with indignation and outrage, anger palpable in the hush of the early morning. Eimear glanced at Tommy and although his eyes flashed concern for her, she could also see his fists clenched.

'Leave me, Tommy, I will contact you, I promise,' and Eimear strode quickly towards her father. The strength of opposition to their friendship was so intense that communication was virtually impossible. Yet such was their yearning to be together that three weeks later they met again, and this was the cause of her father's fury. Asking Mary to help her by taking a message to Tommy was the risk Eimear now had to take. She finally tumbled into sleep confident she could rely on Mary and deliberately ignoring the difficult position she had forced upon her.

The following morning the entire McCarthy family, minus Eimear, were seated sedately at the dining room table for breakfast. The gloom generated by the heavy silence was interrupted spasmodically by the two young girls, Deirdre, and Clare, but otherwise, the air was thick with tension. Meg's eyes caught Mary's as she glanced towards the breakfast room next door.

'Very quiet in there,' whispered Meg and grinned conspiratorially. 'Whatever did Eimear do...'

After a restless night, Eimear had lain in bed, revising her plan, checking for pitfalls, and quietly determined that her father would not thwart her. Her own grandmother had battled and married the man she loved; she would do the same. The morning light gave her confidence a needed boost, and she felt sure Mary would not let her down. She descended the stairs and joined the little group at about 11.30 when they were preparing to set out for their walk. The lack of sleep and the weeping that had drenched her pillow had no effect on her appearance, bar a slight pallor in her cheeks. The youngsters chattered, as usual, arguing over which direction to take, the beach or the playing fields, or even the mountain path. It was Eimear who insisted they walk along the headland which bypassed the local quarry.

'It will be lovely and fresh along the headland this morning. Come on, girls. Sure, it's not often I accompany you.'

The girls ran ahead with the breeze tugging at their jackets, belying the promise of a hot day with the odd sharp gust. At the turnoff towards the quarry, Eimear thrust her letter into Mary's hands and gently ushered her away,

'Mary, please. I know it is a lot to ask but please help me. Tommy will be working near the quarry. You will easily spot him.'

Reluctantly, Mary advanced down the track Eimear indicated. She was unable to shake the feeling she was colluding with an issue that might result in her being returned home in disgrace. Yet, she liked Eimear and was secretly pleased to be helping her. The track to the quarry was muddy and uneven, spotted in sections with manure. Long before she reached the site, her sandals were caked underfoot with a glutinous mixture that made walking treacherous. She paused momentarily to break a branch from a holly bush to ease her path. As she did so an elderly man strode towards her indicating she should turn around,

'Go on back. It is dangerous here for a young lass.'

'I just need to speak to someone. I have a letter to deliver. Tommy is his name.'

'Tommy, Tommy Hanratty, is it?' he queried, stroking his stubbly chin and gazing thoughtfully into the clouds gathering overhead.

'He is up there all right. What do you want him for?'

'I have a message,' Mary replied showing him the letter from Eimear.

'I will give it to him. Ye can't be going up there.'

Reluctantly, Mary gave him the letter, hoping Eimear would not be too disappointed at this turn of events. Although slightly taken aback when Mary explained what had occurred, Eimear was sensible enough to realise Mary had little choice.

'It's all right, Mary. If there is no reply in a few days, we will try again.'

Patting her on the back she walked away leaving Mary to care for the children for the rest of the afternoon.

Mary blushed slightly as she remembered how inquisitive she must have seemed to Eimear. As their friendship grew, she had questioned her about the argument with her father, intrigued by the ensuing drama and tension, and the compelling urge to write about it in her diary. She resisted that urge, aware of the danger if her diary fell inadvertently into the wrong hands. Anyway, Mary could sense Eimear was slightly evasive, obviously feeling torn with split loyalties, and it was some years later before Eimear divulged the full detail of all that occurred.

Chapter 11

A nna lit another cigarette, her third that morning. Ash splattered a dressing gown smeared with more than a few coffee stains, the manuscript now displaying a few smudges of its own. Beth had either absorbed her loneliness and isolation, perhaps her despair, or else Mary understood how to read the desolation that was her daily companion and lay hidden in Beth's account. Either way, Anna's hands shook as she read further, and memories long suppressed welled to the surface.

Anna was exhausted by the time Lily appeared to be winning the fight and with Lily's blessing she took some time to herself. She walked down to the convent that first evening and met with Beth and Eileen. They were excited to see her, perhaps Eileen less so, and although afterward, they commented on her pale complexion, the three, nevertheless, had a pleasant walk to the teachers' house to call on Mary. This pattern was repeated over the next few days as Lily Walshe slowly regained her strength.

Meeting Beth, and even Mary and Eileen, after what seemed endless days of tending to a sick Lily Walshe raised Anna's spirits. The fresh sea air was exhilarating and the chat with her friends renewed Anna's excitement at the prospect of going to England. She found herself humming as she made her way back to the presbytery. The breeze teased her dark hair, returning her curls that had grown lank and lifeless from the long days and sleepless nights. Fr Matthew watched her petite form from his study room window, mesmerized by her shapely womanly curves, emphasised by a dress that clung to her body in a gentle flurry. Anna entered the house and noticed the study door was ajar. Fr Matthew called out to her.

'Come here, Anna, please

Slowly, she pushed the door open further but did not enter. Fr Matthew sat at his desk, obviously in the middle of counting the church collections from the previous Sunday Masses.

'I just wanted to say thank you for all you did for Mrs Walshe.'

'Oh, it was nothing. I was glad to help her.'

Anna attempted to leave but was stalled by a further comment.

'Indeed, and a good job you did too. So, are you off to bed now?'

'Yes, yes, I am.'

'Good, sleep well. Good night now.'

Anna turned away and climbed the stairs, a bit taken aback by the conversation. To an outside observer, he would have appeared quite pleasant, but Anna was not fooled. The speculative penetration of his dark eyes made her shiver and hasten to place a chair at the door to the attic room. It was no protection but at least she would be alerted if he tried to enter while she slept. Sleep was elusive, however, and Anna tossed and turned unable to fully relax, yet the night passed uneventfully. Over the next number of days, Mrs Walshe returned to her old pattern of rising early but was in need of a rest in the afternoon. Whilst she slept Anna completed the chores and then relaxed in the sitting room. Fr Matthew was usually out but she was alert to every sound and quick to run upstairs should he return unexpectedly.

Fr Matthew was praying daily for guidance. He knew Anna had a devil within her that was trying to tempt him to commit the sin of lust. There was a challenge in her eyes that he had seen before in many of the girls who came to the house. So, he stayed out of her way as much as possible, but the image of her young body was always at the forefront of his mind. He knew she listened for him and disappeared upstairs once she heard the front door open. It was always the way with the girls, tantalising and teasing, part of their seduction technique. Today he would thwart her. Silently he opened the side gate and entered the house through the kitchen door. The door to the sitting room was ajar, a precaution, so Anna would hear the front door opening. Fr Matthew stood at the entrance to the room, devouring her with his eyes and inhaling her scent. Alert, not just to any noise, but the slightest change in atmosphere Anna looked up from her book. Startled, she stammered,

'Oh, hello, Fr Matthew, I was just going to attend to Mrs Walshe.'

'Don't lie to me, girl. You were waiting here for me. You think I don't know that?'

Turning, he silently closed and locked the door.

'Come here, Anna. I want to talk to you. Come close to me. I will show you I cannot be tempted.'

Anna took one slow step towards him and paused but he strode towards her, grasping her arm.

'Pray with me, Anna. Kneel and we will pray together.'

The insistent pressure on her arm forced her to move and a reluctant Anna acceded to his demand and dropped to her knees. Fr Matthew knelt beside her and bowed his head. After a few moments, Anna attempted to rise but he stalled her with sinewy arms that clasped her in a tight embrace. His hot breath fanned her cheeks and, as she resisted, he held her tighter clutching at her dress. The more Anna struggled and flailed, the more he hardened his grip, constricting her ability to move. Hot wheezing breath competed with the swish of filmy material as Anna's summer dress was ripped apart. The keening of Anna's anguish echoed in the silent room as insinuating fingers forced a rough pathway inside torn underwear, pushing violently upwards, completing her humiliation.

Anna moaned in agony, but Fr Matthew continued his assault.

'I know it's what you want. I am but just a man after all. Help me, dear God.'

As he murmured these words, he simultaneously held her down and, after fumbling with his own clothing, thrust painfully inside her. Once sated, he again ordered Anna to pray, forcing her to kneel.

'Forgive her Lord for tempting me and forgive me for succumbing to her wiles.'

He intoned continuously until a curtain descended. His eyes fluttered closed and, trancelike, seemingly lost in prayer, he released his grip on Anna. She stumbled but managed to partially rise, before finally floundering haphazardly to the door. Fumbling with the key, an eternity passed before it opened, and she painfully climbed up the stairs.

Fr Matthew continued to pray, yet his ears were cocked anxious in case Anna stopped at Mrs Walshe's bedroom, but she continued on up to the attic. He rose and sat in a seat by the window, gazing reflectively into the garden. The night was turning cold and damp, otherwise, he would have headed off for a brisk walk on the beach. He needed to think and clear his head. He was aware of his frailties, and time and again, he pledged he would no longer fall, but the young girls were too alluring and continually trapped him. He made a solemn vow that night, followed by an *'Act of Contrition'*, or penance to his God. He would not allow these girls to distract him from his dedication to his Lord and once Anna left, he would no longer accept any more girls into his house. He felt reasonably confident Anna would not mention what had occurred. On reflection, she would realise it was her own fault. Sitting alone in his living room every day, Mrs Walshe asleep in bed, it was obvious what she had planned. Yes, he had failed, but wisdom always prevailed, and wisdom dictated that females were always at fault and his God would forgive him. The night silence in the house brought him peace and understanding and he sighed as he felt God's love surround him.

Anna staggered into the bathroom and robotically cleaned and attended to herself unsure where all the blood was coming from, thankful it had now ceased. The attic became a sanctuary as she lay on her bed shivering with shock, unable to comprehend the violation that had just occurred. She stared at the ceiling counting the cracks, anything to stop her mind from focusing on Fr Matthew and her mortification. She tried to push from her mind the idea that it was her fault as he had implied. Anna berated herself for using the sitting room, but Fr Matthew was rarely there, and anyway, preferred his study. The attic was so hot and uncomfortable in the July heat, and she always listened for his return. She had made every effort to avoid him but, maybe, maybe unconsciously, she had given the wrong signal. He was after all a priest, and he knew right from wrong. Barely had the thought entered her head then she dismissed it. Anna physically shook herself at that foolish notion and common sense prevailed. Hadn't he entered the attic before, terrifying her with his creeping hand and insinuations? As exhaustion overcame her, she rejected the idea that she had been the temptress. She also knew she had to get away. Mrs Walshe could not help her and innately she knew Fr Matthew would attack her again.

The following morning, she prepared breakfast as usual. Shock had robbed her of the ability to think rationally and automatically she attended to her chores. Mrs Walshe glanced enquiringly at her from time to time, but Anna did not elaborate or respond. The ability to speak seemed to have deserted her but she managed to request permission to visit Beth and Eileen once all her duties were completed.

'Of course, you can go, but finish the dinner prep. first.'

Mrs Walshe intuited something was amiss, but she was too worn out and tired from her illness to enquire further. Her sleep was always fitful and on no occasion had she heard the scrape of the chair being moved against the attic door. She fervently hoped that Fr Matthew had learned his lesson and left Anna alone.

It was early evening before Anna could get away. She had performed all her tasks as her mind whirled from one solution to another. By the time the convent came into view, she knew what she had to do. Deliberately ignoring Eileen, Anna, forcefully grabbed Beth and dragged her away.

'Oh, Beth, he forced me yesterday evening, forced me, you know what I mean. It was so awful.' Anna shuddered and began to shake, her shoulders heaving in agitation. Beth felt helpless, unable to grasp the enormity of what she had said. An angry retort from Anna broke the silence.

'You don't believe me, do you?'

'I do, I do. It is just so hard to understand. I mean I am shocked, really shocked. The priest? Are you sure he wasn't just trying to be friendly, a bit inappropriate maybe like last time…?'

Beth's voice trailed away, and her face mirrored her confusion as she encountered Anna's look of utter contempt.

Beth could not comprehend any priest perpetrating such action even though she knew Anna had had difficulty before. Like nuns, priests were almost a gender apart, not mere mortals, people of God, and not like ordinary men or women. An ideology instilled by the Church, family and tradition, inculcated a conviction that clergy were chosen by on High and could do no wrong. Yet instinctively Beth knew they were mere men and women. She turned to Anna as an insistent frantic tone now permeated Anna's next words, a plea.

'I can't go back, Beth. He makes me so nervous. I am afraid he will come to my room again. There is just a chair as a barrier and Mrs Walshe is still not fully better. I must get away. Will you come with me?'

Beth was nonplussed, quite stunned at first by Anna's news and now her solution. Anna nodded sagely, guessing Beth's confusion.

'It doesn't matter, Beth. It is not fair of me to ask you, but I am going anyway.'

'No, no, Anna, don't say that. I will help you but what will we do for money?'

'I know where I can get some,' said Anna and stared at Beth for a moment, while a strange, guarded, slightly calculating wave, fleetingly animated her dull features. 'A decent amount.'

This new determined, but seemingly disconnected Anna, was unnerving and a further surge of anxiety rushed through Beth. Her young friend, usually so needy, was displaying an assurance, that was both unsettling in its singlemindedness, and bewildering because she seemed so isolated and detached from all around her. Beth attempted to break through the shell coiled around Anna and gently took one of Anna's stone-cold hands in hers. Stroking it gently she whispered,

'I will go with you, Anna, of course, I will. But we must plan it properly.'

Huddled together on the beach, Beth, after a few minutes of reflection, outlined her idea.

'I am always up early on Monday morning, around 6 am usually, to clean the church after Sunday Mass. I will meet you at Pier Road. No one will think it strange if they see me up and about a bit earlier than usual and I will not be missed for some time. There is no bus at that hour, but with an early start and maybe a lift along the way, we can make some headway towards Galway. Wait for me if I get delayed. If we can get to Galway, and if we have enough money, we can take a train from there to Dublin. After that, we can decide what to do.

The words tumbled out and Beth could not quite remember afterwards exactly what she had said. She only knew, at the time, that she wanted to connect with Anna and break through the shell that encased her.

'Beth, I told you, we will have enough money.'

Anna kept her counsel and did not elaborate but she had witnessed where the Sunday collection was housed until the bank opened on Monday morning. She knew how to get enough money for their trip. Anna stood up, brushing sand from her skirt.

'I will wait an hour for you, Beth, but I better go back to the presbytery now. We might not get a chance to talk again so, see you Monday morning, early. Remember I will only wait an hour. After that, I will go on alone.'

As dawn broke the following Monday, and after a sleepless night, Beth gingerly crept out of bed so as not to disturb Eileen. She had already packed her few belongings.

'Where are you going?' mumbled Eileen with one eye open from under the covers.

'Just for a walk before I clean the church. Stay there, I won't be long.'

As arranged, Beth was to meet Anna on the outskirts of the town and together they would make their way towards the train station. In hindsight, a journey that sounded a lot easier in the planning than the actuality.

Beth slid out the side door of the convent and hurried down to the pier. The wind whistled around her, blowing sand in her face, twirling her hair in numerous directions but, simultaneously, invigorating her. Anna had promised to wait an hour at the allotted spot, but Beth felt an urgency and hurried along, anxious not to be late. Anna's final words rang in her ears, and she was nervous in case Anna's impatience made her set off on her own. She pacified her nerves with a mantra she had recited ever since she heard Anna's news.

'*So, what, if we leave Mayo a bit early?*' she thought.

'*We must go in about a month anyway. I love Anna as a sister, I promised to take care of her.*' Acknowledging it would not be easy did not sway Beth's resolve. She had made her decision and was confident that together they would be able to manage. Now she jauntily battled the breeze, making plans as she marched along, determination in every step.

'*I won't say anything to Eileen. She has enough issues of her own without me adding to them,*' she mused, '*but I will send a message to her once we are safely away, and she can let Mary know.*'

Anna placed the manuscript on the table. It was soggy and stained from the endless splashes of tea and coffee, imbibed while she read. She felt demeaned and violated once more and sat unmoving as sorrow and humiliation took their turn to torment.

Rage took its time but surged through her with a ferocity once it seized hold.

'*How dare Beth reveal such personal details to Mary. How dare she break what was a sacred confidence. It was not her story to tell.*'

Anna threw herself on the bed, quivering with the forceful memories that overcame her.

Chapter 12

L unch at the hotel reinforced how Eimear had been very much on the periphery of the little group, thought Mary. If nothing else, Anna's almost bitter words emphasised that fact.

'She was really just my friend,' she murmured to herself. 'The others barely knew her, but she is part of my story, so I cannot exclude her.'

On an impulse, Mary opened the letters Eimear had religiously sent to her over the years and placed them on the table beside her manuscript. She had finally written in detail of all that had occurred, but Mary wanted to double-check to ensure her story was accurately portrayed.

The tension in the McCarthy house, although still noticeable, appeared to ease somewhat over the next week. Eimear re-joined the family for meals, even volunteering at times to address her father. Regularly, she joined Mary when she went walking with the children and that fledging rapport between both young women gained more ground, perhaps from the unspoken secret they shared. Eimear confided that she had received a reply from Tommy but furnished no details. In some ways Mary was relieved not to know too much, worried the knowledge could rebound negatively at some point. Conversely, she itched to know every detail and to revel in the intrigue. Regardless, Eimear and Mary talked endlessly about everything and nothing, and days that could be very long with just the younger girls' chatter, slipped easily by.

The first indication that all was not as it should be, was on Thursday of the following week, a full fourteen days after Mary's aborted visit to the quarry. Eimear did not appear that morning but that, in itself, was not unusual. Her non-appearance at lunch sparked a query from her mother Jean, who instructed Meg to knock on her bedroom door and enquire if she was unwell. A flustered Meg returned within an instant brandishing a letter which she thrust at Jean as though it were red hot. Pandemonium erupted, as first Jean and then Joe, read the contents. Colour gradually suffused his cheeks until, almost purple with rage, Joe heaved himself upright and rushed from the room. Jean, followed, wringing her hands.

'She will not get away with this,' he roared. 'I am going first to Fr Matthew and then Sergeant Kelly. This is going to be stopped.'

Eimear had slipped from the house early Thursday morning as dawn was breaking. She had no time to look at a sky that was bursting with colour as the sun rose over the green fields and glistened off the water in the distance. A sky streaked with red, and gold bore no fascination, her entire focus was reaching the crossroads where Tommy awaited. Spying him in the distance she threw caution to the wind and ran the last few yards into his waiting arms. The enormity of what she was risking was not lost on Tommy. Reluctantly he pushed her away and once more gently asked,

'Are you sure, Eimear, are you sure? It is not too late to return home and I will understand.'

'Tommy, unless you don't want me, I am not going anywhere unless it is with you.'

Eimear's hand reached up and gently stroked his face before pushing his slight fringe back from his eyes.

Tommy smiled at her, a smile that lit up his face, crinkling his brown eyes.

'Come on so, I'll help you up.'

Tommy had procured a cart and donkey and Eimear clambered aboard, carelessly throwing her bag into the back.

'I must leave the cart at the station. My brother Jimmy will collect it later today,' intoned Tommy, as he directed the donkey in the direction of Ballina town.

The train from Galway left for Limerick at 9 am or shortly afterwards. By 8.30 both Eimear and Tommy were sitting in a carriage anxiously awaiting its departure, scanning the street, which was clearly visible from the small train station, in case Joe McCarthy appeared.

Eventually, the train jerked forward. At the first indication that it was about to move, Eimear clutched Tommy's hand. He squeezed hers in return as he whispered how he loved her.

Eimear's eyes welled with tears and her voice trailed away, requiring Tommy to lean even closer, to hear her murmur, 'I love you too, Tommy, but you know...'

'I know, Eimear, but once we are married, things will settle. Your father, but especially your mother, will accept your decision. They love you too much. They will be angry for a while, but it will pass.' 'Tommy, I so hope you're right. It is the only blight on my happiness.'

Eimear lay her head against his shoulder and as the train picked up speed she fell into a light doze, the gentle cadence of a slight snore, music to Tommy's ears. As the train rattled along, worry assailed Tommy. Eimear was undertaking all the risks of reputation, family, and friends, maybe her future. Most people would consider she was out of his league, that he could only damage her, but he was determined to prove them wrong. He loved Eimear with every fibre of his being and no matter what he had to do, he promised to give her a good life and a happy life.

Smothering his cough so as not to disturb Eimear, his thoughts drifted to his youth and the small holding he called home. Nestled by a small wood, the cottage was not much bigger than a barn. Wild, yellow roses rambled over flaking whitewashed walls, mismatched windows, and ineptly secured front door. The roses gave a hint of the beauty that lay buried beneath the chaos inside. His mother and father had treasured each other and their children, but with little money and rocky, barren soil, creature comforts were minimal. Love though was abundant, as were books. The spring and summer months, in particular, when daylight was plentiful, his father and mother read each night to all six children. His father usually read to the older cohort and his mother the younger. Afterwards, the entire family knelt and prayed together before bedtime. The books inspired Tommy.

I wanted to build. Design and build, see my creations come to life, but working in the quarry is the nearest I have gotten so far.

The untimely death of his father had crushed his dreams for a while. As the eldest, the necessity to earn for his mother and younger siblings overpowered all his hopes. His fledging participation in community groups encouraged further interest in local politics, but meeting Eimear ignited that fire again to achieve, and become the man his father dreamed of. Jimmy was now working and able to contribute. Soon Maria and Jack would have jobs and his mother would not be so dependent on him. The urge to cough was suddenly overwhelming and shook Tommy's body in a violent spasm. It scarcely disturbed Eimear at all.

It was midday when they reached a very busy Limerick as the market day was in full swing. Pushing through the crowd they located the local hotel for needed refreshments before returning to the train station to purchase tickets to County Cork. Their plan was not clear, the necessity to get as far from Mayo as possible, the main priority, and busy Cork City seemed like a good option. It was late evening when they eventually arrived in a damp town, overshadowed by grey scudding clouds and air, tainted with smog. Tired from the journey and the tension of the day, they nevertheless walked aimlessly for some time before seeking directions to a nearby hotel. The hotel was really a boarding house, but it was well-lit, with a peat fire blazing in the hallway. Money was not an immediate issue, but neither was it something they had in abundance. Yet, the allure of a comfortable lodging at least for one night was too much and they booked a double room as Mr and Mrs Hanratty.

Eimear sat shyly on the edge of the bed but when Tommy lowered himself down beside her, she lay her head on his shoulder. Taking Eimear's hand in his own, Tommy murmured,

'I hope you have no regrets, Eimear. I am asking so much of you, leaving your family, maybe even your reputation in our small town.'

There was no answer and when he turned to face her, he saw her eyes flutter and knew she had heard little, if any, of what he had said. Exhaustion had overwhelmed following such a long arduous journey. Gently he laid her down and removed her shoes. He placed a blanket over her before he lay himself down beside her. Tommy knew this was a most precious moment, one impossible to repeat, the trauma in the days ahead unavoidable.

Eimear awoke to the coo of wood pigeons and light streaking through a gap in the curtains. Tommy lay gently snoring. After easing herself off the bed, she padded over to the window. The sun was beaming on a rain-soaked garden awash with cascades of flowers, coloured petals turned towards the sky and welcome warmth. Tommy stirred, and rising, moved behind her. Eimear gazed back beaming.

'Tommy, I love you, I always will.'

She moved into his open arms, and they locked together, passion sweeping over them both. No ceremony overseen by any priest was more affirming of their desire or love, their commitment to each other complete.

Mary hoped she had captured that moment between Eimear and Tommy when the world stood still and a future was possible, the trauma that followed unimaginable. Still restless, but a further turn around the garden impossible now that there was an incessant downpour, Mary made another cup of coffee. The intimate details shared by Eimear never failed to astonish. She could not imagine describing her own private moments with her husband, but she had come to realise over the years, that Eimear needed a sounding board. Perhaps her own friends from school and college were too close or, perhaps, she valued Mary's counsel far more than Mary herself realised. Either way, Eimear had written regularly, and Mary settled herself comfortably to read the rest of her story.

Chapter 13

Mary had mixed feelings about how Anna was presented in her story. Her information had all been gleaned from Beth who wavered between compassion, hurt, and anger whenever she spoke of Anna. As Mary began to read, so did Beth.

Beth wondered how Anna would remember their escape to Dublin and its aftermath. If it was possible to pinpoint a day when Beth noticed a change in Anna, Beth would instantly choose that first day they fled the convent. Yet, she knew the catalyst was Fr. Matthew and how a greater knowledge, gleaned over the last many years, might have made a difference, given her perhaps a better understanding of Anna's trauma.

Beth and Anna had only a vague idea of the direction they should take. Ballina was the nearest large town and it seemed sensible to make their way there. It would be some time before they would be missed, so if they were lucky and were able to hitch a lift, they might reach the town before they were spotted. Anna said she had some money, although where she obtained it had Beth a little perplexed and more than a little worried. She hoped it was a loan from Mrs Walshe but something in Anna's demeanour made her doubtful that this was the case. Anna was in good form, totally unlike the nervous and emotional wreck of the previous days, so Beth did not press her for answers. They rambled along the dusty road in companionable silence, well used to long treks. The early morning sunshine promised another hot day and a mile or two quickly sped by before they heard the unmistakable racket of a cart. The wagon rumbled up beside them with a salute from the driver and a snort from the pony.

'Mornin' to you, ladies,' and a doffed cap was accompanied by a friendly grin.

'Any chance of a lift?' piped Anna.

'Where might ye be goin' now?'

'Ballina,' replied Beth.

'Well now, I'm not goin' that far but, sure, I am going that way. Clamber aboard if you like.'

Beth and Anna threw their bags up first and then hauled themselves up onto the cart.

'The name's Barney.'

'I am Beth, and this is Anna.'

'Grand so, we'll be off now.'

Barney was quiet, puffing his pipe contentedly, and a faint aroma of sweet tobacco lingered in the air. His rosy cheeks grew ever more ruddy as he ushered his pony along with a soft whistle, a man quite fulfilled with his world. Anna and Beth sat in silence, not wishing to impart any information that could subsequently be relayed back to the convent. Barney showed little interest in eliciting information so for two hours they jogged along quietly. He muttered the odd comment about the weather and the scenery but seemed totally uninterested in why, or where, they were travelling. A small turn-off was reached, little more than a track.

'I'm headin' up this way now. If ye keep walkin' for about forty minutes ye will come to the town. Busy place. Take care now.'

'Thanks, Barney,' responded both girls in unison.

'My pleasure,' and Barney disappeared up the laneway.

Their first impulse was to source a natural spring as the dusty drive had them both hot and thirsty. Mayo had an abundance of springs from ever-present rainy, downpours. Fresh water burst forth from saturated hills, cleansed with stone and gravel, before flowing into ditches and seeping into treacherous, marshy pools. Beth and Anna left the roadway and scrambled over a gate, skating and sliding over muddy sludge, careful not to slip in the slimy ooze, until they reached some higher ground. There, fresh water gushed over a rock, bathed in a variety of hues from the summer sun. Sunshine sparkled off Beth's red locks, a shimmering rainbow in the afternoon heat as she bent forward to drink, its beauty lost on Anna as she waited impatiently for her turn. Gingerly, one by one, grasping hands, they each leaned forward and drank their fill.

Back on the roadway, they waltzed silently along, each contemplating their next move. They knew their behaviour had sullied any chance of completing their English practice. Their flight had also ruined any forthcoming assistance to aid the journey to England and find placement or work. If they were caught, they would immediately be returned home in disgrace. Despite that fear, there was a freedom and exhilaration in being together and in charge of the future ahead of them. Their euphoria soon dissipated. Threatening clouds darkened what had begun as a bright, sunny day. A veil of mist carrying a drizzle, light as a feather, descended, increasing quickly in intensity, soaking through the girls' light clothing. Each step towards Ballina became more of an endurance than an adventure as rain dripped down their necks and water squelched in well-worn boots with soles thin as blotting paper. But they were island girls and hardships were not unknown. They trudged along in silence, knowing there was no other route for them now. Barney's forty-minute walk, obviously, a most optimistic forecast.

The one dependable fact about Irish weather is that it is ever-changing. An hour after the rain began, it stopped, and the sun peeked out from behind the clouds. As the first few cottages heralding the outskirts of Ballina came into view, Beth and Anna's spirits rose along with the steam from their sodden clothes. By the time they reached the centre of town with the train station in sight, they were once more happily chattering.

'Anna, I asked you before, but you never gave me a proper answer. How much money do you have? Is it enough for two train tickets and where did you get it anyway?'

'Don't worry. It is mine. I earned it. It is enough, more than enough, for the train.'

A frown creased Beth's forehead, her features displaying her puzzlement, as she attempted to understand Anna.

'Anna, why can't you be frank with me? I just want to be sure we will be all right. We have a long journey ahead of us. I have no idea how much it will cost.'

Anna did not meet Beth's eyes but gazed at the ground as she muttered, perhaps with a touch of belligerence,

'I spoke to Mrs Walshe. She told me how much we would need, between tickets for the train and boat and even lodgings and food. I have enough.'

Exasperated, Beth halted Anna as she proceeded to march ahead. Holding tightly onto her sleeve, Beth made Anna pause in her stride.

'Once more, Anna, where did you get so much money?' she demanded. 'Did Mrs Walshe give it to you? I am not moving until you tell me.'

A truculent Anna replied, her tone quarrelsome,

'I stole it, happy now? I stole it from that priest, and he deserved it for what he did.'

A shocked Beth could only stutter, 'From the Church, Anna, you stole from the Church?'

'No, just from him. He kept it in a box in the living room. I will pay it back, anyway, once I am earning. Come on. If you are coming.'

Anna began to walk away, her pace gathering speed, so Beth had to run to catch up with her.

'Anna, Anna, wait.'

Beth caught up with her, pulling her sleeve once more to make her pause.

'Anna, of course, I am going with you. We have no other choice now. But, Anna, promise me, I mean really promise me, that when we are both settled, we pay it back, every penny.'

Anna shrugged, 'Of course, Beth, I already said I would. Whatever you want, just come along now, before we miss the next train.'

Their disgruntlement soon disappeared when they entered the train station. They listened in awe to the wheeze and rattle emanating from the puffing train, before darting to the ticket station.

'Is that train going to Dublin? Two tickets please,' roared Anna, anxious to be heard above the lively commotion from all corners of the station.

Beyond a slight indication that signalled 'yes', two tickets were sold in total silence as though the seller did not wish to add even a murmur to the general mayhem. Excited now, Anna and Beth boarded the train, the first experience for both. Hugging each other in delight, they settled down in the carriage, all difference over the stolen money forgotten for the moment. They were still a bit damp from the rain but that was just a mild irritation, easily ignored, as the train, with a loud whistle and a squeal, moved slowly out of Ballina Station. Despite their exultation, the strain of the day and the sonorous clickity-clack of the train, soon had both girls dozing. By the time they reached Kingsbridge Station in Dublin, they were well-rested but had no idea where to go. They left the station, wandering outside into a dark and unfamiliar city, totally bewildered, as to which direction they should take.

A flock of seagulls, screeching and diving, drew Beth and Anna towards the River Liffey. The overhead dissonant squawking was just a faint distraction from the overpowering whiff of the river. Neither girl was a stranger to the variety of nature's smells, but the stench from the river took them aback. Nevertheless, the river gave them some direction and they walked steadily along beside it until they reached O'Connell Street. It was a busy street even with the shops closed and the late hour of 9 o'clock. Everyone seemed aware of where they needed to go and what they needed to do. Confused, and not a little frightened, they followed the crowd towards Grafton Street. They passed by Trinity College and the old House of Parliament, now a prosperous bank, without any recognition, relief only dawning momentarily when they spied a church with an open door. Beth and Anna entered, hastily pulling scarves over their heads.

The scent of incense instantly assaulted their nostrils, and they realised Benediction was underway. Attending the service gave them some respite, even a little rest, but once the ceremony was over, they had to source help. They waited until the crowd had dispersed before approaching an elderly nun who had assisted the priest. She was now tidying the altar and checking the church before locking up for the night.

'Please, Sister, begging your pardon, but can you help us?' enquired Beth. 'We have just arrived from Mayo and are totally lost.'

It was quite apparent from the nun's expression that 'offering assistance' was a most unwelcome request at such a late hour. Christianity, however, overruled her unwillingness and she bade them sit in a pew.

'Well, I am not sure how I can help,' was the weary response. 'Have you any money to pay for lodgings?'

'Yes, yes, we have, but we don't know where to go.'

'Right,' and with a sigh, depicting a very definite reluctance, she announced,

'wait here while I finish tidying. I know the owner of lodgings in Gardiner Street, and I am sure she will provide a bed for you. I can direct you or, if necessary, walk you over there. It's not far though. I am sure you will be fine on your own.'

It was obvious the nun hoped the girls would decline her offer to accompany them. They felt awkward, sensing her lack of enthusiasm, yet they were now very weary and needed help. It was Beth who answered.

'We would be very grateful if you came with us as we have no idea of Dublin, and it is getting very dark. Maybe we can help you finish here first?'

Pursing her lips, and swiftly hiding a flash of disappointment, the nun, whose name was never volunteered, replied,

'That won't be necessary. It is indeed getting dark, and very late, but I will do what has to be done.' Muttering about missing her dinner, the nun sauntered away to finish her tasks.

The girls arose, refreshed, the following morning despite the stuffy airless room they had been allotted. They were jubilant as they walked down towards Dublin Port to purchase tickets to Liverpool. Beth had been well primed for this part of the journey by her father, a trip he had undertaken on two occasions. Beth's aunt, her father's younger sister, Sheila, had departed for England about 5 years previously. Seanie, Beth's father, had only volunteered a vague idea of what had transpired but Beth's grandmother now lived with Sheila. Beth remembered both women well and was comfortable with the idea that Anna and herself begin their English adventure in Rochdale, where Sheila was now settled. Purchasing the tickets with Anna's stolen money had not been part of the original plan and Beth could not shake a sense of dismay as she handed over the necessary money. Anna seemed blithely unaware of Beth's discomfort and chatted first with an elderly couple, and then with rather over-familiar abandon, two young men in the queue.

Once aboard and settled, Beth began to relax and read the directions, painstakingly written by her father, for the balance of the journey to her grandmother and aunt. Anna on the other hand had ceased her chatter. Her milky skin turned an even paler shade, something Beth had assumed was impossible. As the journey progressed Anna dozed between bouts of nausea that had her bent, time after time, over the side of the boat. Once the ship docked, Beth had to assist a weary and exhausted Anna to disembark. The grim and busy docks, the harsh racket and commotion accompanied by a strange cacophony of accents were all the more unwelcome because of the steady downpour. A sheet of rain relentlessly descended and rendered the entire area dull and gloomy even though darkness had not yet fallen. There was little attention paid to the girls at the Customs Gate and they exited onto a busy street. Anna, at last, had perked up and welcomed Beth's suggestion they find a café and procure some food. Before long, they came across a Lyon's tearoom and once again utilised Anna's stolen hoard.

Revived by tea and stewed lamb with mashed potato, they secured directions to the train station from a friendly waitress. A sense of adventure suffused both girls once more, and ignoring the continual drizzle, they set off to the train station which, fortunately, was not too far of a walk.

Beth put down the manuscript and closed her eyes. Nostalgia for a time when anything seemed possible overwhelmed her. Her eyes mirrored the sadness inside for the Anna she once loved mingled with regret, at how the course of their lives had diverged.

Chapter 14

Mary distinctly remembered the commotion that emanated from the dining room, and she could almost recall the argument between Joe and Jean McCarthy verbatim.

'Leave it, Joe. Eimear has always been headstrong. Keep it quiet, just between us, and when she returns, we can move on as though nothing has occurred. No one else needs to know.'

'Don't be daft, woman. Nothing can be kept secret around here. Everyone will eventually know she has been with Tommy Hanratty. She will be forced to marry him. We need to get her back home before the, the...inevitable occurs.'

Joe McCarthy pounded the table startling Jean before marching from the room. His roar shook the entire household.

'She will not get away with this and that blackguard will regret he was born when I catch up with him.'

After slamming the study door, Joe stomped around the house struggling into his jacket, muttering under his breath. A frenzied search in his pockets followed before he finally located his car keys.

'I'll be back soon. I am going to the priest.'

Jean's eyes followed the car as it swerved out the gate and down the road.

Disconsolately she returned to sit at the dining table digesting the contents of Eimear's letter and the effect her actions would have on the entire family.

What have you done Eimear, and why?

Jean looked helplessly around the table as though one of the younger children could supply an answer, but silence was the only response.

Meanwhile, Mary and Meg huddled in the kitchen. Meg was flushed with excitement at the drama unfolding but Mary was anxious, quite sure if her part was discovered, she would be banished back home.

'Imagine, running away like that,' gasped Meg. 'I wonder what will happen?'

'Be quiet, both of you,' ordered Mrs Donegan. 'Get on with your work. You, Mary, go and fetch the children and bring them out for a walk. They shouldn't be around today, in the middle of all that tension.'

Mr McCarthy had one of the few cars in the village. Eyes turned as he sped along, and tongues wagged as he screeched to a halt outside the presbytery. The fiery glare he thrust at the few onlookers only piqued their curiosity even further.

Without any preamble, Joe McCarthy outlined the bare facts to Fr Matthew.

If anything, Fr Matthew was even more incensed than Eimear's father.

'Young Eimear, a regular mass-goer, to be tempted that way,' he stuttered, 'and by that young villain, that criminal, Tommy Hanratty.'

His venom was such that even Joe was astonished and surprised himself at his own initial inclination to defend Tommy. Common sense reasserted itself as he needed Fr Matthew's assistance. Tommy Hanratty was, if not a criminal, totally unsuitable, so he forbore to correct the priest. Fr Matthew continued to point out the natural result of the two young people spending the night together.

'You know she will be ruined, Joe, a young man like that, he will take advantage of her. What he will do to a young girl like that, I mean he will...'

Joe's expression made Fr Matthew pause, his salacious interest perhaps appearing a little too obvious.

'Fr Matthew, that's enough for now. Come along, we need to get Sergeant

Kelly and maybe Willie O'Dwyer. Yes, you go and get the sergeant, I'll have a word with Willie.'

Fr Matthew disliked taking orders but in this instance, he felt it wiser to follow instructions.

'We will meet again in an hour at my house and be prepared for a journey.'

Joe went directly to the local pub where Willie O'Dwyer lived with his parents. He had long felt that Eimear and Willie would make a good match. Two teachers, two comfortable backgrounds, a perfect combination. Joe loved his family and wanted to see them all settle well. His daughter Eimear was a source of pride, well-educated, very pretty, not to mention talented and intelligent. He firmly believed someone like Tommy could never make her happy, too uncouth and with no qualifications. How could he ever satisfy someone like Eimear? It was just his appearance that attracted her, and when that faded in the course of time, what could they ever discuss? He had a staunch conviction that without proper qualifications, no man or woman could properly understand the intricacies of the world. The idea of his daughter married to a labourer with no ability to form a coherent thought, was anathema.

He rapped sharply on the pub door and entered before his knock was answered.

'Is Willie there? I need to speak to him,' he roared as he marched rudely past Willie's mother, without any acknowledgment.

'Willie,' she shouted up the stairs, her voice tinged with a frisson of excitement, Joe's whole demeanour inflaming antenna always alert for gossip.

'Joe McCarthy is here and needs to see you.'

Willie trundled downstairs with a puzzled expression that did nothing to enhance his features. A tall, thin man, he bent ever so slightly, as if to minimize his height. The slight stoop caused his glasses to slide down his rather long nose, so his arms were in perpetual motion as they continually pushed his glasses back into position.

'Yes, Joe,' he queried as, simultaneously, his father, Mike, appeared down the hallway.

'Joe McCarthy, the Lord save us, whatever is the matter? Come this way, you too, Willie,' and taking command Mike led them into the sitting room at the rear of the public house. Now that he was here, Joe was slightly daunted and unprepared to voice his wish.

'Whisht, man, what has upset you so?' continued Mike. 'It's a drop of this wee stuff is what you need,' and he poured a generous dollop of whiskey into a glass for Joe. Automatically, as if in a daze, Joe took a sip and as the warmth coursed through him, he knew he had only one option to save Eimear. Words flowed from his lips with the courage garnered from every drop savoured from the glass.

'Willie,' he began, 'I think you have always had a soft spot for Eimear. Am I right in that?'

Poor Willie blushed and as he attempted to stammer a reply, Mike rushed to insist.

'Sure of course he has. Wouldn't any young fella have an eye for a young woman like your Eimear?' Willie nodded; his face now suffused with a reddish glow.

'Well,' continued Joe, 'a match between both of you has always been a wish of mine. Two teachers, two families well suited. Wouldn't you agree, Mike?'

Mike nodded vigorously as his eyes strained to leap from their sockets.

'I have a proposal for ye. Now things are a bit delicate, but with ingenuity, I think we can sort things out.'

Joe paused and looked at Willie ponderously for a few moments, wondering if he was indeed about to embark on the right course. Even he could see that Willie was not the most handsome man. His height was no problem, but Joe wished he wouldn't droop so much, and his demeanour was more than a little off-putting. Willie seemed to have a habitual grimace of distaste regardless of the subject being discussed. As these thoughts made Joe pause, he studied his glass ruminatively, and then, reluctantly continued, unerringly sure he had no other option.

'Willie, if you are willing, I will endorse marriage between you and Eimear. But you first must know she has run away with Tommy Hanratty. They left early this morning and I have no idea where they are. My guess is they made their way to Galway, and I am going there soon with Fr Matthew and Sergeant Kelly to bring her back.'

'Early this morning you say?' muttered Mike. 'You won't get them tonight. Ye know what that means, Joe, don't ye?'

Mike's eyes glittered and Joe felt a twinge of discomfort.

'A marriage now, between my son and your daughter. There must be more for Willie than just marriage.'

Mike's words appeared to strike a chord with Willie, and he looked at his father with understanding. A flash of cunning fleetingly replaced his habitual expression which, in turn, was swiftly replaced by an unusual sense of purpose, reminiscent of his father.

'Quiet, Da, this is between me and Joe. Yes, Joe, I will go with ye and bring her back. I have always had a fondness for her but...'

Wille paused for a few seconds, rubbing his chin and a canny expression suffused his features.

'I will help you, of course, Joe, but I never thought to marry any woman that was 'damaged goods.' I will need extra for that. A nice house maybe, one near your own as befits two teachers.'

The crafty demeanour had not gone unnoticed, and the naked greed took Joe aback, but concern, anger and whiskey, overrode his normal intuition and common sense. Believing it was too late to change the flow of events, now that both the men in front of him knew what had occurred, he reluctantly nodded his agreement.

The listener at the sitting room door smiled to herself. Her one and only child deserved the best and the status acquired by connection to the McCarthys would be well worth tolerating a 'used' wife.

Good on ye, Willie. If you are taking on that spoilt hussy, Eimear, you need a good payment.

Her only regret was she would have to keep the news of Eimear's transgression from the knitting club, for a while anyway.

Joe McCarthy, accompanied by Willie, drove back to his house where Fr Matthew and Sgt Kelly were ensconced in his study drinking tea. A heated discussion followed.

Mary's walk with the children was cut short because of a heavy downpour. The children were quite content to continue a game upstairs but needed refreshments, so Mary wandered down to Meg in the kitchen. Meg put her finger to her lips indicating Mary remain quiet.

The loud voices emanating from the study were impossible to ignore but, in his haste to sort matters, Joe McCarthy hadn't closed the door properly.

Sgt Kelly seemed taken aback at Joe's plan and the part he was expected to play.

'Joe, we don't know where they are gone. Of course, I will go with you to Galway and make enquiries, but the local Garda can take over after that.'

'No, this stays between us. I am not having all and sundry knowing my business. This stays between us, the four walls, and the few others who, of necessity, need to know.'

Fr Matthew rose from his seat and struck a thoughtful pose as he leaned against the fireplace.

'So, tell me, Joe, am I correct in understanding that you are willing to accept your daughter's return, despite her disgraceful behaviour, on condition she marries Willie here? And you, Willie, are you content to marry and, if I may be delicate here, a young woman who has been intimate in such a manner with another man and committed such a grave sin, and still retain respect for her?'

Willie nodded, quickly smothering the slightly belligerent look that had started to form, and piously responded,

'Yes, Father, I am willing to marry Eimear. I have always been fond of her and will do my utmost to respect her going forward, with the help of prayer, of course.'

Fr Matthew blessed himself with the 'Sign of the Cross'.

'You are a good man, Willie. A credit to your family and God will reward you for your graciousness.'

Joe stood abruptly, irritated by the false piety.

'Enough. We are all four going to Galway in my car, immediately.'

Sergeant Kelly reluctantly sat beside Willie in the rear of the car. Teachers and priests held sway in all small Irish towns, and he knew he had no choice but to fall in line. His sneaking compassion for Eimear was well hidden in front of the three men bent on a mission of salvation.

Galway was a bustling town, a fledgling city, but the intimacy of Ireland still existed.

'Aye, I saw a young couple about 12 o'clock or was it 11? Let me see now,' and the station clerk rubbed his stubbly chin as if in deep thought.

'Pretty lass she was. They struck me as a bit worried, anxious maybe, might be the ones you are looking for. I did think it was an unusual time of year for a day's holiday. Mind you, Limerick can be nice anytime, not as much rain as we have. Now, I always like a day in Clare myself. Not too far and lovely countryside. If the sun is shining…'

'Limerick. Did they take the Limerick train?' an irritated Joe interrupted, reacting testily to the ponderings of the clerk. 'What train did they take? Answer me, man.'

Joe's face reddened, and as his hands clenched aggressively, Sergeant Kelly intervened.

'Now, Joe, let me just chat a bit. You sit over there.'

Joe and Fr Matthew retired to a bench. Willie paced restlessly back and forth glancing impatiently towards the clerk and Sergeant Kelly in animated conversation. After a few words, quietly and earnestly spoken, Sergeant Kelly re-joined them.

'They took the Limerick train at midday, but he thinks they were heading to Cork. They sat on a bench near him, and he overheard their conversation.'

'Why all that palaver so? Could he not just have said that immediately?' and Joe stomped off to buy tickets for the next train to Limerick.

Sergeant Kelly ran after him.

'Joe, I cannot go off and leave Kilford without a guard. When you arrive in Limerick go to the nearest station and they will give you any help you need.'

Sergeant Kelly was forceful for the first time in his career and did not back down from the strength of Joe's glare.

'Right then, I have no time to waste,' and Joe stomped off. As it happened there was no further train to Limerick that evening so, with great reluctance, all four men trooped back to the car for the return drive to Kilford. Joe, Willie, and Fr Matthew made arrangements to reconvene early the following morning.

Compassion for Eimear swamped Mary. Eimear may have been better educated and considered of a higher class than herself, Eileen, Beth, and Anna but she had still been just as powerless. Mary was not the only one reading about Eimear, but her reaction was at variance to Anna's.

'Wow, and wow again,' uttered Anna aloud. 'Good for you, Eimear. I never could have guessed how much you were like me. I hope you got away safely.'

Intrigued Anna continued to read.

Beth was also fascinated to read about Eimear, someone she thought had always had every opportunity handed to her. For her part, Eileen was a little scandalized but there was a frisson of excitement coursing through her, and she knew she had to find out what happened.

Chapter 15

A cup of coffee was sorely needed and, as always, Eileen accompanied her coffee with a large slice of cream cake. 'All in moderation, that's the trick,' and once more settled herself to read.

The fire had been lit and the flickering flames brightened the dull wet evening. The windows streamed from the steady downpour, but nestled in her comfy chair, Eileen was at one with her world and returned once more to the convent in Mayo.

Eileen clattered around the kitchen unaware of the pointed looks of irritation floating her way from Sr Francis, the cook, and Sadie and Joan, the helpers from the village.

'Where is Beth?' enquired Sr Francis. 'She has a soft hand with the pastry. You are making it too sticky, and it is too hot.'

Eileen ignored the query. *How could she respond, anyway? Every Monday Beth went out on her own to clean the church. They all knew that. She had no idea why she had not returned and even less as to where she now was. If she were to hazard a guess it had something to do with that one Anna, but they had, as always, kept her out of the loop. Mary probably knew what was going on and maybe she was with them.*

Eileen blinked rapidly, forcing that tingle behind her eyes to dissipate. It always meant tears would follow and once they began, they never stopped until her nose streamed, and her eyes stung. Nothing had changed. Despite feeling she had grown a little closer to Beth, she was always on the outside. Disgruntled, and more than a little peeved, Eileen purposefully grabbed the rolling pin and with a conscious effort stopped herself from bashing the table. It was self-preservation because she knew the exasperated looks from Sr Francis would generate a flow of sobbing, impossible to halt.

It was noon two days later when Eileen was called into the study. Her first knock was soft and elicited no response. The second knock sounded loud and demanding to her own ears and she quaked at the harshness imbued with irritation from the one word, 'Enter.'

Fr Matthew sat in a chair at one end of the desk beside Mother Superior, but Sr Cornelius was stationed by the window. Her stern and disapproving eyes raked Eileen as she slid, gracelessly, through the door.

'Sit,' ordered Sr Cornelius as she took her place opposite the priest.

Eileen sat in a chair in the centre of the room, squeezing her palms with her bitten nails in an effort to stop shaking. The legs of the chair seemed to shake of their own volition and creaked every time she moved, the noise, almost an insult in the solemn silence emanating from her three inquisitors. She had no idea why they needed to talk to her and could not fathom any transgression that required such a formal interview. Eileen tried to keep her head bowed, her eyes on the floor, but their stares were magnetic drawing her gaze upwards, locking with that of Sr Cornelius.

'Now, Eileen, do you know where Beth and her friend Anna have gone? Think carefully before you answer.'

'No, Sister, no, really. I don't know anything.'

'You had better be speaking the truth, Eileen. The actions of those two girls are outrageous, running away like that and stealing money as well.'

Eileen was shocked but also astonished at the priest's expression as well as his intervention.

'Ah, now, Sister, it wasn't too much.'

'Two pounds is a lot of money, Father.'

'No, no, it wasn't two pounds, only two shillings.'

Sr Cornelius pursed her lips, unused to being contradicted, quite sure she was correct but loath to disagree with Fr Matthew.

'Forgive me, Father, but I think two shillings is quite a tidy sum and, regardless, all stealing is a sin.' 'Of course, Sister, you are quite correct, but we must be charitable.'

Eileen listened to this exchange, wishing she was anywhere but in that room. She focused on her lap and cringed with embarrassment. She could see how her thighs stretched her skirt, moulding their shape and cushioning the sides of the wooden chair. Mother Superior now intervened, interrupting Eileen's preoccupation, grounding her in the present once more. Eileen had never heard her speak before and was surprised at her soft tone.

'Eileen, please think carefully. Perhaps something was said over the last few days, something you have disregarded as unimportant.'

'Yes,' interrupted Sr Cornelius. 'Now is not the time, Eileen, for false loyalty.'

'Please, Sister,' admonished Mother Superior, gently. 'Let Eileen have some time to reflect. You see, Eileen, the safety of the girls is paramount. Their parents will have to be notified and will be worried. We need to be able to reassure them that they are in good hands. Also, we will be shamed as we are responsible while they are in our care.'

Turning to Sr Cornelius, Mother Superior continued, 'Am I correct that Eileen is now here alone, although there is another girl, I understand, who came with them from the islands?'

'Yes, Mother Superior,' responded Sr Cornelius, 'That other girl is staying in Mr McCarthy's house. I believe she will be travelling to Dublin in a week or two.'

'So, is it possible Eileen can accompany her?' and to Eileen, 'Eileen, we will have to discuss what is best for you. You may leave, now. Anyway, it is almost time for your lunch.'

Eileen stood up awkwardly relieved to be dismissed and anxious to leave the study before any more questions were asked. Her chair scraped the polished parquet boards, teetered precariously for a second, and then crashed noisily to the floor. Stooping quickly, Eileen righted it as speedily as possible and then with minimum grace left the study.

Sr Cornelius followed Eileen, pausing her with her usual sharp tone.

'Go to your room, Eileen. You need to fast for the rest of the day, to reflect on whether you have told us the full truth, and also to pray for guidance to direct your future course. I will ask Sr Monica to bring a tray up to you later on.'

Eileen went immediately to her room, glad to escape the study and lay down on her bed. She was curiously calm and although hungry, for the moment, her thoughts were elsewhere.

She wished she knew where Beth and Anna had gone. If she knew, it would mean they had confided in her, perhaps liked her, maybe were her friends. And Mary, she had to try and contact her. She was really more of a friend than the others. It is possible she might know where they had gone. Maybe one of the daily convent workers could get a message to her.

The afternoon dragged by, and Eileen remained in her room. Her pillow became more sodden as the hours slowly passed, but Sr Cornelius' instructions to pray were ignored.

Unceremoniously, without even the semblance of a knock, the door was suddenly pushed wide open.

'Come downstairs at once, Eileen,' ordered Sr Boniface. 'Nothing will be solved by you sulking away, especially when there is work to be done.'

Reluctantly, Eileen dragged herself from the bed and followed the nun downstairs. Dinner was being served. Beth usually assisted Sr Francis, but Eileen was instructed to take her place.

'Put on this apron and don't drop anything.'

Eileen did as she was bid and managed to complete the task with only a few minor splashes.

The promised tray was not forthcoming after all and her own meal was served, instead, in the kitchen. Yet her appetite remained lacklustre, and she returned to her bedroom as soon as she was allowed. The evening was warm and bright, and the sun streamed through the window. A disconsolate Eileen sat on the window seat and the twittering of birds, as they teased a stalking cat, distracted her for a while. She could also see the distant roadway through the window and was disappointed to see Mary walking away from the convent.

'*She must have called to see me after all. I bet that Sr Cornelius turned her away.*'

Risking Sr Cornelius' wrath, she sneaked out and waited in the gloom of the dimly lit corridor. Luckily before too long she spotted Maria, one of the daily cleaners, as she was about to leave for the evening.

'Maria, please, can you stop at the teachers' house and give this message to Mary?'

Slightly exasperated, as Maria was anxious to get home, she nevertheless agreed. She had a soft spot for Eileen, a slightly ungainly, obviously awkward girl, a reminder of herself at that age.

Eileen closed her eyes and once more became that shy, nervous girl. That feeling of isolation, of being totally outside all that was happening, overwhelmed her again. For the next few minutes, she mentally castigated that young self for her passivity and dependence but, as always, common sense came to the fore, and she continued to read the events that led to her staying alone at the convent.

Chapter 16

M ary smiled; her anxiety of the past few days slightly eased as she read about those far-away days. She remembered her teenage, self-conscious self, the crush she had on Eoin.

'How I liked Eoin,' she mused, 'yet I was always totally tongue-tied when I met him.'

As Eimear's story began to further unfold, the tension that developed in the McCarthy household enveloped Mary once more.

Mary worked through the day, restless and agitated. Her usual diligent attention to the younger children was haphazard at best. She alternated between regret at assisting Eimear and hoping she got away safely. In between she worried her own part might be discovered and she would be sent home in disgrace. Yet, genuine concern for Eimear and what the future might hold for her, overrode all her meanderings.

Eimear's mother was nowhere to be seen, having gone to her room with instructions to have her lunch served upstairs. The afternoon drifted slowly by and the children, sensing the strain in the house, were difficult and demanding. Once tea was over, Jean reappeared and released Mary from her duties.

'I will see the children to bed this evening. You have had a long busy day,

Mary, like us all I might add. Anyway, relax now. Walk over and meet your friends.'

It was still a little early to go to the convent, so Mary sat on her bed and did her best to accurately describe the day's events in her journal. It was not an easy task as she had to resist the impulse to describe, in detail, all that had occurred with Eimear. She needed to outline enough that her memory would be accurately jogged in the future but, should her diary fall into the wrong hands, Eimear's name and personal trauma would not be revealed. It was important to describe her own feelings and recount her worry over Eimear, what the future held in store for her, and how it might affect herself. Writing was akin to a release. It helped her put everything in perspective and ease her anxiety. Afterward, Mary donned her cardigan and sauntered over to meet with Beth and Eileen. It was a balmy July evening, and she relished the peace and quiet as she rambled along. Neither Beth nor Eileen was available to chat or walk with her, so unusual for her but feeling distracted, Mary ventured over to the presbytery to see if Anna was free. Advised that Anna was unwell by the housekeeper, she disconsolately traipsed back to the teachers' house. It was only in hindsight that she recognised that turmoil that day was not confined to the teachers' house.

Eoin was lounging by the front door, apparently extremely relaxed. Mary knew he must be aware of what was going on, but he gave no sign. He tried to engage her in conversation and glad of the distraction, for once, she responded to his questions. Her initial nervousness when he was around had dissipated and she was now somewhat relaxed in his company.

'What's your plan when you leave here?' he queried. 'Is it off to England with the other girls?'

'Well, that is the idea. When we are all sufficiently fluent in English, passage will be arranged to a convent in Liverpool or London. I have no wish to go there though. I intend to go to America. I have family there.'

'I would like to emigrate too,' replied Eoin, 'but I must finish my education first. Be a teacher I suppose.'

The depressed tone of his voice made Mary query, 'Is that what you want to be?'

'Not really. I think I would like to be a vet, but I doubt I will obtain a good enough matriculation.' Mary was unsure how to respond to this. Her own education had ceased at fourteen and the intricacies of secondary school, never mind university, were alien to her. Conversation lagged and Eoin muttered something Mary couldn't catch before he began to walk away. He turned, lingering, as he reached the gate,

'G'night, Mary, I hope Eimear and Tommy get away and make a new life for themselves.'

Mary nodded, 'I hope so too, Eoin.'

Relieved the subject had been broached, and that Eoin was not in sync with his father, Mary felt a little more at ease. At a loose end, she retired to her room, but sleep was elusive. She spent a restless night wondering about Eimear, trying to analyse what her father might do. Thoughts of Eoin intruded, how nice he was, and how she would be considered as unacceptable as Tommy. A flush of disappointment suffused her, and she resolutely forced herself to turn over and think of home and America.

The McCarthy house was busy from 6 am the following morning. Joe McCarthy had arrived back late the previous evening and arose early the following morning refusing, unusually for him, any breakfast. Commotion in the hallway heralded the arrival of his companions and he ushered them into the study. Indistinct voices, that were nevertheless sharp in intensity, emanated from the room, their loud voices travelling easily up the stairs to where Mary lay contemplating the day. By the time she made her way downstairs for breakfast, they were already on their way to the train station. Lunchtime saw them installed on the train as it moved sluggishly out of Galway Station heading towards Limerick. Fr Matthew removed his breviary from his surplice and began to read. Joe was restless and alternatively shook his newspaper, although he never appeared to read a word, and paced the corridor. Willie dozed and seemed quite at ease. The intention was to proceed directly to Cork, but Joe, exhausted from such a demanding day and endlessly questioning his own actions, decided to delay until the following morning.

'Tomorrow is another day, and we will start afresh,' he stated as he ordered a taxi, refusing to catch Fr Matthew's eye. Sensing Fr Matthew was about to expound on the intimacy another night entailed, Joe held up his hand to interrupt him before he began.

'Enough, what is done is done. We will have some dinner now and start early tomorrow to look for them. They have little money and will have sought directions at the station. We will do the same, but, we do it tomorrow.'

Joe hailed a taxi, and the three men were delivered to the nearest hotel for the night. They sat quietly around the dinner table. Fr Matthew delicately picked at his food whilst Willie swallowed his meal with gusto, flecks of food gathering on his moustache, a myriad spray of the repast coating those sitting nearest. Joe found he had no appetite, consumed instead with debating the wisdom of his decision, aware that delaying the journey a further day was simply prevarication. Memories of Eimear as a small child coursed through his mind and he worried their relationship would forever be broken. Yet, he could not bring himself to veer away from the course he had set. He unquestionably knew Tommy Hanratty would bring her nothing but unhappiness, but as he stared across the table at Willie O'Dwyer, he shivered with misgivings. With a terse 'goodnight' he said he would see them both at 8 am in the morning.

Early Friday morning the three went directly to the station and boarded the first train to Cork. On their arrival, they hastened to the nearest Garda station. An obsequious Sergeant McVeigh, his scapular plainly visible, agreed to accompany them to the nearby hotels and boarding houses to seek answers. They were not as easily forthcoming as the answers received in Galway. Nevertheless, there was only one obvious direction for those on foot seeking cheap lodgings on a dark wet evening. Painstakingly, the local sergeant called to each premises, which he believed was within their budget, and by mid-afternoon, the registration of Mr and Mrs Hanratty was located. The landlady was overwhelmed by remorse to have harboured such illicit behaviour on her property.

'Oh, my goodness,' she exclaimed. 'Well, I never. It is scandalised I am, totally scandalised. Oh, Lord, save us, to have such wanton behaviour in my house.'

She readily agreed to all three men tackling the situation immediately.

Eimear and Tommy lay in ignorance sprawled across the bed. Desire had been quenched and reignited and sated once more with their lovemaking. They lay with limbs entwined and hands clasped, encircled in a bubble of unadulterated joy. The harsh banging on the door shifted them from their reverie and instantly back to reality.

'Eimear, open the door immediately,' roared Joe, quickly followed by Fr Matthew's appeal.

'In the name of God, abandon Satan and his evil and come out to your father, Eimear.'

Tommy slowly opened the door and confronted the four, flushed and angry, men. In the background the landlady scurried away, blessing herself in agitation.

'Mr McCarthy?' Tommy inclined his head politely, as he queried, 'Can I help you?'

'Help me,' expostulated Joe McCarthy, as the sergeant stepped forward and placing his hand on Joe's shoulder, announced,

'Hanratty, you are under arrest for abduction with further charges to follow.'

Non-plussed, but not in any way cowed, Tommy responded,

'Don't be absurd. I am here with my wife Eimear. Please leave us alone.'

Eimear now appeared beside Tommy. Willie took a step towards Eimear and made a half-hearted attempt to clasp her arm, abandoning the effort once he encountered Eimear's sneer of derision. Turning she addressed her father.

'What is going on here? I am not returning home. I explained it all in my letter. I love Tommy. And what are these men doing here with you anyway?'

The appearance of Eimear had taken Joe aback for a moment but finding his voice, he now entreated her to leave.

'Eimear, you are coming home with me. You did not marry, and you will certainly not be marrying this man, despite what you say. Fr Matthew will hear your confession and young Willie here is willing to overlook your indiscretion and save your reputation.'

As Tommy attempted to close the door the sergeant grabbed hold of him.

'Young man, you are coming with me,' and deftly handcuffed Tommy.

Tommy was tall with an easy strength, but the swift action surprised him, and with hands tied, he was no match for the bulky sergeant who hauled him down the corridor to a vacant room.

'I'll stand guard here Father while you assist Mr McCarthy to sort that young lassie. The landlady is contacting the Garda station for some additional help. We will keep him locked up for the day. However, best be on your way to the train station as quickly as possible and take the next seats back home.'

The pressure from her father and the insinuations from Fr Matthew was too much for Eimear. The triumvirate of the Church, male power, and dominance disregarded Eimear's thoughts, desires, and needs. To a certain extent, she could understand her parents' disapproval of Tommy, but it was impossible to accept that her wishes, not alone had no value, but were not even considered. The idea that two others, the priest and a neighbour, colluded in her humiliation was mortifying at the very least. That Tommy was detained under threat of arrest if he impeded her departure was all too much to bear and she marched ahead of all three men to the train station. She did not utter one word to her father, Joe, and studiously ignored Fr Matthew and his attempt to wrap his arms around her in comfort. As for Willie, Eimear could not abide him or bear to look at him. By 3 pm she was on a train to Galway and by 10 pm that night she was back in Kilford.

Eimear went directly to her room once they reached home and tossed and turned all night, missing Tommy, and unable to reconcile how her father had not only dragged her back but, seemingly, had a prospective husband lined up. The idea that this man, Willie O'Dwyer, someone she had known since childhood but with whom she had no connection, had travelled with her father to haul her back home, was inexplicable to Eimear. It appeared her relationship with Tommy did not deter this man. On the contrary, from his look of disdain and disapproval every time he caught her glance on the return journey to Galway, he appeared to despise her. These thoughts pounded through Eimear's head as she lay restlessly in bed, degraded and humiliated. She was over twenty-one and a primary school teacher, a source of pride to her father. Yet, that pride did not allow Joe to grant his daughter autonomy. Eimear realised that simply because she was a woman, it was acceptable for her father to treat her as a possession to be bartered.

There was a recognition within Mary that her conversations with Eimear had broadened her own horizons and given her a perspective on life and of where women were placed. Beth, Eileen, and Anna never got to know Eimear as she had and viewed her as a privileged, educated daughter with the world at her feet. They never realised how she was as positioned and regulated by society's rules as they were themselves, albeit with a little more power.

Consequently, Eileen, Anna and Beth had mixed reactions to Eimear's fate. They had not been close to her, and she had seemed to always hold herself aloof.

Eileen shrugged. Eimear's upbringing had no connection to her own and anyway, her own trauma and distress had been paramount at that time.

'A silver spoon and still she moaned,' thought Anna.

Beth allowed a little sympathy for Eimear to shine through her puzzlement at how a well-educated woman could have acquiesced to her father in such a way.

Chapter 17

M*ary shivered; the McCarthy household had seemed such a safe haven when she first arrived. How quickly things changed. Mr McCarthy's anger leaped off the page, but also his ambivalence. Eimear quickly sensed his obvious quandary at how he had manipulated her life. Yet the rift between them grew ever wider as his initial righteousness was replaced by sorrow the more he witnessed her distress.*

It was also strange how Beth and Anna disappeared around the same time. It was through Beth that she learned of their adventures, and again that flicker of concern gnawed, as she wondered how Anna would view her story through Beth's eyes.

Beth's grandmother Nellie, and Aunt Sheila lived in a tiny, row cottage on the outskirts of Rochdale within the county boundary of Lancashire. It was similar in appearance to a hundred others, built to house workers in the local cotton mill. Tiny cottages in neat lines of similarly, blackened, brickwork that needed pointing. Sagging windowsills and creaking front doors adorned each little home, indistinguishable one from the other, save for the state of the lace curtains. Where one house had pristine and daintily dressed windows, another had grey and often torn mismatched remnants. Sheila greeted the girls warmly, leading them into a clean if dowdy, living room where her mother sat quietly knitting by the fire.

Beth remembered them both well. Sheila had been her playmate as a child, taking her by the hand, building castles on the strand, teaching her to swim. She had left six or seven years before, treading the same path as Beth and Anna, eventually settling first in Manchester and then moving to Rochdale where she secured employment in a cotton mill. Now, inexplicably to Beth, *why would anyone want to work with nuns?* Sheila worked as a cleaner in the nearby convent. She looked much older and heavier than Beth recalled and, despite being only ten years senior to Beth, her hair was greying fast and scraped into a bun, giving her a severe, weary look. Only when she smiled, as she was now doing, did a glimmer of the old Sheila breakthrough. Beth's grandmother was exactly as Beth remembered, small and thin, wiry, with flashes of Beth's own red hair sneaking through the grey. Widowed fairly young, Nellie had been a steady rock, keeping her family together. When the time came, she helped Beth's own mother with her children.

Nellie visited Sheila in Rochdale about four years ago and never returned. Beth now sat down beside her, and Nellie's fingers curled around Beth's, mini talons, displaying a surprising strength.

'How are your father and mother and the other children? I miss them and keep promising to return but it is a long journey at my age.'

'We miss you too, Grandma. We were all surprised when you wrote to say you were staying on in England,' replied Beth.

'Ah, that's a story for another day. Now, tell me about yourself and your friend Anna. What are your plans? We were expecting you of course but not for another few weeks.'

'We both plan to get jobs and as soon as possible, our own place.'

'Your own place? Well, we will see about that,' was the cagey response. 'For now, help Sheila with the bed.'

The cottage was small, containing one main room and two tiny bedrooms. The small backyard contained an outdoor toilet. Washing facilities were undertaken, in turn, in a back scullery. Anna and Beth were to share a bed in a section of the main room. A corner had been strategically cordoned off with a heavy curtain that could be drawn open during the day. While Beth was chatting to her grandmother and assisting Sheila with the bed, Anna was gazing vacantly out the window. She was totally oblivious to the scrutiny Beth's grandmother, Nellie, now gave her as she turned from the window to ramble around the small room, selecting the odd ornament to examine before replacing it again, usually slightly askew. Sitting in her chair, wrapped in a blanket, Beth's grandmother's general appearance belied a shrewdness born of hard work, struggle, and the experience of a long life where she, of necessity, had taken control. She had also known Anna and her family and was aware of the misery that was a constant companion in the house. She drew herself upright, discarding the blanket, and patted the stool beside her.

'Come here, Anna. You chat to me and tell me all your news while the other two settle the bed.'

Reluctantly, Anna sat in the allotted place. She had always been fond of Nellie and remembered how, as a young child, there was always a welcome in her sturdy arms, sinewy from work on the farm. But she was older now and knew that young timid girl was forever gone. Nellie was only a reminder of the unhappiness she had left and the bleakness that had now found sanctuary inside her. Nevertheless, she had no choice and dutifully chatted to Nellie until she could comfortably escape.

That first night, Beth lay beside a gently snoring Anna, unable to sleep. She had a tingle of excitement at what the future might hold, aware she was on the cusp of her adult life. Yet, her mind kept returning to her home and her parents and to when her grandmother had lived with them. She seemed unchanged but at the same time out of place. Her grandma had seemed such a solid part of the island, like one of the numerous rocks, an unaltered part of the landscape. Beth's father had worried about his mother when she left for England, apprehensive as to how she would cope on such a journey, but certain she would return. When the letter arrived stating her intention to remain, he seemed quite distraught. Around the fireplace on a stormy night, his thoughts always turned towards her. He was emotional when he mentioned her name, his admiration and love shone through as he regaled them with stories of his youth.

'My father was bedridden for so long that my mother took over the running of the farm,' he would say. 'She would be up early, at sunrise, putting on the porridge. We had to get ourselves to school as she would leave while we ate and spend the rest of the day, hoeing, planting, harvesting, whatever was needed. At night, after we had eaten, she would spend about an hour mending or knitting and then she would settle Da in bed, before building up the fire. The four of us took turns sitting on her knee but, Sheila, being the youngest, usually shared with everyone. Then she would sing all the old ballads. No wind could compete with her lovely voice and the noise we made.'

The same reminiscence every time and the same glassy-eyed glint would glitter in his eye, but the stories were like a blanket that warmed the family and shielded them from the harsh work of the everyday.

Beth turned restlessly, a furtive tear of her own squeezing from under her eyelids quickly dried to a stain on her cheek. Her father's voice resonated once more, dredging memories that threatened to overwhelm.

'The islanders looked to Ma whenever there was trouble, especially the women. You know, Beth,' her father intoned, 'island women, maybe all women, but certainly those here, they have a special bond. They talk and support each other but there is always a central rock. That was your grandmother. If there was a death, she was called on to wash and lay out the poor soul. If there was trouble in a family, usually from drink or perhaps hungry children or a woman who received a clout, it was your grandmother who found some food to spare or whose tongue lashed the man who was too handy with his fists. And, of course, when I married, and as the eldest she passed the farm to me, she stayed on helping out. She got on well with your mother but perhaps she felt a bit useless because she was no longer in charge. I know she missed Barry and Sadie when they went to the States, but I think Sheila leaving, her youngest, really upset her.'

Eventually, all these thoughts jumbled in Beth's mind and, as evenings by a fire transposed onto windswept mountains with sheer cliffs dropping to the screech of gulls into a roiling sea, lulled her finally into sleep.

Anna slept well and was calm and composed the following morning. Her tacit agreement with all suggestions made it difficult to understand what she really thought. Leaving her island home, followed by the trauma in the presbytery and the all too speedy departure to Dublin and Rochdale, had a strange effect on her spirits. In turn, she seemed to be docile followed by spurts of volatile activity that seemed somehow frenzied. Her erratic mood swings gave Beth pause but the need to find employment pushed any worry to the back of her mind. Sheila suggested they should call up to the local cotton mill nearby and see if they were hiring.

'They are usually busy this time of year, already preparing Christmas stock and I hear the pay is good.'

'Did you work there when you first arrived, Sheila? I thought Dad said something like that.'

'Aye, I did, for a while but then things changed.'

Sheila turned briskly away, clearing the table of a handful of crumbs, slightly distracted.

'Anyway, try your luck there this morning,' she reiterated over her shoulder.

Anna and Beth dressed in their best which consisted of just skirts and sweaters that had seen too many years. The mill was a daunting edifice, grey, austere, with billowing smoke, and steam. Thundering noise from the machinery reverberated in waves as they entered a side door labelled, 'delivery'. The air, thick with dust, invaded Beth's mouth sucking the moisture from her tongue, clogging her nostrils and ears. Through a suffocating blanket, Beth roared at a man holding forth inside the entrance and could only lip-read his response. His waving arms indicated a route to another entrance. Anna stood placidly, not engaging, and then turned and followed Beth to the next building. It was Beth who approached the desk and reddened when the thin, sour-faced gentleman, seated behind a vast typewriter, snapped,

'Speak slowly, girl. I cannot understand that brogue.' And almost as an afterthought, continued, 'Bloody Irish, can't even learn the King's English, yet come in droves looking for work.'

Smarting, Beth enunciated as clearly as possible,

'We are wondering if there are any positions available?'

'Wait here.'

After some time and the completion of forms, the girls were dismissed but, nevertheless, received confirmation that they could start the next day. His attitude rankled with Beth, unsettling her, dimming any fledgling excitement at so easily obtaining a job. Anna just nodded, impervious to either irritation or delight.

The first few weeks of work were exhausting and a strain, especially on Beth. The women who worked in the mill had their own circles, the English, the Irish, and the others. A common bond was poverty, but nationality bestowed a hierarchy. The Irish were low down on the list, but the Gaelic Irish were lower still. As newcomers, Beth and Anna were allotted the more difficult and monotonous jobs. Their place was at the bottom end of the scale and Beth railed inside against the regime instilled by the employers, but also the other workers. Prudence reminded her to keep her thoughts to herself. Anna, as usual, said little but seemed to accept with equanimity whatever was asked or expressed. One or two of the male overseers paid special attention to her and the manner in which Anna preened disturbed Beth, but she was at a loss to explain why. The first morning Anna refused to have lunch with her was unusual and further irritated Beth.

'Sorry, Beth, Jack, the overseer, asked me to finish this piece.'

'You're entitled to your lunch break, Anna. Thirty minutes won't make much difference.'

'Hush, I know, but we are new. Best I do what is required.'

Beth shrugged and sat outside eating her sandwich and drinking her milk, now a little sour from the heat inside the workshop. She sat alone on a bench in what passed for a garden although one girl, passing by, gave her a nod.

A few days later when she went to collect Anna she was nowhere to be found. Outside, leaning against a tree, Beth spotted her smoking with Jack, the overseer. Anna waved and called her over, but Beth declined. Something in Jack's stance and the way he leaned towards Anna gave her pause so Beth shook her head, declined the invite, and finished her lunch alone.

'You seem to have become very friendly with Jack,' was Beth's opening retort on the way home.

'I like him, and Andy, too,' responded Anna. 'They're fun. The only thing fun about this place.'

'We have only just arrived, Anna. We will make friends. Things will improve but we need to settle first. Since when have you started to smoke anyway?'

'I always liked a fag. You know that. I just never had any money.'

'You still have no money and don't forget that promise to pay back what you stole.'

'Oh, Beth, you are such a fusspot. Anyway, Jack and Andy give me the cigarettes so stop your nagging.'

Both girls finished the trip home in tense silence, the strain not lost on Nellie when they entered the cottage.

Beth was also reading about those first few days in Rochdale and, not for the first time, murmured aloud,

'I was too young myself to realise how deeply traumatised Anna was after the events in the presbytery. Only now do I understand how those events coloured all her actions and how her carefree attitude was just a veneer.'

Eileen was totally engrossed in Beth and Anna's adventures. At last, she was reading about their experiences after they ran away but, unfortunately, she had to read about herself too. That familiar surge of inadequacy niggled in the background when she read the opening lines.

Morning came and with it, as per usual, a gnawing hunger. Eileen could not understand how she was always the one who craved food and yet looked like she needed it the least. She hoped Maria had delivered her note to Mary and maybe she might see her that evening. Dressing quickly, she descended the stairs to the kitchen.

'There is a pile of vegetables to be prepared,' greeted Sr Francis, 'but you won't be up to much without some food. Butter that soda bread and carve a few slices of ham. Not too many, mind you, it is needed for lunch.'

Sr Francis turned away and busied herself at the stove. Eileen sat down and gulped the food; almost afraid it would disappear before she had an opportunity to consume it. The morning passed in a busy haze. Guests were expected that evening but there were also meals to be prepared for the other nuns and packages for the poor and destitute in the surrounding area. Through the window, Eileen saw Fr Matthew and Sr Cornelius greet the teacher, Mr

McCarthy. The three were to eat with Mother Superior in the private dining room. Sr Monica served them first, but Eileen was ordered to bring in the tea and cake.

'Come in, child,' was Mother Superior's soft response to Eileen's knock.

The tray wobbled precariously as Eileen entered, milk splashing liberally forth onto the starched, white, tray-cloth. The convent's fine bone china tinkled in tune with her trembling hands, and she blushed quite crimson as four daunting characters watched mutely as she rattled the tray onto the table. Eileen forcefully closed her ears to the symphony of clinking and clattering from the cups and saucers. She could feel the heat emanating from her face and knew her underarms must hum after a long day in the stifling kitchen. Her hands were clean, but the bitten nails and cuticles were unsightly.

'Thank you, Eileen. That will be all. We will ring if anything else is required.'

For the first time, she was glad to hear instructions from Sr Cornelius and scurried back to the kitchen.

Eileen, of course, was unable to hear any of the ensuing conversations, otherwise, her ears would have joined her scarlet face.

'Quite a pleasant child,' was Mother Superior's opening comment.

'Mmm,' was Fr Matthew's less than interesting response.

'I will be totally frank,' said Sr Cornelius firmly. 'Eileen is an impressionable girl. Contact with the other two, Beth and Anna, will have left a mark that might not be easy to erase especially if she is on her own.'

Mother Superior now addressed Mr McCarthy.

'Mr McCarthy, am I correct in stating your young girl, has now gone to Dublin?'

'Mary? Not yet, Sister but we are arranging for her departure in the next few days.'

Mr McCarthy spread his palms as his voice trailed away. His own problems at home were at the forefront and it had been with great reluctance he had agreed to this meeting. However, he had tremendous respect for Mother Superior and didn't want to seem unhelpful in any way.

'Well, is it possible Eileen could accompany your girl to Dublin if we have her ready on time?' continued Mother Superior. 'Eileen cannot be allowed to venture alone to Dublin, never mind England. How sensible is your student, Mr McCarthy?'

'Mary seems like a very practical and reliable girl. I will enquire from my wife, Mother Superior, and see what arrangements have been made.'

He stood to leave but was forestalled by Sr Cornelius. Imperiously, she waved for him to be seated.

Reluctantly, Mr McCarthy resumed his seat, but his thoughts began to wander as Sr Cornelius got into her stride.

'I firmly believe God creates us all for a purpose. I believe Eileen will be too easily influenced by those of an easier virtue. When I look at her, her ungainly physique, and her apparent inability to avoid the temptation towards gluttony, I am led to the conclusion that she was directed here by our Heavenly Father so we could look after her. Mr McCarthy, I propose that you find her a match. A congenial farmer with a small bit of land will suit very well. Eileen will be called to the higher purpose of producing many young souls for the Church.'

Mr McCarthy's response was slow as he was reluctant to get drawn into Sr Cornelius' plans, he had enough on his own plate. Her stare demanded an answer, however.

'Sr Cornelius, I am aware of my reputation as a 'matchmaker', but it is not something I like or wish to engage in too often, especially with such a young girl,' was the less than enthusiastic response.

'In fact, I would not like to intervene without the girl's parents being involved.'

Sr Cornelius pursed her lips, and a frown creased her already deeply indented forehead, before attempting to continue. She was precluded by Mother Superior gently intervening and, irritatingly, patting her hand.

'I am not always confident that it is up to us to direct the future of these young girls in so definite a manner, Sister. Prepare them for the world, yes, instruct them in God's ways, yes, but to confine them so totally because of our own convictions makes me concerned.'

Her words faded into the ether as Sr Cornelius stood up abruptly, her chair teetering perilously before stabilising, as though bowing to her dominance.

'Yes, Mother Superior, I totally agree, but in this instance, I think God is directing us in a very precise manner. Do you not agree, Fr Matthew?'

There was no response from Fr Matthew. His relationship with the teacher was strained after the episode with Eimear and he did not feel it prudent to take sides. Why there was such a strain was beyond him as he had only assisted in the prevention of further sin, but there was undoubtedly tension between himself and the teacher.

Without waiting for Fr Matthew's reply, Sr Cornelius bowed her head.

'Let us all pray for guidance.'

After the required few minutes, Mr McCarthy rose from his seat.

'Mother Superior, Sr Cornelius, and Father. I have some pressing business to attend to, but I will bear in mind your request. Should a suitable man come to my attention I will contact you. In the meantime, I need to return home.'

He left abruptly and was not privy to the heated discussion that ensued between the three left behind in the study.

'I hope we are all in agreement?' The enquiring look from Mother Superior to Sr Cornelius and Fr Matthew received a lacklustre response.

'I agree, Mother Superior, that we should meditate and pray for guidance before making any final decisions. In the meantime, we should also contact Eileen's parents and advise them of all possible plans for Eileen's future.'

Without waiting for any response, Sr Cornelius with pursed lips finally reached for the bell. The instruction that she was required once more in the study unnerved Eileen.

What is it now, she thought, *I have no idea what Beth and Anna planned or where they have gone?* Three solemn faces once more scrutinised Eileen as she entered the room. Sr Cornelius took the lead.

'Eileen, we have been discussing your future, praying in fact for guidance. It is our responsibility to ensure the girls entrusted to our care are adequately prepared before they leave here. We have assessed you and considered your needs. There is a calling for each and every one of us, some to higher office, others to the Lord's work, others to ensure there are children born to bear witness to the Church. Mother Superior, Fr Matthew, and I have watched over you the past few weeks since you arrived here and have come to a decision.

We believe there is a certain path that God has designed for you. Over the next week, we will pray to ensure we are making the correct choice. We will then write to your parents to advise them of the arrangements we will have made. Hopefully, they will be in a position to join us for such a celebration. That is enough for now.'

Totally confused, too nervous to query whatever they were discussing, Eileen rose, glad to be dismissed, and scurried from the room. Her spirits had lifted when she received the news her parents might possibly arrive to see her in the convent but, at the same time, confusion reigned over why.

After Fr Matthew departed, Mother Superior gently admonished Sr Cornelius.

'Sister, let us both spend some time this evening praying for the right solution for Eileen. Our own preferences and wishes should not impede our duty to ensure she is prepared for a future she can choose herself.'

Sr Cornelius bowed. 'Of course, Mother Superior. You are quite correct. I have though, been praying for some time as Eileen has troubled me since her arrival. I firmly believe Our Almighty Father is guiding my hands.'

The eyes of both women locked, supportive colleagues they may be within religious life, as women, ambitious adversaries within the limits of advancement in the convent.

Eileen was impatiently pacing around the grounds that evening, desperate to see Mary and becoming quite convinced she had also let her down.

'Hey, Eileen,' panted a breathless Mary, running to catch up to her.

'Oh, Mary, I am so glad to see you.' And Eileen hugged her tightly.

Somewhat taken aback at such an effusive greeting Mary, nevertheless, responded in kind.

'What's up, Eileen? What is so urgent? Sorry, but I couldn't get away before now. I did call over the other evening, but I was told you were unavailable by Sr Cornelius.'

Eileen rolled her eyes.

'Yes, I thought I saw you and assumed that old bag sent you away.'

Mary grinned at Eileen, unused to hearing her criticise any religious person for fear of damnation.

Eileen now blurted her news, overcome with frustration at the long wait for Mary.

'Beth and Anna have run away. No one knows where.'

'When? Where did they go?' was the surprised retort.

'No one knows where they are gone. It happened Monday morning. It was Beth's turn to check the church had been properly cleaned but she never returned. It was a few hours before we realised anything was amiss. I checked our room, and her clothes were gone. Do you know, Mary, I knew something was up. Anna only called here a few times but every time she arrived, well, you know as well as I do, it was always dramatic. Yet the last time was extremely strange. She was not crying exactly but I could tell she was distraught about something, although she tried to hide it from me. She seemed sort of distant, totally unlike her usual self.'

Mary shrugged. Anna was unpredictable but she was surprised to hear that Beth had left so suddenly.

'What did the nuns say?'

'That is what is so strange. When Sr Benedict realised Beth was missing, she went down to the presbytery. On her return, she just snapped at me to get on with my work. I was called into the study and questioned but I knew nothing about their plans. Nothing has been said since, but no one seems to be looking for them. I heard Sr Benedict whisper to Sr Cornelius that Mrs Walshe didn't seem surprised that Anna had left.'

Eileen paused for breath before, in a hushed tone, she confided further,

'I think there is money missing as well. Do you think they stole it?'

Mary was as mystified as Eileen and more than a little scandalised at the idea of stolen money. After the trauma in the teachers' house, she could do without any more tension, but she recognised that this problem affected Eileen more than herself.

'What I don't understand is why they would run away now. Sure, we will all be going to Dublin soon anyway.'

Eileen nodded sagely as she whispered.

'I think Anna must have caused some trouble and they were going to send her home. She must have persuaded Beth to run away to prevent that.'

Mary nodded, acknowledging the possibility. After all, she had no idea herself and, anyway, she wanted to discuss her own plans for Dublin and not waste time on Beth and Anna. Yet, Eileen's own issues were now taking precedence as she outlined to Mary her meeting that morning in the study and the possible, imminent arrival of her parents.

'I have no idea why they might be coming here. I hope they are not going to send me back home.'

'Surely not,' comforted Mary. 'You haven't done anything wrong.'

Eileen nodded in agreement but continued to fret, describing the uncomfortable atmosphere in the study when she delivered the tea.

After some time, even Eileen ran out of further words and Mary was able to let her know her own news.

Eileen lay the manuscript down on the table and closed her eyes. Her naivety was one thing, but the manipulation of her life had been so wrong despite its eventual outcome. Her emotions were always near the surface and ready to flow and she allowed free rein.

Chapter 19

'*H*ow unprepared we all were for the world,' thought Mary. '*None of us were mature despite the fact we were heading into the world as adults. Our immaturity just presented itself in different ways.*'

Pausing to sip her coffee, she contemplated to herself.

'*Was Eileen more vulnerable than the rest of us? She certainly seemed needier but perhaps she then received more consideration. Beth and Anna appeared so confident but maybe that made them more vulnerable, more in need of protection.*'

Shaking off these disquieting thoughts, Mary once again began to read.

It wasn't the first time Mary felt that Eileen was clingy and, in some ways, self-centred. Her news and her feelings of inadequacy were always paramount. Mary's plans had to wait until Eileen was finished expounding her woes.

'Eileen,' she eventually interrupted, 'I am leaving early for Dublin because of the situation with Eimear.'

'What situation? What is the problem with Eimear?' queried Eileen inquisitively, and rather querulously, thought Mary. Calmly, in order to pacify Eileen, Mary uttered softly,

'Do you know in all the confusion I thought you had heard. But then we haven't met over the last week. Sorry about that. I just couldn't get away and then, of course, Sr Cornelius wouldn't let me see you.'

Eileen appeared intrigued and strangely curious but a reluctance to give too much detail overcame Mary, perhaps out of loyalty to Eimear. She had no wish to reduce Eimear's romantic, maybe misguided action in running away, to salacious gossip. Yet, Eileen was now eager to hear all the details, her prior peevishness forgotten. Mary answered her questions as sketchily as she could.

'It has something to do with a proposed marriage and Eimear is not happy about it. It has been a little stressful in the house over the past couple of weeks with arguments and so forth. Whenever I could, I escaped with the younger children down to the beach to avoid all the tension.'

Despite Eileen's prompting, Mary refused to supply any more details to satisfy Eileen's unusual fascination with Eimear.

Mary could not elaborate further without feeling uncomfortable as though she was betraying a trust. Anyway, how could she articulate how the return of Eimear had cast a depression over the whole McCarthy household? Mrs McCarthy said little, beyond instructions to Mary to deal with the children. They were irritable, sensing all was not well, and fearing their father's wrath might turn on them. It was not for Eileen's ears how the daily arguments between Eimear and her father were both embarrassing and unproductive. It was not necessary to relate how Willie O'Dwyer was a constant visitor, but Eimear was steadfast in her refusal to see him, enraging Joe even more. Those details were locked away, sealed in a special compartment, until Mary felt free to enter them in her journal. Eimear had confided how her heart ached for Tommy and almost daily asked Mary to enquire if Tommy had been spotted in the village. All to no avail. The trust Eimear placed in Mary drew both girls ever closer and strengthened a bond that was to endure.

The easy companionship that had developed with Eoin was also not for Eileen's ears. Twice he joined the little group on the strand playing with his younger siblings. Mary had come to realise that all Eoin wanted was company his own age, and with that knowledge, came a fledgling friendship. Eoin's obvious interest no longer confused her, in fact, he stirred a glow inside her that she relished when she was alone in her bed at night. There was no way she was going to share that secret with Eileen. The young man that Mary initially thought cosmopolitan and from a different, wealthier world to her own, now seemed vulnerable as he too struggled with the new tension in his home. He sat with her on the beach most days, listlessly scooping handfuls of sand, only to let the grains drift through his fingers once more.

'What do you think, Mary? Would it be so awful if Eimear were to marry Tommy?'

Mary was unsure how to respond. Part of her felt Eimear had been reckless to run off and another part loved the romance of it all. Yet, she could understand the boundaries of class. Had she not felt the same when she first noticed Eoin's interest? She would be no more acceptable a partner for Eoin, than Tommy was for Eimear. She shrugged off the question and ran towards little Clare struggling with a bucket of water.

Mary's journal was her lifeline and a refuge from the troubled household. At night she described how a hot July was sliding closer to an even warmer August, how the long humid days were draining, and the endless monotony of the beach enabled a dull lassitude to creep in. How such tedium seemed impossible to shake and had begun to depress her. This introspection Mary kept to herself and her journal. When Mr McCarthy called her into his study and proposed she leave early she was relieved.

All these thoughts jumbled around in Mary's head even as she posed her question to Eileen. 'Eileen, we always planned to go to Dublin together. Now I must leave in a few days, so will you come with me? It is only a little earlier than planned.'

'No, Mary, I cannot, not yet anyway.'

'What? Why ever not?' responded Mary, taken aback. 'Are you staying here? There are only a few more weeks agreed?'

'I am not sure what is happening. As I said, my parents are supposedly coming in a week or two. They, all the nuns I mean, have some plan but I am not sure what it is. I cannot leave until I meet my parents.'

'I don't understand, Eileen. What has changed? I know Beth and Anna are gone but you and I should be able to go ahead with the original plan to go to Dublin, at first anyway.'

Eileen shrugged but stayed quiet.

Mary had arrived at the convent fully expecting they would be making plans together for their forthcoming trip. The news she would be travelling alone was unsettling and a bit frightening, but all her persuasions fell on deaf ears. Aware they were both about to travel on separate paths, conversation flagged and there were no words left to bridge the widening gap that their futures foretold. After some further desultory chat and promises to write, Mary hugged Eileen, wished her well, demanded she write,

'Write care of the teachers' house. They will know where I have gone.'

As Mary sauntered back Eoin fell into step beside her.

'Have you been to the convent to see your friends?'

'Yes,' responded Mary but she did not elaborate. Silently they walked together to the house, each immersed in their own thoughts.

A fledging plan had hovered at the edges of Mary's mind over the last few days and was cemented after her conversation with Eileen. Her fluency in English was greatly enhanced from her chats with Eoin and excitement at her pending departure to Dublin, which had palled after her chat with Eileen, began to flicker once more. She decided she would not go to England but would stay in Dublin and obtain a job in order to save for the States. Turning to Eoin she enquired,

'Eoin, do you know anyone living in Dublin? I will be leaving for there soon.'

'Yes, so I heard, and as a matter of fact, I do know someone who hails from Dublin. One of my friends from school lives there, his family has a restaurant or hotel or something. Are you wondering about work? They are always looking for staff if you are interested?'

'Oh, Eoin, yes, I am. Could you give me the address?'

'No problem, Mary.' And timidly, 'I will miss you, Mary.'

Without warning, Eoin awkwardly leaned forward to kiss Mary on the lips. Flustered she turned slightly, and he grazed her cheek.

'Sorry, Mary, I don't know what came over me.'

Mary smiled and taking his hands she responded, 'I will miss you too, Eoin.'

Leaning forward she closed her eyes, and this time Eoin found her lips and they were all that he ever imagined.

'I wish I could go with you or,' and he smiled, 'at least go to Dublin, but there is no way I could leave at the moment with the trouble over Eimear.'

Mary nodded, not wishing to upset Eoin by responding.

'He has no idea how fortunate he is,' she thought, *'to have a secure future ahead of him with no need to worry about earning money to help provide for his parents. He thinks leaving for Dublin is an adventure.'*

Mary smiled encouragingly, saying little, as Eoin prattled on about how he envied her, her freedom. They trotted along side by side, Eoin, tall and gaunt, almost gangly, hair falling slightly over his eyes, his innocence shining through his anticipation at the excitement, he believed, was ahead for Mary. *'For all his education he is very naïve,'* Mary mused, but silently to herself, aware his contact in Dublin might become useful in the future.

A week later, on a wet humid day in August, as expected, Mary was presented with a train ticket to Dublin and instructions on how to find her way to a nearby convent. There she would spend the night and passage would be arranged for Liverpool as soon as possible. Carefully secured in her bag was the address of Eoin's friend and an introduction to the family.

Mary had not long departed for Dublin when Willie O'Dwyer arrived once more at the teachers' house. This time he had been summoned and he was optimistic that Eimear may have come to her senses. In this he was correct. Eimear realised she had no option but to marry Willie. She had not heard from Tommy and Mary's enquiries had been fruitless. Eimear now had more than an inkling she was expecting Tommy's child. Crushed with that knowledge, she had bowed to the inevitable. Although Eimear kept her growing suspicion to herself, her agreement to marry Willie resulted in hastily made plans for a quiet wedding before she changed her mind. Her mother seemed totally disconnected from the whole process. Beyond patting Eimear's hand and issuing platitudes, she was totally uninvolved with her daughter's distress. Eimear thought she would scream if she heard further pronouncements on the lines of,

'*Everything works out for the best,*' or, '*God works in mysterious ways.*'

The letter she received from Mary produced a surge of envy and she was unable to respond adequately. She knew Mary would understand that she wished her well, but she was in such inner turmoil, she could not write anything but the vaguest of replies. In a state of deep depression, she accepted her fate, and linking her arm in her father's, she walked slowly down the aisle to Willie.

Chapter 20

E *motions swirled through Anna. She was angry at Beth and at how she was portrayed, but other uncomfortable, suppressed memories, threatened to overwhelm her. The details of what had occurred were fairly accurate but did not reflect the pain she had kept well-hidden and that had now resurfaced. Fortified once more with a gin and tonic she lay back against the pillows and continued to read about herself through the eyes of others.*

Beth and Anna left Mayo in August and it was now October. A cool wind howled heralding the winter to come. They had little spare cash after contributing to food and rent in the cottage, but they had saved enough for two winter coats. That day in Preston trying on coats, and even dresses and shoes, anything at all in fact, followed by fish and chips and large mugs of sweet tea, became an enduring memory for Beth. The following morning Anna was queasy.

'Must have been the fish,' murmured Beth, 'I feel a bit odd myself.'

'Mmm,' said Nellie, 'we will see.'

Anna was unwell all week and on Saturday morning, Grandma Nellie asked her directly.

'Are you expecting, Anna? Is that why you left Ireland earlier than planned or is it one of those lads you keep talking about from your workplace?'

Anna reacted as if scalded. 'Expecting, me? Never.'

Yet, Beth knew instantly her grandmother was right. Anna had been complaining of tiredness, to an extreme in Beth's viewpoint, and she knew from her own mother that sickness was a real indication of pregnancy. Anna stood to leave, her very stance indicating a rage at such a suggestion. Grabbing her coat, she roared,

'Never, not me, ever,' and slammed the door behind her.

Anna walked towards the mill, her brisk pace fuelled by the seething anger inside her. As she neared the factory gate a voice called to her.

'Anna, Anna, over here.'

Andy was leaning against the factory wall, puffing away, his companion adding to the cloud of smoke that surrounded them. Anna walked across slowly, unsure if she wanted company, yet glad of a distraction from the three busybodies in the house.

'Andy, hello. What are you doing here on Saturday?'

'There is always something for the managers to do, even at weekends.'

'Manager, a likely story,' retorted Anna and all three laughed.

'Have a fag. This here is Charlie.'

Tension oozed from Anna as she took her first puff from the cigarette. She knew Andy admired her, had asked her out in fact but she had little interest in him. She could sense Charlie staring at her, sizing her up. She caught his eye and grinned, preening a little.

Andy is good-looking enough, she thought. *But perhaps a little heavy around the middle.* She could imagine him in a few years, fat with a bald head and his ears do seem to protrude. *He will look a little like a bull,* she surmised. *Now, Charlie, he will look elegant. Slim and tanned but also nicely dressed.*

Her short time in the cotton mill had given her an appreciation of varying types of weaves and the quality of clothes produced. Anna surprised herself by recognising that Charlie's jacket looked well cut and a grade above the standard of the lads around. She wondered what Charlie did for a living.

'I don't recognise you from around here, Charlie. Do you work with Andy?'

'No, I work for myself. I have my own business,' he pronounced with obvious pride.

Anna tried not to show she was impressed but it was apparent to Charlie he had piqued her interest. He also liked what he saw. Anna's hair was now long and flowing, curls framing a face that at once seemed innocent but, somehow, also all-knowing. It was her smile, sensual and enticing, while her youth appealed for protection. Charlie was intrigued.

'Andy and meself are going for a bite to eat. Want to come?'

With no hesitation, Anna agreed and the three of them went down to the local chip shop.

'Have a beer?' insisted Charlie and Anna, who rarely drank any alcohol, eagerly agreed. An abandoned streak seemed to have taken possession of her, and as the evening wore on, that wildness, changed to a certainty that she had found new allies and new friends.

'We will walk you home, Anna,' said Charlie. 'It is dark out there. Can't be too careful.'

The icy, night air hit Anna with instant shock, and she clung to Charlie as she felt her legs give way. Andy grabbed one arm and Charlie the other and both men supported her as they led her towards the woods. Anna had no idea where she was going but sang lustily as they went, further and further into the darkness.

She awoke sprawled against a tree. Dawn was breaking and the rosy glow promised a bright day to come. Within seconds she was vomiting into the dewy, wet grass. She felt as though her entire insides were emptying but, eventually, the heaving subsided and she took stock of where she was and how she got there. She remembered Charlie and Andy and leaving the pub but after that...

Leaning against the tree, she closed her eyes, but that made her head spin even more and once again she was sick. Her energy was sapped but after a few moments, the dizziness eased, and cleared enough for Anna to realise her clothes were soggy and wet and her new coat was speckled and stained with vomit. Disgust washed over her as, in flashes, she remembered what had occurred. The mirage she had found new friends, their concern to lead her home, and then her mind refused to go further.

'Later,' she thought, 'later, I will think of that. For now, I need Beth. She will be frantic with worry.'

Anna easily found her way out of the forest, a small wood really, that was no way dense in the morning light. She raced down the hill and found her bearings within a few minutes. A fifteen-minute trot and she recognised her road.

'Beth, Beth,' she roared as she banged on the door.

Grandma Nellie opened the door wide and seeing the state Anna was in she held out her arms and folded the sobbing girl inside, rocking her to and fro' as she soothed,

'A stór, a stór, tar isteach, tar isteach.'

The Gaelic language of Anna's youth, 'Oh love, love, come inside, come inside.'

Nellie filled a basin with water. Gently she removed Anna's clothes before sponging her down as though she were a five-year-old. Smothering her in her own old dressing gown, she led her to the fire and fed her some soup, all the time, muttering in Gaelic. Anna relaxed in fits. Comforted by Nellie, she dozed, only to jerk awake as memories of her stupidity tumbled in a rush, crashing through her consciousness.

'Beth and Sheila are out looking for you. They will be back soon. Do you want to talk to me first?' Anna did, but she flushed with shame.

What will Nellie think of me? A tramp. That's what she will think.

'Hush, Anna, hush. Whatever happened can be sorted. We all make silly mistakes.'

But Anna was unable to bring herself to open up to Nellie.

An old woman, how could she understand? It was far from a silly mistake. First the priest and now those other two.

The thought of work in the mill the following day also filled her with dread.

Would Andy tell everyone?

Once again, she cringed with remorse.

Now, instead, she uttered what she had been trying to ignore but what Nellie had already guessed.

'I am expecting, Nellie. You were right. I am sorry I yelled at you.'

Nellie patted her hand. 'We will work something out, never fear.'

Beth returned first and on seeing Anna, and receiving assurance she was, indeed, all right, left again to find Sheila. When Beth and Sheila returned once more Anna was in bed, asleep at last. Nellie confirmed what they had all suspected and together they formulated a plan. Nellie's small frame had always belied a strength of mind that had enabled her to survive life on a wild island in the Atlantic Ocean, off the west coast of Ireland. Fortitude, perhaps, was innate to many women who lived on those islands.

'First, I am going to make us all a hot, nourishing meal and then the four of us will talk. I have no idea where Anna spent the night, or even if it was alone, but the most important thing is to sort out her forthcoming child.'

Their voices penetrated Anna's troubled slumber and the tenor of the faint mutterings in the room indicated they were discussing her. She gave no indication she was awake. Inertia had enveloped her for a while, possibly a protection against recalling the events of the previous night, but once she was fully roused, the memories were insistent. She recalled the feeling of camaraderie, how she enjoyed the admiration of both men, especially Charlie. She remembered them on either side as they walked through the town and towards the woods.

I didn't care where I was going, she realised. *I just didn't want the night to end. I liked when we stopped, and Charlie kissed me. His tongue caressed my lips before sending shivers down my spine as it circled around inside my mouth. And Andy, I could see him watching. I could see his hand move under his belt and down his trousers. I knew what he was thinking, what he was about to do.*

Anna groaned and rolled over in the bed, shoving her head into the pillow and digging her nails into her own thighs in a futile attempt to block out the insistent flood of memory.

I caught Andy's eye, and he came over and knelt down in the grass. And Charlie, he was kissing my neck and at the same time helping me to lie down.

Anna remembered she was glad to stretch out because she felt unsteady, but even in that drunken haze, she murmured 'no, no' as Charlie reached forward to unbutton her blouse. Andy bent over and kissed her mouth roughly, stalling her protest. As Charlie pushed up her skirt and lowered her stockings, Andy stroked her breasts. As Charlie's fingers explored inside her, Andy, stifled her cries with his hand on her mouth. And he kept his hand there while Charlie removed his fingers and his erection forced its way inside her, violating her until he was spent. But not for long, because he switched places with Andy. Anna could smell and taste herself on Charlie's fingers as he clamped her mouth shut, while Andy, quickly, took his turn. She must have passed out because she awoke lying prone against a tree with no memory of anything else. She stifled the fleeting thought that somehow there was a part of her that had enjoyed the encounter.

My private pain laid bare for all to read. And Anna wept, shuddering and shaking, anguished sobbing steadily streamed in a river of pain.

Chapter 21

E ileen donned her coat, in need of some fresh air before she read the next chapter. It was disturbing to read about Anna and Beth and an hour's reflection sauntering along the beach was essential to bolster her courage to read further. She had happily written to Mary about her own journey and all that had occurred after Mary left for Dublin. She hoped Mary had written sensitively and that her story was not in such graphic detail as Anna's. She recalled how once she had adjusted to her changed circumstances it was a relief to relate all the events and it had helped her put everything in perspective. Yet reading about that period in her life was not going to be any easier, just because she had moved on.

'The walk will do me good,' she muttered aloud. Closing the door behind her, Eileen set off at a brisk pace, the more than vigorous breeze aiding to clear the jumble in her head.

Eileen had no idea why her parents were coming to the mainland, an arduous journey at the best of times, never mind the expense, but Sr Cornelius had assured her they intended to make the trip. She was exhilarated at the thought of seeing them. Lately, with Beth gone, she had double the number of chores and no energy at night to do other than go to sleep. She missed meeting Mary already, even though she was only gone a few days and hoped she would write soon. Eileen assumed at some point in the future she might join her in Dublin.

It was Friday noon when Sr Cornelius requested her presence once more in the study. Eileen wondered what her latest transgression was and if it required punishment. Her only joy was food and Sr Cornelius seemed to sense this and withholding it was her penance of choice.

'Sit, sit, Eileen,' she ordered. 'Don't look so woebegone. I have some good news for you, but we must wait a few moments.'

Eileen relaxed, presuming it was news of the day her parents were to arrive. A sharp rap on the door was the precursor to chasing that illusion away. Two men entered the room and Eileen looked quickly away, shy in their presence.

'Eileen, I think you met Mr McCarthy before, our local school principal,' and with a wave of her hand, Sr Cornelius indicated the taller of the two men.

'You might not be aware, but he is also our local matchmaker.'

The significance of this statement did not dawn on Eileen as she was too engrossed in making herself invisible.

'Sr Cornelius, lovely to see you, as always.' And turning to the gentleman accompanying him, Mr McCarthy continued, 'And, Sister, this is Mattie Doherty.'

Sr Cornelius nodded, her eyes assessing, even as she waved her hand at Eileen.

'Yes, indeed,' responded Sr Cornelius. 'Eileen, manners, please. Say hello to both gentlemen.'

Eileen peeked out from behind her curtain of hair. 'Good day, sir, sirs,' and retreated once more behind her shield.

Both men sat in chairs that had been placed at each end of the desk. Eileen, once again, found herself sitting alone in front of three intimidating adults.

'Now, Fr Matthew should be along shortly. It is not like him to be late,' continued Sr Cornelius. 'Look up at me, Eileen.'

Eileen raised her head only to find Mattie Doherty staring intently at her. For a moment she was distracted before she rapidly looked away. His stare penetrated and surreptitiously she registered a man of about forty-five with black hair rapidly receding.

He will soon be bald, she thought to herself, even as she took in the brown suit. The shiny knees on the trousers and the patched elbows spoke of a long life. The blue shirt looked clean but had missed the iron.

'Eileen, are you listening to me?'

'Sorry, sorry, Sister, of course, I am.'

'Then kindly show me some attention.'

Turning to address the two men, she continued,

'Perhaps we should start. Fr Matthew must be delayed. Now, Eileen, as I indicated, Mr McCarthy is our local school principal but also a valued matchmaker. Now, you are just sixteen? Is that correct?'

'No, Sister, I was seventeen last month,' interrupted Eileen.

'Well, really? You don't look it but in fact so much the better. However, you are still young and extremely immature. Added to that, you are now alone. The three girls who came over with you, and were supposed to travel on with you, are now gone. Anyway, two of them were obviously too flighty and a bad influence. Mother Superior and I have prayed for guidance. We have also spoken to Fr Matthew, and we are now all in agreement. I wrote to your parents outlining the current situation and received their reply a few days ago. They are delighted with what we have decided.'

As Sr Cornelius droned on, Eileen was barely listening. The study was stifling, and she could feel a trickle of sweat under her arms. She guessed her face was flushed and the sun, streaming in through the window opposite her chair, made it difficult to focus on the three adults facing her. The scrutiny from Mattie Doherty was disconcerting and Sr Cornelius' words barely registered.

'In the absence of suitable companions to travel and, bearing in mind your own particular personality, we believe a match is the best solution for you. I wrote to your parents and they, as you know, weather permitting, will arrive next week. Mr Doherty is anxious to meet them and gain their approval before the marriage goes ahead.'

Eileen gaped, not entirely sure of what she had just heard and too panicked to ask for it to be repeated.

Surely, they weren't suggesting she marry that old man? Her parents would never agree.

Even as she thought this, she knew they might. They worried about her going away and knew she was distressed at leaving. Yet there was no future on the island. Here was a husband willing to take her on and it meant she could stay in Ireland.

'Eileen, Eileen, answer me.'

'Sorry, Sister, what did you say?'

'I said this is an opportunity for you. Your own home. Mr Doherty has a small farm. It is near the sea. You will like that.' Sr Cornelius smiled gently. 'This is right for you, Eileen. Now thank Mr McCarthy and shake hands with Mr Doherty and we will all meet again in a week's time after your parents arrive. Go now and pray.'

Eileen automatically did as she was bid, apparently acquiescing, but turmoil was building inside. The tranquillity in the small, convent church did nothing to calm the confusion inside her. She bowed her head and tried to connect with the heavenly figures she had been taught to believe looked out for her welfare. The mantras of her youth had no meaning, 'Hail Marys,' and 'Our Fathers,' even in Gaelic, had no relevance to her predicament. She felt adrift, flotsam to be collected and discarded at the will of others who felt they knew better. The stillness in the church seemed to mock her, at odds with the fever raging inside her, for which she had no expression.

Eileen had been unable to eat her dinner that evening, and a restless night followed. Her dreams tormented her, startling her awake every thirty minutes. Mr Doherty looming over her with a pike, being lost in a fog in London and unable to find her way, Fr Matthew leering at her while Sr Cornelius tempted her with food, only to snatch it away as she tried to take some. She awoke numerous times through the night bathed in sweat with her heart thumping. Clarity came with the morning light. Eileen knew she could not marry that old man and had to find the courage to say so. Being alone had always scared her but the thought of marriage was even more frightening. She could not return home because that meant returning to a life of nothing. There was always the nunnery, but she knew it was not for her. She could not contemplate spending her life in a convent with the likes of Sr Cornelius or even the mild-mannered Sr Francis. She had to persuade her parents to let her travel to Dublin and to

Mary. It was mid-afternoon when Eileen summoned her courage and knocked on the study door to speak to Sr Cornelius.

'Enter,' was the imperious response.

Hesitantly, Eileen opened the study door.

'Oh, it's only you, Eileen. I will talk to you later. I am busy here with Mrs Walshe. Run along now.'

The glare from Sr Cornelius shattered the last vestige of courage in Eileen's possession and she scuttled away, more degraded than ever.

The day was surreal in many respects. Mrs Walshe had reported Fr Matthew missing. It seemed he had not returned from his walk the previous day. The housekeeper was quite distraught when questioned by Mother Superior. Her recent illness had left her weak and, apparently, a bit confused.

'He went out, as usual, yesterday, Mother Superior, to walk the beach and pray. I knew he had a meeting with yourself, so I wasn't expecting him back until later. In fact, I left him a cold plate in the dining room and went to bed early. I have been sick, you know, and with Anna gone, the work is just too much for me. The presbytery is large…'

'Yes, yes, Mrs Walshe but Fr Matthew. What happened?' was the impatient response.

'Well, I don't know. He is missing. When he didn't appear for breakfast, I assumed he had been called away to attend to a parishioner. By lunchtime, I was getting a bit worried because Paddy Murphy had arranged to meet him in the presbytery at eleven and I had also noticed the plate in the dining room was untouched. There was no sign of him anywhere and no word which was very unusual. So, I spoke to Sergeant Dwyer. He is organising a search as we speak. He told me to come here and let you all know.'

The convent throbbed with a mixture of concern and excitement and Eileen heard snippets of what was going on. She knew no one would listen to her worries until Fr Matthew was found. The atmosphere in the convent was frantic and everyone was ordered to the chapel to pray for his safe return. Later that evening news was received that Fr Matthew had been located among the rocks and four local men were dispatched with a stretcher to retrieve the body. Further news filtered through slowly but there was no doubt Fr Matthew was dead and had possibly been attacked. The realisation dawned on Eileen that any opportunity to persuade Sr Cornelius to change her mind about the matchmaker had disappeared. She would have to wait until things calmed down, talk to her mother when she arrived, and persuade her to intervene on her behalf.

The town was buzzing with the news of Fr Matthew's death. Lurid stories abounded, one more sensational than the other but no perpetrator was found. The convent was shrouded in mourning and early Tuesday morning the entire community of nuns, accompanied by any resident staff, walked down to the village church. Eileen, of course, was among them. Fr Matthew's remains were carried in a slow procession through the village and into the church. They would lie there for the next two days before the funeral on Friday. Silence and prayers for his eternal soul continued into Wednesday and Thursday. No one had time to listen to Eileen and she bubbled inside with resentment and frustration that she was unable to voice her fears and refuse to marry Mattie Doherty.

On Saturday morning she donned her coat and walked down to the pier. It was a wet, windy day but she barely noticed. It should have been a happy time, seeing her parents after so many weeks, but she felt twisted and turned, manipulated. When her mother and father disembarked, for a few minutes, delight surged through her. They were still the same. Dressed in their Sunday best, her father clutching his cap tightly in his hands, her mother, smoothing her skirt, holding it against the breeze, joy suffusing both faces. They took turns to embrace her, one more impatient than the other. A measure of comfort bathed her as she thought,

They will sort things. They love me. As these thoughts floated through Eileen's mind, her mother, totally oblivious, blurted happily,

'Oh, Eileen, Sr Cornelius wrote to us. You are to be married. I cannot wait to meet him. Oh, my love, I am so happy. Now you will not have to go away. You will be near enough to see us every so often.'

Enveloped in a hug, Eileen's muffled retort went unheard.

'Mammy,' she stammered, even as her father kissed her cheek and murmured,

'I am happy for you, Eileen. I believe he is a good man. A little old, maybe, but settled. He will know how to treat you right. If not, he will answer to me. I am near enough to be sure you are well cared for.'

A stream of good wishes and of congratulations, a tidal wave of joy, swirled around Eileen. Caught up in the maelstrom, Eileen was unable to utter the word,

'No.'

Eileen's parents were welcomed by Sr Cornelius who informed them of the recent tragedy.

'Our wonderful Parish Priest, Fr Matthew, was attacked and left lying among the rocks. The scoundrels have not been apprehended and we fear they never will be. However, we will not allow this sadness to interfere with the celebrations for Eileen but, of course, it will be a quiet affair. A temporary curate, Fr Sullivan, has been appointed and he will conduct the ceremony.'

Gently, Eileen laid the manuscript on the table and closed her eyes, refusing, in vain, to allow any memories of that young girl to haunt her sleep.

Chapter 22

Mary groaned aloud. Anna could easily object to her portrayal. More importantly, was it accurate? Had Beth's own bias coloured how she viewed Anna and her actions?

'It is possible she will ask me to remove her story from the manuscript or, at best, rewrite it,' thought Mary. 'How important is accuracy? Is it daft to fabricate Anna's story but leave the rest as fairly authentic?' Mary paced the floor, no longer surprised that anger between Anna and Beth still simmered.

It was as well Mary could not see Anna. She wanted to rip the manuscript in half but yet had a compulsion to see how the story unfolded. The indifference she had displayed at the lunch table could not be sustained. Alone, there was a fury that surged inside her and threatened to overwhelm her, no matter how she attempted to suppress it. Sipping a gin and tonic did nothing to calm her as she began to read once more.

In her cosy house across town, Beth was also reading. Lost in nostalgia, her grandmother's face swimming before her eyes, it was some time before the blurred images on the page made any sense.

Anna struggled out of bed, dreading the talk that lay ahead but knowing there was no way to avoid it.

'Glad you are safe, Anna,' said Sheila. 'We were worried about you.'

Beth looked enquiringly at Anna, but Anna shook her head and mouthed that she would tell her later. Anna had no intention of telling Beth anything later and vowed to herself to never divulge what occurred to anyone. As she approached the table three sets of eyes stared expectantly at her. She sat down, poured herself some tea, and taking the 'bull by the horns', Anna started the conversation.

'Beth, your grandma, Nellie, was right. I am expecting a baby. But, Beth, you know how that happened. Nellie, Sheila, it was the priest where I was staying.'

Sheila gasped, her hand automatically covering her mouth, 'The priest? Never, Anna.'

Forcefully, Beth interjected.

'Sheila, it was the priest, and you can understand how difficult it is for Anna to admit it because no one believes a priest capable of that.'

For a moment Sheila appeared chastened and lowered her head, yet her eyes exhibited open disbelief.

Nellie countered. 'Sheila, believe me when I say, he's not the first priest and won't be the last. Unnatural, that celibacy lark, if you ask me.'

This remark caused all three women to look astonished, Sheila openly shocked, but Nellie continued,

'Anna, you will have to leave work soon. They will never keep you on at the mill once you start to show. There will be talk because you are unmarried. Now talk won't kill you but, once the management hears, you will be told to go.'

'Will I, eh, will I have to leave here?' stammered Anna.

'Sssh, no. I will deliver the baby meself. Did it many a time. No, you can find something to do when you have to leave. Take in washing or something like that.'

Anna was visibly relieved and all but gasped.

'Oh, thanks, Nellie, thanks, and Sheila, is that alright with you? It is your house after all?'

'Well, it is not my house,' retorted Sheila. 'It is Nellie's, but anyway, it is all right with me too.' Heaving a large sigh, Anna continued,

'Afterwards, it can be adopted. Your convent can sort that, Sheila, can't they?'

Beth could not fail to notice the looks that passed between Nellie and Sheila, but Anna, like a child, felt her problems for the moment were solved. It was Sheila who spoke first.

'No, Anna, if you have the child here, it will stay here. No adoption.'

Anna was nonplussed, a spanner in what she had presumed was a perfect solution.

'But why? I don't want it.'

This time Nellie intervened.

'Anna and Beth, let me tell you a little story. When Sheila, my youngest, left the island I was distraught but, more than that, I was lonely. Of course, there was you, Beth, your brothers and sisters, your mother, and my son Seanie, but Sheila had always been mine. My other children were gone away, and I accepted that. You see, Sheila came late in my life, and I was able to enjoy her in a way I was unable to enjoy the others. I loved them with all my heart but there was little money and a lot of hard labour. Your granddad was very disabled with a bad leg, so I had to undertake a lot of the farm work. When Sheila came along, your father, Beth, was old enough to take over much of that work. When she was about two, my husband, your grandad, died, so I only really had Sheila to care for. When she left, and I know there is no other path for a girl unless you marry, I missed her so. Your family, Beth, were able to manage quite well without me, maybe even better.'

Nellie laughed and waved at Beth as she attempted to demur.

'Ah, Beth, I know we all got along well but married couples need their space. Anyway, the post was always irregular, but Sheila's letters had become very sporadic, and I was worried something was amiss. I decided to travel over and check on my Sheila, my baby...'

Nellie beamed as Beth and Anna grinned in concert at the idea of Sheila as a baby.

'As I was saying, I travelled over to see Sheila...'

Beth waited expectantly for Nellie to continue but Nellie was watching

Sheila. Sheila caught Nellie's eye and an unspoken communication appeared to pass between them.

With a slight movement of her head, Sheila paused Nellie, and continued herself.

'When Mamma found me, I was in the convent,' continued Sheila. 'I had given birth to a little girl just four weeks beforehand. She had already been adopted. You know, many girls underestimate their mothers, and I was guilty of that. I should have trusted her and told her what was happening. We both cried, and we spoke to the nuns, but there was no going back. My little Nora was gone, forever. Well, at the time, Mamma was in a lodging house but when she decided to stay, she rented this house for the two of us. I stayed on at the convent cleaning. In the beginning, it was to work off the debt I owed for the help I received in delivering the baby, and then they kept me on because they needed a cleaner.'

There was silence in the room as all four absorbed the story. Anna and Beth with new eyes and ears, Sheila, and Nellie, with renewed sorrow over Nora. Beth was full of questions.

'The father, Sheila. Who was he? Where did he go?'

Sensing Sheila's discomfort Beth's voice trailed away but Anna, perhaps less sensitive, attempted to interject but her question was nipped in the bud, by Sheila's raised hand.

'Beth, Anna. No more. I have told you all I can for now. Maybe some other time.'

The hollowness in Sheila's tone combined with the agitation playing across her features quietened both girls. It was some time before Beth had the courage to continue.

'Grandma, if Anna keeps the baby, and of course it is up to her, how will we manage? I mean you must feel the cottage a little cramped since we arrived and with a baby...?'

Her voice trailed away as Nellie responded.

'A baby is never a bother, Beth and Anna. They are a blessing. Like Sheila, I cannot bear to see another mite brought into the world, this house, and see it disappear to who knows where.'

Although Anna remained quiet, her expression displayed an array of churning thoughts, quickly camouflaged. Whether it was relief, pragmatism, or just to buy time, Anna acquiesced.

'That is fine with me. I will work in the mill until I show. The money will be needed. Now, if none of you mind, I am going back to bed.'

Anna rose without waiting for a reply. She was, of course, still in the same room, but with the curtain drawn, there was a semblance of privacy and Anna could hear the conversation continuing uninhibited.

'Thank you, Sheila and Grandma,' continued Beth. 'It really was not Anna's fault what happened with the priest.'

Sheila pursed her lips, still unable to believe a priest capable of such an act, but Nellie nodded.

'As I said, not the first time that has occurred.'

'Can I ask something else?' queried Beth. Without waiting for a reply, she continued,

'How did you manage to get this cottage, Grandma? I thought you had to work in the cotton industry to get one? Does the management not own them all?'

'Ah, they used to, built them in fact, but then they began to sell them to private landlords. Many an Irishman bought them, and so when I decided to look for a place, I put on my Gaelic hat. A man called John Casey owns this street. His family hailed from Mayo, although he himself was born in Manchester. It was that connection that clinched the deal. I suppose the antipathy towards the Irish lingers on even if generations have passed. It makes the Irish, and not just the Irish, all nationalities, stick together and look out for each other.'

Beth interjected, 'Some of the girls at work mentioned something about the Irish always getting drunk and fighting. I think that is why they dislike the Irish so much and why Anna and I found it difficult, at first, to make friends. It is easier now.'

'Well, after the Famine,' said Nellie, 'there were a lot of Irish who fled here for work out of hunger and desperation. I suppose such a huge influx of people in such dire straits created antagonism. Add to that, the few who always cause trouble, and everyone is tarnished by association. However, never forget it was the English who decimated our people, impoverished them, not just with necessities like food, the almost obliteration of our language, but with the withholding of education and the right to prosper. So, you know that connection with Ireland never goes away, and I used it to my advantage with Mr John Casey. Anyway, I got the cottage and Sheila moved back here but, sadly, without Nora.'

'I am sorry to hear about your baby, Sheila.' Beth rose and hugged her aunt before turning stealthily to wipe her dampened cheek, wet from the stream of Sheila's silent weeping.

Moving aside the curtain she attempted and failed to cajole Anna out of bed for a walk.

It was Beth who appeared more anxious at work the following morning, worried that Anna's condition would be instantly recognisable, but there was no remark passed. Anna was serene, blithely unconcerned, and as the day wore on Beth relaxed. This pattern continued for the next week and Beth truly believed Anna understood her position and was content to let Grandma Nellie and Sheila help her. Nellie had no such illusions. Shrewdness, born from age and experience, enabled her to sense the turmoil hidden underneath Anna's calm exterior. She reminded Nellie of the deceptive currents that ebbed and flowed around her native island. On the surface, the sea invited the unwary. Indolent waves sluggishly danced towards the shore, but only a strong swimmer could escape the treacherous undertow that encircled the careless. She watched Anna and was not deceived.

Meanwhile, on the following Monday, Beth had an issue of her own. The regimen in the mill dictated toilet breaks and shortly after she returned to her station, she knew she needed to visit the privy again. The cramps in her stomach were a sure indication that her monthly period had arrived, the wetness now seeping between her legs a very definite confirmation. Mr Russell, as they were required to address the foreman, was not receptive.

'Mr Russell, sir, may I be excused for five minutes?'

'Certainly not, you had your break. Continue with your work.'

'But, Mr Russell, I need…'

'Quiet. Either continue or leave. But if you leave, you leave for good. Do not address me again.'

As he strode away, a flag of pomposity, Beth fumed. She was uncomfortable and dreaded the embarrassment should her condition become obvious. More than that, there was a seething resentment inside her that a natural condition of womanhood was not recognised, and toilet breaks were at the mercy of an arrogant male. Restricted by the necessity to work, especially now with Anna's baby on the way, she returned to her bench. As soon as the lunch bell rang, she raced out to see to herself. On her way back, she paused. In the distance she could see Anna sitting on a low wall, swinging her legs nonchalantly, smoking, and chatting to Jack. Already in an agitated state, she was further unnerved. It was not so much Anna's actions, more the way she held her head or bent to whisper in Jack's ear. Unable to tackle any more controversy she turned away, clenching her fists, in a vain effort to control a further flare of anxiety in an already tension-filled day.

Finally, after a stressful week, Saturday arrived. It had become the custom for both girls to ramble into town in the late afternoon, once work was completed. They had little money to spend, even less now, as it was essential to put as much aside as possible. Yet, the atmosphere in the shops and the music from the bandstand in the centre of the town generated a carnival mood and drew both girls like a magnet. On the way home, it was obligatory to buy fish and chips for all four women for tea that night. It was one of those Saturday evenings as they walked home with arms linked, that their old closeness resurfaced, and shrouded in the familiar intimacy known since childhood, Anna hesitantly told Beth the full story of what had occurred in the woods.

'Oh my God, Anna,' Beth gasped, horrified. 'How could you let that happen, how could you, knowing you were expecting as well?'

Beth's hand clasped her mouth, eyes wide, unable to conceal her disgust. Shame flooded through Anna and, soiled again, she reacted, as usual, with anger.

'You are so perfect, Beth. We cannot all be like you, you know. How does it feel to have a tramp for a friend, living with you, sleeping with you?'

Anna marched off, her stride quickening with each step. Beth followed slowly doing her utmost to digest what Anna had confided to her. That evening the atmosphere in the confined cottage crackled with tension and the small, shared bed made sleep impossible. The strain was palpable the following morning and both Nellie and Sheila knew something was amiss but neither girl confided the reason. Yet, the heightened friction could not be sustained, possibly from sheer exhaustion, and slowly, over the next two weeks the animosity between the girls eased, and their shared history fought its way unsteadily back to a semblance of normality.

Nellie examined Anna and guessed she was now about 20 weeks pregnant, but no one would have guessed as her lithe frame concealed any sign of pregnancy. Her sickness had passed, and Anna, of all the four women, seemed the least concerned at her condition. The girls' usual Saturday outing continued but was disrupted a few weeks later when Anna spotted Jack near the bandstand. She pulled and dragged a very reluctant Beth into a position near enough so Jack would notice them. See them he did and introduced Anna to his friend, Freddie, while turning questioning eyes towards Beth. Anna and Freddie quickly became engrossed in a deep discussion, while Jack, after a few awkward minutes, queried,

'Do you work with Anna? Don't think I have seen you there. What did Anna say your name was, again?'

'My name is Beth, and yes, I work at the mill too,' replied Beth quietly.

'Wow, I cannot believe I haven't seen you and it is hard to miss that hair! Anna is quite something, isn't she?'

Beth could only shrug, unsure if his comment on her hair, never mind Anna, was meant as a compliment or not. Beth and Jack stood side-by-side for the most awkward and uncomfortable fifteen minutes that Beth could ever recall. Unable to stick it any longer she insisted they leave. Anna was not only displeased but quite annoyed and they walked home in tense silence once more, only communicating about the type of fish to buy on the way. The discord eased once again over the next few weeks, and even though Beth continually remonstrated with Anna over her now, continual, smoking, Anna was in better form, more relaxed, and at last beginning to talk about what she should do when she had to leave the mill.

Beth was unsure how Anna would react when she read this account. Anna had told her in confidence but, Beth, probably from anger, recounted it all to Mary.

'I am sorry, Anna. I blamed you and made you feel demeaned,' she murmured aloud. 'You didn't deserve to have your secrets betrayed,' and Beth felt her cheeks flush with regret.

Anna was also flushed but it was with anger, red hot anger.

'How dare Beth! And Mary, how dare she think she can publish intimate details of my life. No way will that happen.'

The manuscript, already battered, once more, hit the wall of the hotel room.

Chapter 23

A sense of unease enveloped Mary as she read her own manuscript. She wondered what effect it was having on Eileen, Beth, and Anna. She knew it was important to include details of her own journey, that it would be a dishonest account if only Beth, Anna, Eileen, and, of course, Eimear's stories were heard. Her own personal trauma was always lurking in the background, and she dreaded bringing it to the fore once more. Reluctantly, she began to read about her life in Dublin.

Mary found her way to the convent quite easily, the instructions clear and concise. Her few meagre belongings were packed into a battered case that had seen many a better day. A profound sense of loneliness overcame her as she believed she was the only one of the original four girls to make it to Dublin. Her promises to write to both Eileen and Eimear would be kept once she was settled but, for the first time, she believed writing would not dissipate her isolation. Deliberately she pushed the last image of Eimear from her mind. She had too many issues of her own to deal with and focusing on Eimear's distressed and ravaged face just disturbed her. Eileen's uncertain future was another cause for concern and another letter that had to be written. Where Beth and Anna were, was anyone's guess.

The address in Dublin was easy enough to locate which was just as well. Although she had few possessions, Mary's bag was bulky, and the strong east wind tugged the case in a variety of directions while simultaneously steering her in another. She bashed and clattered her way from the train station clutching the map drawn by Mr McCarthy. Her hair, grown long over the summer, blew in her face and she felt bedraggled as she rang the bell on the heavy oak door of the convent. 'Welcome, welcome,' smiled a kindly face and Mary gratefully handed over her letter of introduction.

'You stayed with Mr McCarthy? A lovely man, I am sure you learned a lot. Come in, come in out of the cold and I will get you some tea while we wait for Mother Superior.'

Mary politely followed the kindly nun into a spacious dining room with floors of highly polished dark, brown oak. The mahogany table was the largest she had ever seen and was surrounded by twelve ornate chairs upholstered in a deep royal blue. She sat on the edge of the nearest one, intimidated by the plush surroundings.

Her friendly nun brought her tea and scones and told her to relax.

'Mary, dear, don't look so worried. Mother Superior is a gentle soul and we have seen lots of young girls pass through here. She will look after you and make sure you are properly sorted. Enjoy your tea now, she won't be too long.'

A flurry outside the door announced the arrival of Mother Superior. Her more than ample girth shook the chair as she seated herself. Chest heaving, reddened cheeks growing ever more crimson she puffed and bellowed instructions.

'You are to remain in the convent in Dublin for two weeks and then accompany Sr Ignatius to Liverpool,' she wheezed. 'In the meantime, you are free to explore the city, but you must be careful to stay on the main thoroughfares. Otherwise, enjoy your few days here in the capital. I will get Sr Dominic to show you to your room.'

Exhausted by the exertion required to utter the few words, Mother Superior leaned forward on the table in order to haul herself to her feet, her chair shuddering and creaking beneath her. Mary sat immobile unsure whether to assist or not, terrified such a well-upholstered woman would topple at her feet.

The next day Mary wandered down O'Connell St., thoroughly in awe of the magnificent statues and the imposing buildings. She had committed the address Eoin had given her to memory, but she faltered in her step, surprised, when she suddenly stumbled across Sackville Place. It was a small side street abutting O'Connell St., but it was just as busy. Mary could see that it was mainly a creamery but in two parts. The frontal section was unobtrusive and obviously a very refined, restaurant and café. The second section was only barely visible, bounded as it was by a high wall and gates, but the sign above was distinctive. 'Mountcarrick Creamery'. The restaurant appeared to be just a small part of a very busy enterprise. There was no conscious decision, Mary's feet just began to move of their own volition, and before she knew it, she was at the entrance to the café.

'Would you like a table, ma'am?' enquired a friendly voice and Mary stumbled a reply.

'Well, I have an introduction in my bag, if by some chance you are hiring. I have a recommendation,' rushed Mary, the awkwardness of her reply making her blush to the roots of her fair hair.

'Sit here and wait a few minutes. I will be back.' Mary did as she was bid.

'Good day. I am Mr Higgins. How do you do?' uttered a voice that seemed to emanate from the ceiling. Mary, still sitting, gazed up at a man so tall and thin, he towered over all present in the restaurant.

'Come with me.'

Obediently, Mary followed the gaunt individual into a small office.

'May I see your reference, please?' he politely requested.

'It is not a reference, not really. An introduction letter,' stuttered Mary. 'From Eoin McCarthy. He has stayed here... he is friends with...'

'I know Eoin,' interrupted Mr Higgins, 'a nice lad. How do you know him?'

'I stayed in their house, minding his younger brothers and sisters.'

'Ah, yes. Mr McCarthy, the teacher.' Mr Higgins thrust out his hand for the letter. 'Now, let me read it.'

Mary tried her best not to fidget while Mr Higgins took an extraordinarily long time reading the letter. 'Mmm. Where are you staying at the moment?'

'The Sacred Heart Convent.'

'Are you intending to go to England? Would a position here be just a stopgap? It takes time and money to train young girls properly.'

'Oh, no, Mr Higgins. If I had a job, I would stay here. I much prefer to remain in Ireland.'

'Very well then. I will get Mrs Maxwell to show you around, explain the duties expected, and if that is acceptable, on the basis of this letter, we are happy to employ you for a probationary period of a month. After that, we will see. It will also be necessary to obtain approval from the convent before you can commence work.'

Mary nodded and waited while Mr Higgins scribbled something on a notepad. He then rose and opened the door, calling to a young girl in another side office.

'Miss Kelly, please take this young lady, Mary O'Connell, down to Mrs Maxwell and request she be shown around with a view to an introductory position. Also, hand this note to her. Tell her to call into my office if she has any queries.'

And turning towards Mary he reiterated,

'Please remember this position will only be temporary until we are satisfied you are suitable to work here.'

'Thank you, Mr Higgins. Thank you,' gasped Mary and followed Miss Kelly.

'My name is Linda. Linda Kelly. Nice to meet you, Mary. I am going to take you to meet the manageress Mrs Maxwell and she will let you know your duties.'

Linda made the necessary introductions before leaving Mary with Mrs Maxwell.

'All girls start in the creamery and that is where we are going now. The restaurant was Mrs Comerford's idea. She is the owner's wife. It is very popular and always busy, but the creamery is the main business.'

After leaving the back entrance to the restaurant they entered through a side gate into a large courtyard humming with activity. Horses and carts were lined up as milk churns were loaded and unloaded and instructions barked before they moved quickly on to make way for the next cart. The noise and the clatter indicated mayhem, but Mary soon discerned that everyone knew what they were doing. They crossed the yard, taking care not to step in the ample mounds of horse manure, and entered a large three-storey building.

'Now this is where you will work.'

The large, bustling kitchen was steamy and hot and redolent with the scents of roasting meat and baking bread. Except for a nod from a very rotund woman, quite likely the cook, no one paid them any heed, so intent were they on tasks in hand. Mrs Maxwell pattered on.

'The creamery never really closes but the main activity commences at 4.30 in the morning. You will need to be in the kitchen by 4 am in order to prepare food for the men's breakfast. Now, you look a bit shocked but never mind, you will have lots of help. At 10 am the men will be fed again, which amounts to dinner, and then at 2 o'clock, there is a light tea provided before most depart for the day.' Glancing at Mr Higgins' brief note, Mrs Maxwell continued, 'Now, I believe you are currently staying in the convent, is that right?'

'Yes, yes, it is,' answered Mary.

'We do our best to make life as easy as possible for our staff,' replied Mrs Maxwell.

'On the third floor, we have lodgings for the female workers. Many girls do not live here but opt to stay when they are on an early shift. Those from outside Dublin find it quite reasonable and pleasant to stay permanently. So, follow me and see what you think.'

Mary returned to the convent that evening rehearsing what she would say to Mother Superior. Mrs Maxwell had shown her the restaurant but advised her she would not be working there yet. Whether the creamery would be acceptable as a place of work, with the number of rough, albeit, kind men, was questionable. It took some persuading but eventually Mother Superior said she would visit the creamery and then make a decision.

'I have to be sure you are being well looked after. Mr McCarthy and Fr

Matthew expect nothing less. I will call into the creamery tomorrow and then we will see.'

Mary followed both women into the kitchens and around the yard, Mother Superior's girth and flowing habit, making progress lumbering and laboured. The raucous and often strident tones from the unkempt and shabbily dressed men almost overpowered the clatter and racket of the yard. Questions were posed and answered before Mother Superior and Mrs Maxwell eventually climbed the stairs to the staff quarters. Mary only released her breath when she saw both women smile and shake hands. Once the final blessing had been received Mary returned to the convent with Mother Superior.

'You are to start next Monday,' she puffed. 'On Saturday you can move into the creamery lodgings.'

In many ways the creamery was the start of my life's journey. It all seems so distant now. I was so young, so hopeful…

Chapter 24

Despite her anguish at what she considered Beth's betrayal, Anna *was intrigued to learn of Eileen's fate. Had Eileen gone ahead with the arranged match, or had she refused at the last minute? Anna settled down to read, wondering how she had fared.*

'Almost there now,' grunted Mattie as the cart turned up a bog road. Treacherous ruts and holes were avoided as practice, born of experience, enabled him to steer the cart without too much discomfort.

Eileen was unable to make up her mind. *Was she glad to have arrived after such an awful day or was there worse to come?*

The events of the past week had swept her along with little heed to her wishes. Sr Cornelius was insistent that the wedding take place, despite Fr Matthew's death, while her parents were visiting and her mother, her lovely mother, was only too happy to comply. A dress was supplied by the convent, one that Eileen would never have chosen. Besides being too tight, a fresh wash had not eliminated a musty smell that still lingered in her nostrils. Her father had walked her down the short aisle in the convent church. Eileen stood beside Mattie Doherty, a man she viewed practically as elderly as her own father, but a man soon to be her husband, and wondered if she would always be adrift, her desires swept away by other plans. Sr Francis had prepared a small wedding breakfast but even the sight of the cake, specially baked for Eileen, could not raise her spirits. She felt unable to swallow, her mother's words choking her as they lingered, reluctant to leave.

'Remember, Eileen, you might not like it at first, but it gets better, easier. You will relax and enjoy it later on.'

'It? She knew what her mother meant, and the thought terrified her.'

'Let me help you down from the cart, it's a bit boggy here,' muttered Mattie, but Eileen refused, and jumped off quickly, landing in a pool of soggy peat. Stumbling, but determined to try and maintain some control, Eileen responded,

'Thank you, but I am fine. Maybe just carry in my bag.'

The darkness was like a shroud, the night sky shedding no light on the farmyard. It was difficult to see any path to the front door or even make out the shape of the cottage. Despite herself, she was glad to feel a guiding hand on her elbow as she picked her way forward. Inside the door, Mattie lit a lamp and led the way over to a well-banked fire that smouldered in a grate. He poked it with an iron rod, twisted and blackened from use, and flames flickered into life.

'Get yourself warm first while I put the kettle on the hook. You can make some tea when it's boiled. That's a lovely fire,' continued Mattie, holding his hands to the blaze. 'Good neighbours are a wonderful blessing. Now, you make your hot drink and relax and rest here. I need to see to some of the animals.'

Mattie headed back out into the night carrying the lamp. Eileen looked around the room dimly lit by flames that danced and shimmered across the floor and the walls. The water soon boiled and, as instructed, she made tea and then examined her surroundings. The cottage was basically one central room with a bedroom on either side. She opened the door of one room and then the other, but the firelight did not penetrate, and it was a hopeless task to attempt to see anything. A pressing need made her realise she had no idea where the outhouse was.

Was there one indoors, unlikely, so it must be outside? she muttered to herself. Eileen opened the front door but without a lamp, it was impossible to get her bearings. Apprehensive, taking small steps, guided more by instinct and need, than knowledge, she located a secluded spot. The hastily chosen bush revealed itself to be heavily endowed with thorny prickles. Ignoring the barbs, she hastily lowered her underthings and relieved herself as quickly as possible. She returned to the seat by the fire and finished her tea. The heat and the long day did their work and by the time Mattie returned Eileen was fast asleep. Mattie watched her for a few moments from the doorway before attempting to rouse her.

Eileen woke with a start, confused as to where she was, and who was the strange man diffidently leaning over her. Realization quickly dawned and she clasped her coat around her, eyes wide with terror.

'Hush, now. It's only me, Mattie.'

Slowly, Mattie eased Eileen to her feet and guided her into the adjoining bedroom.

The creeping dawn, through dusty windows unadorned by curtains, woke Eileen from a deep slumber, the most relaxed sleep she had experienced in a long time. Instantly she knew where she was and glanced to either side expecting to see Mattie, her new husband. It was apparent, that not only was she alone, but that he had slept elsewhere. She lay fully clothed on an old, well-used, but clean-smelling quilt, her coat tucked around her. A heavy woollen blanket, its bright tartan colours a murky grey in the early dawn, lay across her for warmth. The room was shabby, its dark walls casting a gloom, and the heavy wardrobe and chest of drawers in the far corner created further shadow. To the right was what appeared to be a new door. Curiosity aroused; Eileen walked quietly across the wooden floor. She turned the handle cautiously, heedful of disturbing the morning silence, and peered around a door that squeaked in protest. A new indoor closet had been installed, complete with a wash-hand basin and a large towel sporting a few threadbare patches. It was little more than a lean-to, and there was a strong draught whistling through some ill-fitted boards, but Eileen smiled to herself with pleasure. After washing and changing her clothes, she ventured into the main room. Mattie was nowhere to be seen although the pot of porridge was still warm. Hunger pangs assailed her, and Eileen helped herself to a large bowl. Refreshed, she wandered outside.

The morning was dull and misty but promised heat later on once the haze was burnt from the sky. There were a few cows in a nearby field and several sheep in the distance. Otherwise, Eileen was entirely alone, surrounded by endless fields, stone walls, and the distant shimmer of the sea. Where Mattie was, she had no idea. Returning inside, she tidied, pleased enough with the small cottage. An attempt had been made to clean it, and although it was sparsely furnished, it was reasonably comfortable and warm. It was not too dissimilar to her island home, and pangs of homesickness overcame her, fighting with an odd sense of belonging.

Turf was stacked to the side of the front door and Eileen now built up the fire and placed a copper pot on the hook to heat water. She was restless, unsure of what to think or do. She had dreaded the first night with Mattie, yet now she wished it had happened and the ordeal was over. She appreciated how he understood she was tired, but her stomach clenched once more at what lay ahead. To distract herself she checked the other bedroom and could tell that Mattie had slept there. She opened cupboards and presses and examined the supplies in the pantry. Finally, the water was boiling, and she washed her clothes from the day before and the few things of Mattie's she found on the floor. She assumed that these were the expected wifely duties, but she shuddered as she collected his under-things, the intimacy, something she refused to contemplate. Finally, Eileen decided to organise some food, aware Mattie would probably be like her father, up before light with only porridge to sustain him until twelve noon. He would most likely return after some hours labouring in the fields, looking for a hot meal. She peeled and boiled potatoes, chopped carrots, and onions wondering what Sr Francis would add to make it more appetising. It was most likely some herbs, maybe bacon or mutton, but nothing like that was to be found.

And so, Eileen's days settled into a rhythm of cooking, baking and cleaning. Mattie would return and eat his midday meal before once more heading off to the fields. His words were sparse. He expressed a grateful 'thank you' for whatever Eileen managed to cook and she was well aware it wasn't always tasty. The weather was the main topic. A sick animal generated a spate of words, his intensity as he spoke, displaying a well-hidden tenderness. His watchful gaze was disturbing but not uncomfortable. She got used to it and was able to ignore it. If that were all he ever did, she could live with it. In some ways, Eileen was content. The cottage was her space, and while the weather was still good, she walked the fields every day, finding little boreens and hidden glades and a secret track to a small sandy beach. That beach made her think of home and frolicking in the sea with her brothers. It beckoned to her, but it was too cold now and she was still too unnerved to swim. From time to time, she wondered about Mary, Beth and even Anna. She resolved each day to write to Mary, but the evenings slid one into the other without pen seeing paper.

Eileen shivered, recalling the powerlessness, coupled with an aching loneliness that dominated that time. It was months before she could write to Mary. For a time, she was filled with self-loathing as though she was responsible for her circumstances, as though her lack of physical attraction made her less than anyone else.

'How dare they?' she said aloud, twisting her wedding band in agitation.

'How dare they to presume to know best and leave me no choice?'

As quickly as her anger flared, it died. The emotions now aroused in Eileen made her restless once more and she knew she would not be able to read further until the next day.

'Bloody hell,' muttered Anna aloud. 'How did she allow that to happen?' Yet, even as Anna spoke those words, she realised she had been just as powerless. Her own vulnerability had led to a recklessness that affected every aspect of her life.

Chapter 25

Mary's admiration for Beth swelled within her every time she read how she had stood her ground and refused to be daunted, despite being a relative newcomer in England.

I am not surprised, she thought, but I never had such confidence at that age.

Strangely, Mary ignored how she had forged her own path, not giving credit to the independence she herself had displayed.

Two events occurred in quick succession.

The first disruption was Anna. She fainted at her station and Rosie, who worked alongside her, roared at Mr Russell when he barked,

'Get her up and outside, and then get straight back to work. Hurry up and be quick about it.'

He then rushed over and grabbed Anna by the arm.

'Leave her be to rest a minute. Can't ye tell she's expectin'?' was Rosie's angry retort and, in turn, tugged at Mr Russell's own arm.

Mr Russell flushed red with anger and batted her away. 'Is that so? Well, watch yourself, Rosie, or you will be getting the sack as well as that one. Help her up and out the door. Her sort is not wanted here.'

Beth had seen the commotion and now moved to help Anna to her feet. Grumbling, Anna stood unsteadily but then rounded on Rosie.

'Ye said you would keep that news to yourself, Rosie, that's why I told ye.'

'Sorry, Anna. It was yer man, coming over like that.'

Anna ignored her and looked at Beth.

'Stay, Beth, I will be fine. No point in both of us losing our jobs. I will see you back at the cottage.' Anna walked out the door, head high.

The second disruption occurred shortly afterwards. Cotton mills were disappearing from the Lancashire landscape as the 20th century progressed. Exports declined during WW1 and many countries developed their own industry. The mill within which Beth and Anna obtained work was archaic in its practices and struggling to keep afloat against better-resourced and more modern methods. As such, some of the old machinery lingered, much of it no longer of use and balanced precariously on old workbenches, or discarded carelessly against the walls. Some vigilance was needed when moving from one area to another. Jenny was a large girl and the gaps between the workbenches were narrow. In her haste she knocked over an ancient, rusting, handloom and screeched as it clattered to the floor, gashing her leg severely in the process.

'You, stupid woman,' roared Mr Russell. 'You will pay for that.'

'Please, sir, it wasn't my fault,' whispered Jenny, as she ineffectually tried to staunch the flow of blood from her leg. Beth was nearby and could not restrain herself. Perhaps it was the dismissal of Anna or the memory of her own humiliating experience with that odious man, but regardless, she piped up,

'Mr Russell, look at that cut on Jenny's leg. Are there no first aid supplies here? What if someone was really badly injured?'

'You watch yourself, Irish, or you will be out the door like your friend.'

'And you,' to Jenny, 'go and clean up. If that machine is damaged, the cost of repair will be docked from your wages until it is paid for.'

Jenny stumbled away, cheeks wet, her distress obvious. Calm was restored to the workshop, but it was uneasy, as eyes skirted away anxious to avoid Mr Russell's attention.

The rest of the day seemed endless, but eventually, the whistle blew, and Beth was first out the door. Preoccupied with thoughts of Anna, she almost passed Jenny without noticing her as she marched along.

'Hello, Beth,' mumbled a shy voice interrupting her reverie. Beth turned around on hearing her name.

'Oh, hello, Jenny, sorry, I was lost in my own world there.'

She was tempted to give Jenny a wide berth and carry on alone, but Jenny's dejected demeanour made Beth pause. To her surprise, Jenny's eyes welled with tears, not for the first time, as her red-streaked cheeks and snivelling nose gave testament.

'Jenny, whatever is the matter? Mr Russell will have forgotten all about you by tomorrow. Anyway, it was just some old junk you knocked over.'

'Maybe, but if the machine is broken, he will dock my wages.'

With an enormous sigh, Jenny added, 'It is hard enough to manage as it is. Me da is dead and me ma is sick, and I have three younger brothers. We all depend on my wages.'

Beth was unsure what to say so just hugged the young girl. Silently they walked along together, a small part of Beth's brain registering a vulnerability that Jenny's large frame belied. That frame, hidden in the voluminous clothes she always wore, disguised a gauntness that obscured how there was more bone than flesh.

'Jenny,' Beth ventured, 'remember, the machine was not in use and possibly was broken already. He is just being petty.'

As she spoke these words a surge of anger suffused Beth. *Even if it wasn't broken why should Jenny have to pay for it, stored as it was in such a dangerous position?*

Suppressing that thought but placing it in a compartment to be considered at another point, Beth found herself suggesting,

'Look, Jenny, there is no way they can insist you pay for that rusty bit of a machine. If they do, I am going to ask the other girls for a whip around. Anything at all will help. We will get you through this.'

Jenny gazed at Beth in wonderment, both at the idea that she would stand up to Mr Russell but also the generosity, something she wasn't used to.

'Thank you, Beth,' and with a watery smile, she answered, 'the suggestion is more than enough. No one has money to spare so best not to say anything to anyone. Just being able to talk to you is a help. As you say the machine is useless anyway. I think I am just so tired of the drudgery and being shouted at.'

They reached a crossroads, but before they headed in separate directions, Jenny squeezed Beth's hand.

'You're a good person, a good friend, Irish.'

As Beth wandered home, she realised that both herself and Anna were accepted by the other girls. Rosie had stood up for Anna, Jenny had called her, friend. They were part of a community now, one that Beth was delighted to be considered a member. She arrived at the terraced cottage drawing a deep breath as she opened the door, hoping Anna was in good form.

The three women sat around the fire drinking tea. It was 9 o'clock and there was still no sign of Anna.

'I told you already, Beth, Anna hasn't been here all day. If, as you say, she left the factory at about noon, there is no way she returned here. I would have seen her,' reiterated an exasperated Nellie. 'It's not the first time either that young lady has gone off on her own, worrying us.'

Anna was, in fact, on her way home. After leaving the factory she wandered into town. Restless, but not too disappointed at having to leave the job, she decided a ramble around the town centre would cheer her up before the endless questions back at the house. She made her way to the small park where the bandstand, now standing idle, was situated. Anna removed her gloves, her only pair, as she had no wish to dirty them. With one or two swift movements she brushed the leaves blown from a nearby oak tree off the bench, before settling herself down to smoke and think. She had developed a habit of keeping a few cigarettes, never more than a loose three, in the pocket of her overcoat and enjoyed a quiet smoke when she was alone. That was a rare occurrence because, if not at the mill, she was usually in the cottage with either Nellie or Sheila, fussing around.

'Pick up your skirt, it will be trampled on if you leave it on the floor. Don't throw your coat on the chair. Someone will want to sit there. Are they your stockings? They need a wash.'

Beth's quiet displeasure was nearly worse, and the way she picked up her things without a word, was irritating at best.

The sooner I have this baby and get away from there, the better, mumbled Anna to herself.

'Well, if it isn't little Anna. I would recognise those curls anywhere.'

Anna looked up into the assessing eyes of Freddie. His scrutiny unnerved her slightly. On the surface, he seemed quite amiable, brown hair, perhaps a bit too long, nose the same, and a wide mouth that was, in turn, attractive or appraising, depending on the smile. His eyes were a deep brown with flecks of yellow, by far his best feature but, again, seemed to be constantly evaluating. The wariness Anna felt in his presence was exciting, the type of sensation she imagined one would feel if embarking on a journey into the unknown.

'Hello, Freddie,' she replied calmly, her inner turmoil not apparent. 'How come you are here, no work today?'

'I might ask the same of you, little Anna,' he countered.

'Oh, I got the sack,' retorted Anna with alacrity. 'I am sitting here just contemplating my future.' 'Did you now?' he laughed. 'And why was that?'

'Never you mind. Would you like a fag?'

'Don't mind if I do.'

They sat in a comfortable silence puffing away, broken by a request from Freddie.

'Fancy joining me at the pictures? Good Western showing.'

Anna had no interest in seeing a Western but spending the afternoon with Freddie was a different matter.

'Yes, I would love to.'

Anna arrived back at the cottage shortly before 10 o'clock. There was a faint smell of beer off her breath and a strong smell of cigarettes but, otherwise, she was in good form.

'I hear the works let you go?' enquired Sheila.

'Yes, well it was going to happen sooner or later. Tomorrow I will check around the town, see if there are any jobs going. For now, I am very tired, so I will say goodnight.'

'Come up to the convent with me,' offered Sheila. 'They are always looking for help and there are lots of girls in your condition there.'

'My condition?' Anna raised her eyebrows but answered pleasantly enough. 'Well, I will see. I think I would like to lie in tomorrow morning for a while and you leave so early. In 'my condition' I deserve it. Goodnight now.'

'Just a minute,' interrupted Beth. 'Where were you all day? We were worried.'

'Why?' was the sharp retort.

'Well,' faltered Beth, but Nellie continued.

'Because, Anna, you are expecting and you are a young girl in a new country, and because if nothing else, we care about you, and you should appreciate that concern.'

A little chastened, Anna retired without a further word.

Anna pinched her knee, a reflexive action that halted any threatened blubbing. Her protective shell had housed her pain too well. So well, in fact, that even Beth had not sensed how distraught she was inside, how fearful of the future. Beth's memory of that time was not Anna's. But then, how could she have explained to Beth how she needed every distraction to block the revulsion she felt, towards herself?

Chapter 26

Disquiet at how Anna had been portrayed lingered with Mary. The excitement she had initially felt at the possibility of publishing her first book had waned to be replaced by a gnawing uneasiness. She could easily understand if Anna was angry.

'I need to talk to her alone, find out how she really feels.'

Mary's first week flew by, but she was constantly exhausted. On her first free day, she made her way to the convent mindful of Mother Superior's instructions that she keep in touch.

'We have to ensure all is going well as I will need to report on your progress to Fr Matthew.'

Silence, where possible, was encouraged in the convent, but even so, Mary felt an unusual hush as she stepped into the hallway.

'Follow me, please,' murmured an unfamiliar voice and Mary was led into a small waiting room.

Mother Superior bustled in, flustered, her veil flying in myriad directions.

'Oh, Mary, what is the world coming to? Poor Fr Matthew, oh, the poor man,' and Mother Superior made a hasty sign of the cross, 'bless his immortal soul, he depends, used to depend on me to ensure you girls are settled properly.'

Mary was taken aback, unable to grasp for a moment the significance of the words gushing forth in an unbroken stream.

'Mother Superior, did something happen to Fr Matthew?'

'Oh, yes, my dear. But, of course, you wouldn't have heard. No one is quite sure what happened, but poor Fr Matthew has passed away.'

Once more she made the sign of the cross. With great difficulty Mother Superior made to kneel, steadying her journey to the floor by gripping Mary's arm in a vice.

'Perhaps we should kneel together and say a short prayer for the repose of his eternal soul?'

she panted, and Mary found herself kneeling beside a heaving woman, whose breath grew more stertorous with every uttered word of the short prayer. It was with a grateful sigh of relief that Mary eventually left her ensconced in a chair, her heaving breath a very audible sign she was still alive.

Once she returned to the creamery Mary wrote to Eimear and, surprisingly, received a quick response. There was no mention of Fr Matthew despite the number of questions Mary had posed as to what had occurred. In fact, Eimear's letter was vague in detail but indicated, to Mary's astonishment, that she was considering marriage to Willie O'Dwyer. This information gave Mary pause and her brow furrowed with worry as she pondered what had happened to Tommy and what had made Eimear acquiesce to marriage with a man she professed to loathe. Eimear's letter also enclosed a card from Beth with an address in Rochdale. Mary's own letter to Eileen elicited no reply at all. She had nurtured a slim hope that Eileen would be allowed to join her in Dublin, but as the weeks passed without any word, that hope faded.

Perhaps her letter had gone astray, mused Mary, hopefully, as she turned over, feigning sleep, cosy in bed in her new lodgings, forcefully pushing the niggling worry over Eileen from her mind. Today she was not due to start her shift until 9 am but if Fiona knew she was awake she would start nattering. She shared the room continuously with Fiona, but two other girls slept over from time to time. Sneaking a final few minutes, snug under the blankets, she determined to write again that evening to all three friends.

The work was tiring at first, but Mary now felt she was getting into the rhythm of the day and tasks, that had at first seemed onerous, were becoming routine. Initially, the early regime to ensure breakfast was ready was the most difficult part of the day. No matter how early she went to bed, rising at 4 am was torture as was the amount of preparation required. Mountains of bread had to be slathered in butter, scores of rashers and sausages had to be fried, not to mention eggs by the dozen. Four girls, in groups of two, took turns on the early shift alternating every four days. Mrs Corcoran was the cook, and come rain or shine, she was there every morning. For the most part, the men, about fourteen in all, ignored the women, wolfing down their food in relative silence save for the irritating chomp from chewing and the slurp of tea gulped with haste.

There was a pragmatic approach to feeding the creamery staff. The food was viewed as fuel and speed was of the essence. Preparation for the midday meal followed the after-breakfast clean-up. Haste was the priority now as the mound of potatoes or carrots never seemed to lessen. Yet, invariably, it did. The cook tended to the boiling of bacon or the roasting of mutton. Once the men had been served, the girls themselves could eat before once again distributing tea and biscuits. The first three weeks saw an exhausted Mary stumble from the creamery at 1.30 pm, the time when her early shift ended, and fall into bed. Gradually, her aching body got used to the rigorous routine and, although she needed to be in bed by eight if she had an early start, she was able to socialise a little between shift end and bedtime.

The distress Mary felt when she received Eimear's next letter, detailing her marriage to Willie, went unnoticed by all the staff as they scurried about on a chilly October morning. The knowledge that Eimear was expecting a baby did not so much dismay Mary, as kindle a wave of sadness. She was in no position to voice her suspicions that it was Tommy's child, it was Eimear's business after all, and their friendship was still too delicate an affair. She would like to have confided in someone who was not judgemental, but she was aware that, besides shocking her new work companions, it would appear to all that Eimear was lucky to have found a husband. So, putting all worries aside, Mary concentrated on her job. It was three weeks before Christmas when Mrs Maxwell approached her.

'Mary, one of the restaurant staff has not shown up for work and we are very busy. Christmas shoppers, I suppose. Can you help in the restaurant today?'

'Yes, Mrs Maxwell. Do I need to change clothes?'

'Yes, go into the office and Linda will help you.'

The restaurant was as busy as the creamery, but the atmosphere was different. The restaurant's patrons were, in the main, the more well-heeled or middle-class women from Dublin. The 8th of December was Christmas shopping day for many women from rural Ireland and that was the day Mary made her debut. There was a festive feel as she juggled plates of dainty cakes or more elaborate meals that were fussily presented, an alien concept in the creamery. As the days passed, her assistance in the restaurant was required more and more, until she gradually permanently joined the staff there. The busy month of December also provided a distraction from her anxiety over Eimear. The latest letter she received in mid-December was almost a plea for help, but Mary was helpless and in no position to assist her.

'Mary, I am at my wits' end. I know you understand the value of writing down one's thoughts and worries and that somehow perspective is gained by putting pen to paper. I am praying that this happens for me and that a pathway to the future can be envisaged for me and my child. I of course implicitly trust your loyalty and discretion. As you know I married Willie O'Dwyer. He is not someone who ever appealed to me, but Tommy had not made contact and when I discovered I was expecting a baby, I felt I had no choice. Did I wish to deceive Willie by passing the baby as his? I cannot answer that but, perhaps. Certainly, I was in a quandary. I was terrified, and not just for myself. My father and mother, my entire family, would have their reputation and standing in the area destroyed were it to become known I was pregnant and unmarried. Willie was there, knew I had been with Tommy, and still seemed willing to marry me. So, I acquiesced.

So, what of life since the wedding? It has been difficult. From the moment I said, 'I do' Wille has looked at me with profound distaste. There was no deceiving Willie about the pregnancy because he has never touched me. I cannot say I am sorry. He appears to despise me, and I believe he only married me for the money my father obviously promised. Warmth and love glowed within Tommy and drew me like a magnet. I felt safe and secure with him and the few days we had together cemented my love which has not dimmed although I am distraught that he appears to have abandoned me. Willie is the opposite to Tommy, a complex figure in many ways. Outward appearances indicate he is religious and quite self-disciplined, ascetic in many ways. I find him harsh, puritanical, and extremely self-serving. He obviously knows the baby is not his, but for propriety and his own pride, he will never admit that to anyone. An austere man, his public image is highly important. He insisted, with the aid of my father, that we purchase a large house, too large for us even with a baby. Yet, he loathes spending money on furnishings other than the rooms the public might see. I have no need of clothes or personal items at the moment, but I believe there will be a battle for any money when I do need some essentials, especially for the baby. He does not talk to me but watches all I do and checks on my movements. Sometimes I believe it is all he can do to restrain himself from striking me but, so far, he has not done so. Yet, I am tense around him, afraid of the anger that seems to bubble inside. I am worried it might find an outlet when the baby finally arrives. When I sit across the table from him at dinner in the evening, I despise myself for getting into this position. This man I am shackled to revolts me.

Dear Mary, it helps me to know I have a friend who, despite being shocked, is still there for me and for whom I can be honest and truthful. Have a lovely Christmas and write soon. Needless to say, your letters must always let me know how you are but give no indication that you have heard anything, other than the most positive news, from me. I think Willie might read my post.'

It was a relief for Mary to meet Linda that evening. As they chattered and laughed the time flew by and with it, for a short while, her worries over Eimear. Linda was fast becoming a firm friend and invited Mary to her home for Christmas Day. Delighted not to spend the day alone, as the expense of returning to her family was prohibitive, Mary accepted enthusiastically. She spent some time on Christmas morning after Mass bringing her journal up to date. The busy few weeks in the cafe had meant her writing was sorely neglected and she needed to fill in the pages before her memory failed her.

Christmas was a boisterous affair in Linda's home. Her three younger brothers bounced from one chair to another brandishing guns and bows and arrows. Linda's mother carried a continual array of plates from the kitchen to the living room and shrugged her shoulders as her sons vaulted around. Linda's father dozed virtually uninterrupted in his chair by the fire. Mary felt totally comfortable and at home but was not too disappointed when the time came to leave.

It was early in the New Year when Mary met Sean Fallon. She had noticed him on and off, sitting in a corner, scribbling away while drinking endless cups of tea or black coffee. His intensity intrigued her, and she was always a little nervous approaching him, afraid to disturb him. It was a quiet Friday evening when he first spoke to her.

'I can tell by your accent you are from the west. What part?'

'A small island, off the coast of Mayo. No one's ever heard of it.'

'Oh, an islander and a Gaelic one at that. Is as Dún na nGall mé. Cad is ainm duit?'

Mary stammered her name. 'Mary, Is mise Mary.'

'Well, Mary, ba mhaith liom cupán tae agus píosa cáca le do thoil.'

'Of course, what type of cake would you like?'

'Anything with cream,' replied Sean with a grin.

Mary and Sean developed a type of friendship, not least because she displayed such an interest in his writing. He would arrive regularly for weeks on end and then disappear for long periods. Whenever he eventually showed up, he greeted her in Irish followed by a beaming smile. He spoke often of his wife, and she knew his interest in her was the connection to the islands and their shared Irish dialect. It was simply an opportunity to speak and listen in the soft cadence of their native tongue. She had reluctantly admitted that she too liked to write but, despite his efforts, she was too shy to show him her own scribblings. However, he became an unlikely sounding-board for her worry over Eileen. A package containing her own letters had been returned to her through the convent. There was no information as to where Eileen now was or how to contact her. The distress when she received the package had obviously been visible to the discerning eyes of Sean, and after some gentle enquiries, she had spoken of her concerns. There was little Sean could do, or say, beyond offering a comforting few words, but Mary felt some ease at being able to share her anxiety. Her concern about Eimear she kept to herself inhibited by the knowledge that the McCarthys knew the owners of the creamery. A stray word overheard might find its way back to Mayo.

A chilly start to spring translated into a sunny April and Linda and Mary wandered the streets of Dublin, rambling through Phoenix Park and St Stephen's Green, chattering about everything and nothing. A friendship, stronger than either girl had previously known developed quickly. Linda confessed to having a fancy for a young man called Martin.

'I have never met him on my own before and he has asked me out next Saturday. Come with me. I am nervous when I am with him, I don't know what to say. He is from Galway, and he shares a flat with a few friends. Come with me on Saturday, I will ask him to bring along the nicest friend.'

Mary was terrified at the prospect of a 'blind date' but surrendered after two hours of constant pleading from Linda. As arranged, they met under Clerys' clock at 6 pm on the following Saturday evening. Linda introduced Mary to Martin and Martin, in turn, introduced Gerry. After some coffee in Bewley's, they went to the Capitol Cinema. To this day Mary cannot remember the name of the film, so conscious was she of Gerry sitting beside her. From time to time, his arm glanced against her own, and between her startled look and his quick apology, senses were heightened. She found out later that he was glad to leave the cinema and walk in the fresh air where they both relaxed enough to agree on a further date.

Some weeks later, a letter from Eimear was waiting for Mary when she returned from her walk in the park. It contained news of the birth of her child, Kevin, and gave the impression all was well. Mary sincerely hoped, so. Eimear's letter also contained an envelope addressed to Mary that had been sent via Mr McCarthy's house. It was from Eileen. Her letter was full of apology for not having written before.

'I am sorry, Mary. I know you probably tried to contact me, but it is only now I feel able to write and describe all that occurred. I remember the day you left and how you hoped I would join you in Dublin. That was not to be as you will see.'

Mary settled down to read Eileen's letter, anger surging in waves as she read the lonely fate of her friend.

'Two of my group, Eimear and Eileen, now married,' sighed Mary. 'How will Eimear ever be happy married to a man when she can barely bring herself to utter his name? And, I fear for Eileen as well, married off to an old bachelor farmer. How could the nuns allow that?'

Seething with anger, Mary read the letter once more.

Who could have foreseen how their lives would change, thought Mary. Strange the way things transpired.

Chapter 27

Beth blushed with shame.

*   'I owe Anna an apology,' she mumbled aloud. 'Her private experiences should have remained private until she decided otherwise.'*

*   With hindsight, Beth knew it was the hurt she felt at Anna's betrayal that had overrode her usual caution. Yet it was also her story, so she had ownership of some part of it.*

Christmas came and went in the little row cottage with little fuss. Beth was pleased to receive a Christmas card and letter from Mary enclosing, more surprisingly a card from Eileen. Anna showed little interest in their news. Money was tight and all four women in the cottage agreed to forego presents and just enjoy a pleasant meal on the day. Nellie produced a bottle of wine but that was the sum total of their extravagance. Anna was now quite obviously pregnant, but she still continued to disappear on many an evening. She eventually joined Sheila in the convent, and although she stuck at the work, she was a thorn in Sheila's side. She complained about the early start, the late evenings, the attitude of the nuns, the smell in the convent. The advent of snow in January appeared to have a sobering effect on her. Perhaps it was the fear of slipping as her body became more ungainly, but she ceased going out and even her complaints dwindled. Yet, she was not the Anna that Beth remembered from Ireland. She was more than just quiet and compliant, she seemed to hold herself aloof, as though she was waiting for something and was biding her time. Perhaps she was anxious about the birth, scared in case anything would go wrong but Beth sensed there was more. Not wishing to rock the boat, she said nothing. Keeping quiet prevented arguments but it lengthened the distance that was steadily growing between them.

Holding her tongue in the cotton mill was more difficult for Beth. The more she focused on the conditions, the angrier she became. Not only were women paid less than men, but they had to endure conditions that made working life intolerable. The heat and the steam, the lack of ventilation, but most of all, the unsafe working conditions made her seethe inside. She was unable to voice her thoughts too forcefully, aware any mention of unions or working conditions were grounds for dismissal. Instead, she read avidly and spoke quietly to those few women she felt she could trust. Now Anna was gone, she was more inclined to mingle with the others and, in particular, two women called Maggie and Hilda. Both were middle-aged and had worked in the same place for many years. Maggie was widowed but Hilda had never married. Together they urged caution, afraid that Beth's often fiery arguments and the radical ideas she propounded would result in her losing her job. Beth's grasp of English was now so fluent that she could argue comprehensively and with passion without resorting to her native tongue. Fear of getting the sack held her back slightly but a part of Beth determined that fighting for better conditions might just be worth the risk.

Winter snow melted under the onslaught of torrential rain and wind. It was late March 1934 and, as a watery sun peeked through, scattering the canopy of grey clouds that had enveloped the landscape for weeks, Beth begged Anna to join her for a walk. Her intention of using Anna as a sounding board for some of her ideas came to naught. Anna cried off, complaining she was too tired and unsightly, but also because she had absolutely no interest in what her friend had to say. Beth marched on her own, her red hair blowing gently in the soft breeze. She felt exhilarated and alive in a manner that had eluded her since she left Ireland. The fresh air and the walk enabled her to think and focus on the conditions in the mill. Beth vacillated between that growing need to take control of her own life and be instrumental in forcing change, and fear, of straying beyond the carefully delineated lines for a girl of her class. She was not able to articulate why there was such turmoil inside but as she ambled along a growing confidence entered her step. Yes, there may be obstacles ahead, but she could challenge them and overcome them. To continue to work day after day in the same place, hoping for something better to come along was no longer sufficient. After the birth of Anna's baby, she was determined to advance her own life and forge her own path.

Anna went into labour one evening in mid-April. Nellie oversaw the birth, shouting instructions to both Sheila and Beth. There was no fuss. Anna was one of those lucky women who delivered quickly and easily. By 10 o'clock, she was sipping tea in bed with her baby girl tucked alongside her in a cradle Beth had salvaged and, painstakingly, repainted.

'I am not feeding her myself,' announced Anna. 'Have we any bottles?' looking at Nellie.

'Well, I don't know. I just assumed you would feed her.'

'Absolutely not. Can you borrow a bottle? That woman, Mabel, I think she is called, the one who lives three doors down and has about 9 children. Ask her, she must have one,' ordered Anna, this time her focus was on Beth.

Beth looked to Nellie, and receiving a nod, left the house to borrow a bottle. The next morning Nellie once again tried to persuade Anna to at least attempt a feed. Sheila joined in but Anna was adamant. 'No, I already told you. I am not feeding her. It ruins a woman's figure.'

As Beth was out at work every day, except Sunday, she was not a party to a lot of the arguments that ensued. Anna paid little attention to her new daughter, handing her to Nellie to change and feed whenever possible. Whoever came home first, Beth or Sheila then took over. Sheila, especially, was unable to leave the child alone. When she came in the door, at the first whimper, she immediately took her to nurse. At first, she asked Anna for permission but, gradually, there was no need. There was one other additional problem. Anna had not given the baby a name yet.

'Anna, what are you going to call her?' was a daily refrain followed by, 'she has to be christened as soon as possible. She is three weeks old now.'

Sheila looked quite distraught, but Anna shrugged, almost smirked, in obvious amusement at Sheila's distress.

'Oh, I don't know, Sheila. I will think of a name tonight. I like Claudette Colbert. Maybe I should call her after her, or how about Greta or Rosalind or even Marlene?'

Visibly upset, Sheila argued, 'You can't call her after a Hollywood film star.'

'Why ever not? She is my daughter, after all.'

Anna watched Sheila for a few minutes, surprised at how upset she had become. It dawned on her that Sheila had become very attached to her baby, bonded with her in a way that she herself hadn't. Relenting, because in her own way she was fond of Sheila, she said,

'Sheila, you name her. I really couldn't care. Call her after your own baby if you want. Now, I am going out tonight and I assume you will take care of her, Sheila?'

'Where are you going?' was almost a chorus.

'Just out. I deserve it after all I have gone through.'

The following Sunday, Sheila, Nellie, and Beth brought baby Nora to the church to be baptised by Fr Monaghan. Anna had returned late from her Saturday night sojourn and was unable to join them. Nellie's disapproving look was *'apt to turn the milk sour'* whispered Anna to Beth, but Beth herself was disappointed in Anna and never answered. A pattern began that heralded trouble to come. Anna rose late, did the minimum required for Nora, and disappeared as soon as Sheila returned from the convent. It was Beth who took her to task.

'Anna, what is going on with you? You are not contributing to the expenses in the house, yet you seem to be able to go out almost every night. Nellie, Sheila, and I, cannot continue to support you and the baby. That was not the plan.'

'Well, I wanted to put her up for adoption but all three of you wanted to keep her, so you can take care of her now. I have some money saved from that horrendous job in the convent. You can have it all. Freddie pays for me, for everything, and I am going to move in with him.'

Sheila was in earshot and, horrified, interrupted the two girls.

'Anna, Anna, what about Nora? You can't take her away. You just can't take her away to live in sin with that man, a stranger.'

'Oh, hush, Sheila. You do take on so. I am not taking her anywhere. You heard me. You like her, you keep her.'

A strange silence followed this remark until Anna began to snigger.

'Look at the three of you. You are all dumbstruck. Look, I am not as heartless as you think. I know Nora is better off here. I am going to help Freddie in a new club he is starting with some friends. A baby is not part of the plan. I will come and see her often, but Sheila can be the chief carer, for now, anyway.'

Life took an unusual turn for all four women. Anna moved in with Freddie, much to the consternation of the others. She paid the odd flying visit and appeared openly carefree. Any questions were cheerfully evaded. Any attempt to press her ensured a quick departure and a snappy riposte, sometimes followed by an expression that was fleetingly sad and pensive in turn and only noticed by the astute. Nellie studied Anna covertly. When Anna believed she was unobserved she inhaled Nora's sweet milky scent, her fingers caressing her smooth silky skin or fluffy cottonwool hair. Often a fleeting kiss heralded a light-hearted 'goodbye'. Nellie made no comment beyond remarking on how well Anna looked but her brow creased in worry when she glanced at Sheila. She worried how Sheila would cope if, or when, Anna decided to take Nora away.

For the moment Anna maintained her carefree approach to Nora. She appeared beaming, her long dark, curly hair was glowing, usually sporting a fashionable hat that matched a well-cut suit or dress. Sheila too was radiant. She lived for Nora, quite content to spend her free hours holding her on her lap or playing with her. Nellie cared for Nora during the day and freely admitted that, although she loved her, at her age, she found it demanding and welcomed the return of Sheila each evening. Privately, she felt the situation could not continue indefinitely, but they needed Sheila's pay packet, and apparently,

Anna had no interest in her child. Worry continually plagued Nellie. The more she contemplated Anna and her attitude, the more she believed she would eventually claim Nora and break Sheila's heart. Always confident that a child was best left with its mother, she forcefully suppressed a niggling doubt as to the wisdom of that old belief.

Beth too had found a new path. Although she was still employed in the mill, she knew she was on thin ice with the employer. She was viewed as a troublemaker, inciting discontent, and urging the other workers to make demands the employers claimed they could not afford. Yet, there was exhilaration in having a purpose, in realising there was a wrong that needed to be put right. She was not afraid of losing her job as she felt the other workers would support her. Also, she had been approached by the local branch of the cotton union. They liked how she spoke, approved of her goals, and she felt sure there might be a position for her in the Textile Union before too long.

Beth shrugged as she read of her naivety. Yet, her life had taken an unexpected turn and led her to the path she now trod. Although she believed her portrayal of events was accurate, she readily understood that Anna would be angry. She couldn't disagree with any suggestion that perhaps she had spoken out of turn and knew it came from a deep well of hurt. Subdued, Beth lay back on her bed as memories of herself and Anna and all the lost years washed over her.

Meanwhile, Eileen poured herself another cup of tea and began to read once more.

Eileen felt quite certain Anna would refuse Mary permission to publish such private details.

'Sordid details,' she fleetingly thought, anxious now to move on to read about Mattie, wondering if Mary had accurately characterised the man he was. She knew her first letter to Mary after so long apart had presented an image of Mattie, that in hindsight, was not accurate.

E ileen closed her eyes and drifted away, allowing scenes from her solitary adolescent years to float, one by one, lonely frame by lonely frame, through her memory.

Mattie dug his shovel into the bog with unnecessary force. Leaning on the handle he surveyed his land, an action that used to be a sign of contentment. Now, he was quite distracted. Ever since the idea entered his mind to contact the 'matchmaker' he had not been able to relax. Now that Eileen was his wife, he was constantly tense and agitated.

He loved the farm and while his parents, particularly his father had been alive, he had been satisfied with his lot. After his father finally passed away, a feeling of emptiness crept up on him unawares and he realised he was lonely. His younger brother and two sisters were all in America and his older brother, who should have inherited the farm, had died in an accident almost twenty years ago. His mother, probably from a broken heart, had followed him shortly afterwards but his father had just failed slowly over the years. Caring for him had meant there was little time to meet anyone, and anyway, he felt it would not be right to start a marriage while his father required so much attention.

He mopped his brow and wished he knew what to do. He had gone to see Mr McCarthy, a man recommended by his own local priest.

'Great man, Mattie. He will get a good woman for you.'

Mattie believed he had little to offer so he would not be too fussy. A nice woman, a companion, content to live with him and the life he led. Mr McCarthy had indeed been helpful, careful to a point, if rather heedless of the effects any decision might have on the prospective bride.

'I must ask a few questions, Mattie. I need to be sure we get the right woman for you, but I need to be sure you are right for her, too. I was just chatting the other day to Sr Cornelius, in the convent, and I think we may have someone to suit you well. A strong girl used to hard work, and I am sure you could do with some help on the farm. She has learned to cook in the convent, and she looks to me like she could produce a son or two. Between you and me, her English is not too good either, so you won't have to put up with too much chatter.'

Mattie did his best to disguise the sense of loathing that overwhelmed him at these words. He wanted a companion and not a workhorse and had to bite back the suggestion Mr McCarthy was in the wrong profession.

The cattle mart was where he should be working.

Prudently Mattie kept his mouth shut. Having started on the process, he felt he should at least see where it led. But he was filled with misgivings now. He could see loathing in Eileen's eyes and, *Who could blame her?* he thought. *He was forty-two and he could sense she thought him too old. How could he disagree with her?*

When he had approached the matchmaker, he expected any prospective bride to be at least in her late thirties, but Eileen was barely a woman. Yet, when he first laid eyes on her, he was overcome with a desire to protect her. He became totally tongue-tied and knew his expression was far from friendly. He remembered how he had surreptitiously glanced at her silky, black hair falling in a gentle wave, shielding her face from his gaze. How it had glinted in the sunlight beaming through the window and how, despite her best efforts, it could not fully conceal her deep blue eyes cloaked by dark circles. Wet cheeks were covertly wiped away with that sheet of lustrous hair, and with shoulders sagged, she nodded and agreed to a future over which she had no control. She reminded him of a stray kitten he had found one day in the bog. The kitten had escaped from the sack that contained her siblings and sat shivering underneath a bush, terrified of the world around her. He tucked her gently under his jacket afraid he would crush her frail body. That same urge to protect had overpowered him when he saw Eileen. Had he done wrong in marrying her was now the question?

Mattie attacked the soil with a vengeance. Hard work was the only way to calm his whirling brain, to block that enticing image of Eileen dozing by the fire on that first night, her swirling locks enfolding her like a blanket, auburn highlights ablaze in the firelight. Now, each evening once the light started to fade, he would feel a rush to return to the farm cottage, to a tidy house with a fire lit and the smell of the evening stew, perhaps of freshly baked soda bread. But he said nothing, totally tongue-tied. Tonight, Mattie promised himself, tonight.

I will say good evening, I will thank her for the food. I will ask her if there is anything she needs. I will try and put her at her ease.

Eileen and Mattie were now married a little over two months. Eileen had settled into a rhythm of keeping house and was clearing a small section to plant vegetables. She was reasonably content, especially as Mattie left her alone. He had not so much as kissed her. She assumed it was because she was too fat and not very pretty, but that suited her perfectly. The idea of sharing a bed with him was anathema, although she had always hoped to have a baby of her own at some point in the future. To be fair she thought, *He is not unpleasant,* but he was not how she had visualised her future.

Come to think of it, she mused, *I never really gave my future much consideration. Working in England seemed like a big adventure but what it might entail never properly crossed my mind. I never realised how much I would miss Mammy or Daddy until I arrived at the convent. I never realised how big and fat I was until I saw girls like Beth and Anna.*

Shrugging these thoughts away, Eileen bent over the task of clearing the weeds from her proposed vegetable patch.

The weeks sped by, and Christmas was on the horizon. Eileen cheerfully snipped small boughs of holly, heavy with berries, and placed them strategically around the room amongst the few cards from her family. She placed Mary's card on the makeshift mantelpiece, a reminder to respond to her. Shortly after her marriage, she received numerous letters from Mary in Dublin but for a long time she had no heart to reply. Now she enjoyed the correspondence and was pleased she had eventually put pen to paper. She had been worried initially that Mary had left Dublin and gone to England, as originally intended, and was delighted when she realised she had procured a job and was still in Ireland. Now she wrote every couple of weeks with a careful description of life on the farm. She guessed Mary was astonished she was married, possibly horrified to learn it was arranged by Mr McCarthy, but she was too polite to enquire the circumstances, least of all, criticise. She looked forward to Mary's letters, a break from the monotony of the long, cold, wet, winter. The letters were full of details about her new job in the café. Eileen read the missives avidly, intrigued to learn about the big city and, perhaps, how her own life might have transpired had she accompanied Mary.

Picking up her pen Eileen dipped the nib in the little ink bottle and began to write. Feeling it would be churlish not to confide a little of her own life, she pondered for some time, before setting down her thoughts. She did not want to denigrate Mattie in any way, after all, he was her husband, but writing to Mary helped put her thoughts in perspective and she believed Mary would keep her confidences. Sitting by the kitchen range with the wind howling outside, the realisation dawned that she was not unhappy, in fact, quite the reverse.

Christmas morning started the same as any other. Although the first away from her family it was surprisingly pleasant. Even though the weather was miserable, Mattie went out at first light but returned early for breakfast. He presented her with a length of cloth, roughly wrapped in brown paper, promising to take her to the market in the New Year to purchase whatever else she might need. After a late lunch, when the watery sun peeked hesitantly through the scattering clouds, he suggested a walk and they spent an hour hiking the hills in companionable silence. That comfortable ambience continued over the next weeks. A nod of appreciation from Mattie recognising her efforts around the cottage, and the tasty meal each evening, allowed an easy companionship to develop. They sat by the fire in the evening and the odd word passed between them until it was time for bed. An unacknowledged thanks emanated from Eileen that she retired alone each night, and she never noticed or heard the sigh of regret from Mattie. Her letters to Mary described a little of this and Mary surmised a whole lot more.

Hailing from an island in the Atlantic, off the west coast of Ireland, Eileen had been reared to swim in all weathers. Cold was not a problem, only the wild storms that raged and bombarded the island were signals to stay on land. April dawned chilly and wet, and Easter Sunday was a day for remaining by the fire. Easter Monday held a hint of spring, and by the following weekend, a heatwave was underway. Mattie rose especially early as springtime is a busy time for any farmer. Eileen had resumed her daily walks and the lure of the beach could not be ignored. Armed with a towel she made her way across the fields and down towards a rocky shore. She walked along the shore's edge, kicking at the waves, delighting in the sting of the cold salty water. A partially hidden cove drew her attention, and she scrambled over a mound of rock and entered her own private sandy, haven. The silence and the peace, disturbed only by the lap of the waves, were like a magnet drawing her towards the water. After a hasty check to ensure she was totally alone, Eileen stripped down to her underslip. Bracing herself, she entered the water and memory took hold. Quick as a flash she dived under, immediately surfacing with a yell of glee combined with an almighty shiver. The first plunge was always a shock but also the most exhilarating. Stretching her body, she swam, sleek as a fish along the seashore. Fifteen minutes was long enough in early April, despite the intense heat now emanating from the sun. Dressed and warm she lay on a rock. The post had been quite abundant that day. A letter from home and one from Mary. Also, at long last, a letter from Beth. She opened Mary's letter first. She indicated she had met someone called Gerry but there was very little detail, the absence of which quite intrigued Eileen. The letter from home could wait until later. It would contain the usual desultory details about the weather and farming. Eileen turned her attention to Beth's letter.

A very late response to my Christmas card, Eileen thought whilst smiling wryly to herself.

It contained little news beyond the fact both girls were in Rochdale working in a nearby cotton mill.

Someone else to write to, anyway, she mused and tucked it into a pocket to respond to later.

As the fine weather continued, Eileen developed a habit of a daily swim after a long walk. Sometimes she caught herself humming, especially when she returned to the cottage, exhilarated and at ease within herself. Mattie had become like an old shoe. She was comfortable around him. Within reason, she could do what she liked. He bought paint for her to brighten the windows and doors, and even whitewash for the exterior walls. He brought her to the market and made a fuss of the price of material for curtains and cushions, but she knew it was just an act. For some time now he left a cup of tea by her bedside every morning, and when he returned each day for lunch, he made a point of asking her what she planned for the evening meal. Sometimes he brought her home some wildflowers, sometimes an unusual rock and once an injured bird. Together they had come to an accommodation and were forging a companionable life but, for Mattie, there was something missing. He was not a voyeur but at times he could see Eileen as she swam. Her body was now toned and trimmed from her walks and daily dip in the sea, all puppy fat a distant memory. Her hair was long and flowing, shiny with vitality, and her breasts voluptuous and inviting. Her face came alive when she chatted about her flowering plants or her vegetable garden. Mattie listened avidly, afraid to move sometimes in case he disturbed the serenity that had developed between them. He quietened the longing within, to hold her, to run his fingers through her lustrous hair. He purposely refused to think any further. He suppressed the image of Eileen laying across his bed, the swell of her breasts as he leisurely kissed her lips. To envision her cocooned beside him, as the rain beat against the window pane and the wind shrieked in unison was to provoke an unbearable longing. Anyway, he knew who he was, self-conscious and nervous, constrained by years of isolation. Years of taking care of his father, overwhelmed him. Years where he rarely met a woman his own age had made him introspective and critical of his own attraction. He felt old and ugly in her presence, but he realised if all he could ever have was her company, he would be content and consider himself fortunate. Studiously he ignored his bodily demands for more.

Letters were usually a source of joy for Eileen but the latest one from her mother brought sadness. Her father had passed suddenly. When Mattie returned from his day's work, he instantly knew something was amiss. No smoke emanated from the chimney and the usual waft of a dinner underway did not assail his nostrils. Eileen sat quietly with the letter neatly folded on her lap.

'I must return home, Mattie, as soon as possible. My father has died. Already buried, I am sure, but I need to see my mother and my family.'

Without hesitation, Mattie bent down beside the chair and enfolded both of Eileen's hands within his own. Even in her sorrow, Eileen noticed how big they were, paws really, but strong and sure. 'Eileen, whatever you want, we will do. I will make you some tea now, a drop of whiskey maybe?'

While he prepared the drink for Eileen, and also some bread and ham, Mattie continued to chatter. 'While you eat this, I will pop over to Jemmy. He will look after the animals while we are gone.' 'Mattie, no, you don't have to go. I will be fine on my own.'

'Eileen, you are my wife, and, and... you know I have never said it before,' stuttering and stammering, Mattie kept going, 'but, I eh, I do, I do love you, ye know. Yes, I love you, there I've said it. You are not going alone. Now, I will see you in a while.'

Red-faced, his ears aglow, Mattie scurried from the cottage and muttered all the way over to Jemmy. Part of him was elated at his pronouncement and part of him shuddered at what Eileen might be thinking.

'Either way, I have burned my boats now, either way' he muttered aloud.

Eileen and Mattie took the cart to the harbour early the following morning. Tranquillity surrounded them despite barely speaking on the two-hour journey and the discomfort of the cart went unnoticed. Mattie's pronouncement of love lurked at the back of Eileen's mind, but the death of her father was all she could deal with at that moment.

Later, later we can talk, she whispered to herself.

Once on the island, Eileen was overcome with grief when she held her mother. Soon the entire family surrounded Eileen and she mouthed a quiet '*thank you*' to Mattie for enabling her to make the journey to see them all. Of course, they could only stay a few days but that was enough time for Eileen to ensure her mother had sufficient help from her own family and neighbours to keep going. As they boarded the boat to return, Eileen's mother whispered to Eileen.

'Thank Mattie for me, that few pounds will go a long way. I was always worried about you, Eileen, but he is a good man. Look after him.'

Eileen sat alongside Mattie as the boat moved away from the harbour. Taking his hand, she pressed it in her own and leaning forward gently kissed him on the lips.

Mary pondered the news in Eileen's letter. The entire tenor was so different to the letters she was used to receiving. Hastily she grabbed pen and paper and scribbled a reply.

'Eileen, there are no words to express how happy I am at your news. A baby, so wonderful. I do believe from all you have written lately that your life has taken a turn for the better and that you are content. A baby will cement that and bring you happiness, especially after the sorrow of your father's death. Mattie seems like a good man. You should write and thank Sr Cornelius (only joking!) but it seems things have worked out well for you in the end. Hopefully, my Gerry will be as good a man as Mattie. We are getting along so well. In fact, I believe he has become my closest friend. That is all I can say now. Anyway, I must get to work.

Write soon and best wishes,

Mary.'

The endless flow from Eileen's eyes dampened the page but they streamed unheeded.

'Thank you, Mattie,' she sighed, 'for loving me and making me the woman I am. I loved you with all my heart. Thank you, Mary, for writing about him in such a wonderful way.'

Eileen rose and placed the manuscript on the table and enfolded in memory of her Mattie, prepared for bed.

*M*ary knew the next chapter would be a difficult read for herself. It had taken quite some time to put pen to paper as the emotions evoked had been suppressed for so long. The tenacity she brought to all her actions had helped her to unpack those days but, despite her caution, memories had spilled in an unending stream without any format. It had, in the end, been a release but she had no wish to repeat the experience. Reluctantly, she began to read.

Both Mary and Linda became engaged to be married on the 1st of August 1935. It was an important entry in Mary's diary as it represented the start of a new era for both of them. Linda married first as, Eamon, older, and with a good steady job, was able to afford a deposit on a house. Mary continued to work at the creamery, going to tea regularly in Linda's new home always accompanied by Gerry. His job was also secure, but the salary did not leave much spare change to save. Impatient at the long struggle to afford their own home, they decided to marry the following year in August 1936 and moved into a small flat in Fairview overlooking the park. It had the added advantage of being within an easy walk to the seashore. The weeks fled by with long strolls on cool September evenings sliding seamlessly into cosy nights cuddled together by a glowing fire. Nights that cemented their relationship for the hardships to come.

Linda delivered a baby boy shortly after Mary's wedding and was pregnant again within a few months. Mary revelled in the private knowledge that she too was expecting. When she felt the time was right, she excitedly wrote to Eileen who now had a small little boy of her own. Mary gave in her notice at the creamery when she was six months pregnant, anxious not to over-stretch herself in the final months. She was slightly hesitant to do so, as her small salary added to their savings towards that ever-elusive deposit, but work was not just tiring, she was too bulky to comfortably move around the restaurant. After ten days of lounging around the tiny flat and entering the most mundane events in her journal, Mary was open to Gerry's suggestion of a short trip but there was also a slight apprehension.

'Come with us, Mary. It's not a long drive to Wexford and the sea air will do you good,' pleaded Gerry.

With some slight hesitation, Mary agreed. It was not the drive that bothered her but the driver of the small Morris Minor car. Frank was a workmate of Gerry's and made her uncomfortable. It was as though he wanted to continually impress her, and a vague uneasiness unsettled her in his company. Added to that uneasiness were the cramped conditions in the backseat of the car for a woman 32 weeks pregnant. Nevertheless, she agreed to go, and, despite her apprehension, the journey was uneventful. After a walk along the seafront, they settled down to tea in a small café in Rosslare. A sudden dart of pain and a quick intake of breath went almost unnoticed but the cramp that followed could not be concealed from Gerry's ever-watchful eyes.

'Are you all right, Mary?' he queried.

'Yes, yes, just excuse me a moment.'

Mary rushed to the rear of the café where a slightly askew door was adorned with the moniker, 'ladies.' It was a tight squeeze to enter, akin to a cupboard, and Mary was hampered by a trickling sensation that surged to a torrent as she squeezed through the door of the cramped facility.

'Just water, just water,' she moaned to herself, 'just water.'

But as she tried to relieve herself, she noticed a pinkish hue now gracing the ever-increasing flood. There was little Mary could do to stem the flow. There were no toiletries in what passed for the 'ladies.'

Awkwardly she removed her cardigan and with a rising panic threatening to overwhelm her, she stuffed it inside her underwear. Gerry seemed to sense her distress because as she opened the door to enter the café once more, he was waiting on the other side. He threw her coat over her shoulders and aided her outside. Frank paid the bill and then followed them, unsure what the problem was.

'The nearest hospital, Frank, quick,' yelled Gerry.

Although Frank was not slow to comprehend that something serious was afoot, he was not quick to respond.

'Frank, Frank,' yelled Gerry once more. 'Open the car. We must get Mary to hospital.'

At last, the urgency of Gerry's tone penetrated, and Frank did as he was bid. The town was small, so the county hospital was easy to find.

Gerry paced back and forth in the waiting room, the terror on Mary's face wavering continuously in front of him. Frank had left some time ago.

'Have to get back, Gerry. Sorry, but I can't stay here tonight.'

Gerry just nodded, relieved to be left alone with his thoughts. He would sleep on the street if he had to. He just needed to know what was happening. The seconds and the minutes ticked slowly by, and his relentless pacing continued back and forth across the polished wooden floor. The scrape of the ill-fitting door slowly opening, the downcast eyes of the nurse, and Gerry knew the news was not going to be good.

'Mary, how is Mary?' was his frantic appeal.

'I am sorry, sir, but she has lost the baby. She is sleeping now but you can sit by her side for a while if you wish.'

'Is she all right though? Is Mary all right?'

'Your wife is upset but she will be fine. She will have another child.'

A stunned Gerry just nodded; his brain scrambled for words, but he was unable to say anything. Slowly, he followed the nurse to Mary's bedside. He could tell her sleep was agitated but he was at a loss as to what to do or say.

He settled for holding her hand and stroking her face, hoping that the intensity of his love would find a way through to calm her troubled mind.

Mary knew he was there, but she could not form any words as she struggled through the haze of pain that enfolded her.

Margaret, she tried to whisper. *I called her Margaret,* but she knew he couldn't hear her.

I was so afraid, Gerry, I was so afraid that she would die stained with original sin and go straight to Limbo. Our little girl, Margaret, wandering for eternity in Limbo.

A silent stream sneaked down Mary's cheeks and Gerry felt even more inadequate. He was sure Mary was trying to speak to him, but even the urgency of what she had to say could not break through the fog encasing her.

But it's all right, Gerry. The nurse, she helped me. When she saw me crying, she asked what was the matter. 'Don't worry, Mary,' she said. 'I baptised her myself, in the waters from your womb. Your Margaret is safe tonight with Our Blessed Mother. So, sleep now, Mary. You have an angel in Heaven, and you will have another baby before long.'

But, Gerry, I want her here with me. I want my Margaret here with me.

And the stream continued its slow, unending trickle, down Mary's pale cheeks.

Gerry did not have to sleep outside that night but instead sat quietly in the waiting room until the early hours. The following day was Sunday so after a quick check on Mary, he wandered outside. A group of locals dressed in their Sunday best were heading down towards a church and he followed them along the road. He hoped Mass would bring him some comfort, but he sat dazed throughout, surprised when he realised it was over. Tired, he continued to sit on the hard bench, unsure what to do. He had little money on him, but he had to find some lodgings. Monday, he would call to the bank and ring his work for some annual leave but, for now, he forced himself to move and traipsed down the road in the direction of the hospital. After a few failed attempts he finally secured lodgings in a bed and breakfast. The lady of the house offered him a cup of tea, perhaps moved by his story and his need for a bed for a few days. The tea was accompanied by homemade brown bread thick with butter and strawberry jam. Gerry believed he had not dined as graciously in days.

Afterwards, he walked briskly along, anxious to see Mary. His entrance was barred at reception as visiting time was not until 3 pm. However, on hearing his name he was directed to Mr Walker, assistant to the chaplain. A tentative knock and Gerry gained entrance to a small dark study. A red-cheeked, chubby man was perched behind a massive desk strewn with papers. He peered at one page and then another in the dim light before directing Gerry, with a nod, to a seat.

'Well, sir, I understand your wife delivered your first child and the baby has not survived. Please accept my condolences but be comforted that the child is now with God.'

Mr Walker bent his head as if in prayer and Gerry felt obligated to follow.

'So, now,' he continued, 'formalities must be dealt with. I have some papers here for you to sign. A small plot has been graciously awarded to you for a nominal fee. You may collect the poor departed angel tomorrow morning at 8 am. Directions are drawn here to the mortuary and the cemetery. It is but a short walk at the rear of the convent, adjacent to the hospital.'

Gerry, at a loss from grief, and adrift in circumstances for which he was totally unprepared, just acquiesced and signed and accepted the paper thrust towards him.

Mary was asleep when he was finally allowed to see her later that afternoon.

'Don't disturb her,' recommended a kindly voice. 'Sleep is healing for body and soul and, God bless her, she needs all the strength she can get. If she is not awake before you leave, I will tell her you were here. As it is Sunday, we don't allow visitors this evening.'

Gerry sat down and held Mary's hand, but it was cold and flaccid. Lost in his own sadness he did not notice Mary's eyes flutter and open. Her flat emotionless voice disturbed him as it quietly urged him,

'Promise me, Gerry, promise me. Name her Margaret, please.'

The subdued tone and the lack of emotion distressed Gerry far more than any sobbing.

Monday dawned grey and overcast with warm moist air promising rain before long. Gerry trudged slowly towards the hospital not relishing the task ahead. Preliminaries at the mortuary were quickly accomplished. Gerry, carrying his new-born daughter, Margaret, in a small white box walked alone to the plot indicated. As promised, the rain began. A gentle ooze at first turned rapidly to a steady downpour. Gerry's hair was soon plastered to his scalp and water seeped across his neck with tiny rivulets snaking down his back. The rain soaked his woollen cardigan, his only protection, as his coat had lain forgotten on the back seat of the car and was now in Dublin with Frank. Nothing registered with Gerry. The soggy cardigan, the sodden shirt, the rain-plastered hair, all went unnoticed. Instead, he heard the patter on the thin cardboard box and wondered if the moisture penetrated through to Margaret. His wandering thoughts imagined she could hear the tinkle of the drops, his teardrops, as they mingled with the rain. The gravedigger paused as Gerry approached. He leant on his spade and removed his saturated tweed cap. As he bowed his head in sympathy and solidarity Gerry noticed a red necktie peeking from under his collar. Gerry focused on it, the incongruity enabling him to choke back the whimper threatening to burst through and disturb the morning hush. There was to be no service by the graveside as baptised babies did not require it. They were received with open arms straight into Heaven. Gerry laid the precious box down gently and walked hurriedly away before he heard the first thud of earth, praying no sound would penetrate through to little Margaret.

Mary and Gerry settled into a new rhythm. She returned to the café in the creamery and Gerry resumed going to the office every day. Her journal lay untouched for some time, the numerous letters from Eileen, Beth and Eimear tucked, unopened, underneath. When the day dawned that she reached for her pen once more, she could only write of Margaret. How she missed her, how she loved her and wished she had gotten to know her and hold her if only for a few minutes. She also wrote of her relief that the nurse had baptised her. A profoundly religious Mary gained comfort from knowing her baby was not doomed for eternity. Eventually, she renewed her letter writing and found writing, especially to Eileen, brought comfort and soothed the ache inside her.

Eileen always responded speedily, bringing a consolation borne from the ease she now had in her own world. The space between Beth's letters grew longer all the time. Mary could gauge that all was not well but had neither the energy nor interest to enquire further. The same detachment existed where Eimear was concerned. It was obvious from Eimear's letters that she was patently unhappy, but Mary was constantly weary, and she was only able to return lacklustre responses. Mary continued to work but within a year she was pregnant again. Despite the urge they both had to bolster their savings, Mary left work immediately. The baby was due in June, and as Mary's parents now lived in Mayo, Gerry insisted she return and stay with them. Coincidently, his sister, an experienced midwife also resided in a nearby town and agreed to check on Mary and be there at the birth. Gerry wanted to ensure all went well this time. Despite himself he also had great faith in that old adage that 'home air' was healing and Mayo was near enough to Mary's childhood home. In late April Mary arrived home to the delight of her parents and Gerry's sister. Gerry would follow in early June 1938, in time for the birth.

Frost stung Mary's cheeks and the tips of her fingers were numb despite warm sheepskin gloves, a Christmas present from Gerry. She expected the restaurant would be quiet with few venturing out on such a miserable January day. She was taken aback to see Sean Fallon in his usual corner, shoulders hunched, as he concentrated on the page in front of him. She supposed he had been in the café a number of times while she was missing but today was her first time seeing him, in possibly two years. Catching her eye, he hailed her as always.

'Dia dhuit, Mary. I am surprised to see you here today. I thought you would be home looking after any number of young children by now?'

Sean was taken aback at the emotion that instantly welled in Mary's eyes.

'Tá brón orm, Mary. Tá brón orm. I am so sorry. What did I say to upset you so?' and Sean pulled out a chair and pressed Mary to sit down.

'Take your time. Here, over here,' Sean called to another waitress and insisted tea and cakes be brought to the table. Mary looked into his kind eyes, eyes she knew had seen a lot of the tragedy and misery in the world.

'Sean, please excuse me. It is good to see you, but things have been hard for me these last few years.' 'Is it your husband? Gerry, I believe his name is?'

'No, no. He is a good man, but you see we have lost two babies. I don't think I can have any more.' And Mary recounted the tragedy in Wexford and how she went home full of hope when she became pregnant again.

'After Margaret, I thought I did everything right. I rested in my family home, in my native air. But six weeks before my little John was due, he decided to enter the world. It was the same agony, only worse because I knew the outcome. You know I never saw Margaret, never held her, or breathed in her baby smell. After, after, little John,' and Mary choked and stuttered before she was able to continue, 'I insisted my sister allow me to hold him for a short while. She dressed him in doll's clothes because he was so small, and I cradled him for over an hour before he was taken away. Gerry was not alone at the funeral this time, but it was no less of a trauma, for him, and for me.'

Mary's voice trailed away before, with a purposeful shrug, she continued,

'So here I am back again, earning more money than ever but for what purpose?'

'Mary, Mary,' and Sean patted her hand as he took a pen from his ever ink-spotted pocket.

'Now, éist liom. Listen to me. I know a great many people and some of them are well-educated doctors. I am going to write down the names of three of them on this piece of paper and whichever one you choose will help you, I guarantee it. You just need some special care.'

Mary's eyes were now dry because a flicker of hope was threatening to surge within her.

'Thank you, Sean,' she gabbled, afraid she would swamp him with her weeping once more.

'I will do what you say, I promise, and thank you, thank you from the bottom of my heart.'

'And, Mary, despite all your sorrow, I hope you are still writing. The written word is a powerful tool to give strength.'

Brandishing the slip of paper, damp and crumpled from Mary's sweat-stained hands, the argument waged back and forth.

'We have nothing to lose, Gerry, by trying one of these doctors. The middle one, well his name is Dr Carpenter, that must be an omen. Joseph, the husband of Mary, Our Blessed Mother, was a carpenter. I will write to him tomorrow for an appointment.'

Gerry was thoughtful, pensive, as he questioned once again.

'Mary. What do you know of this man Sean Fallon? How can we be sure these doctors are any good?'

Gerry's fear was visible, a naked emotion that could not hide his loss and disappointment, emotions he had always tried to hide from Mary.

'Please, Gerry, please. I have known Sean a long time now, just from talking. He lived in the islands; he knows our ways. He is a good man.'

And Gerry eventually acquiesced for he could not deny her.

Mary murmured a short prayer of thanks. Dr Carpenter had helped her, and she was the proud mother of two girls and a boy. Yet, the ache from the loss of Margaret and John had never dissipated. It surged unexpectedly from time to time, all the more poignant because Gerry was unable to mention their names or share their mutual sorrow. He could only cope by blocking out the heartache, ignoring their existence.

Chapter 30

F riendships have their ups and downs, but most friends come to terms
with their differences, especially as the years pass. Not so with Beth
and Anna. The years had widened a gap that was impossible to bridge
or so it seemed. Anna had a fleeting sense of regret as she read on but, as
always, there was a ready excuse to ease her conscience.

Beth was restless. She missed Anna who now only appeared occasionally. She
flitted into the cottage without warning, always dressed impeccably in outfits
Beth could only dream of. She was afraid to speculate how Anna could afford
them. She never failed to leave some money for Nora, but following a cursory
few words, and a hug at arm's-length, Anna darted away again. The closeness
both girls once had, and the dependence Anna had on Beth, had all but
disappeared. Lately, writing to Mary was a solace for Beth. It helped to ground
her and put her anxieties into context. Originally, she had been reluctant to
discuss all that had occurred since leaving Mayo but the distance from home
made it easier to describe the turmoil that had ensued. Mary never failed to
reply and over time Beth brought her into her confidence and she described her
sadness and worry over Anna.

Beth's restlessness led to a lack of caution in the mill. Incensed about conditions, she wrote to the United Textile Factory Workers' Association. She knew that knowledge about her letter would render her position in the mill precarious, but she had an inner compulsion to highlight what she felt were unfair and dangerous work practices. Her letter went unanswered but the speculative looks from Mr Russell made her wonder if he had heard about her on the grapevine. A troublesome woman, and an Irish one at that, would not be tolerated if her action was discovered.

The Lancashire textile industry was in serious decline by the mid-1930s, so Beth was not surprised to be named among the first group of women to be laid off. Whether her letter to the union had garnered her unwanted attention from management was something she would never know. She had mixed feelings. Her income was sorely needed, but despite the hardship its loss would engender, she was still glad she had highlighted conditions in the mill. Shoulders hunched, encased in a shroud of depression, she trudged up the hill and home that Friday evening. Her last wage packet was in her bag and that glimmer of hope that usually sparked inside her had withered as fear of the future overwhelmed her. Nellie had already heard of the layoffs and hugged Beth as she entered the cottage.

'Lass, lass, don't take on so. You are young and will get settled in a better job. In the meantime, we will manage. It is what we have always done.'

'But, Grandma, we will only have Sheila's wage and I know the rent has gone up recently.'

'Beth, hush your keening, you will wake Nora.'

'Sorry,' snivelled Beth, 'I am just worried. I will go searching for another job in the morning.'

Beth spent the next two weeks hunting for work but there was a lot of competition from many of the local girls. She also helped care for Nora which gave Nellie a much-needed rest.

Nellie loved Nora but her age was against her. Now three years of age, the child's boundless energy left Nellie exhausted each evening, fit only for bed. The years had been kind to Nellie, but arthritis had taken a firm hold of her hands. Stiff fingers daily grappled with the buttons on Nora's little dresses and coats. Legs, hosting a blue hue from bulging varicose veins, failed to keep up with Nora's speedy little limbs. Nellie hid her disappointment well when Sheila broached the possibility of work in the convent.

'Beth, it will just be cleaning, laundry, whatever is needed on the day.'

Beth was hesitant. Such work had no appeal, but they needed money.

'Could Beth work part-time and help me in the afternoons with Nora?' enquired Nellie, her feet resting on a stool, feet too swollen to fit easily into her slippers.

'Possibly, I will check tomorrow,' was Sheila's thoughtful response very much aware of how worn out her mother appeared.

The following morning, while Nora was having a nap, Nellie poured tea for herself and Beth and proceeded to outline her plan.

'Beth, I have been thinking a lot lately about life, the future, choices I suppose. I know I seem a bit tired this past while, probably grumbling too much, but I can manage a while longer. You are my granddaughter and very special to me. I want you to make more of a life for yourself. Believe me, I worked hard all my life and I have no regrets, but there is so much more out there for a young woman today. Sheila is content with her lot, especially now Nora is here, but you, you can become so much more fulfilled. I see it in you, and this country will give you that opportunity if you let it. The whole world is changing so much and there is talk now of war. Without a doubt, war brings untold tragedy, but it also opens up possibilities, in particular for women. You will find your place if you take your time. So, I suggest you take a part-time job in the convent for the moment but figure out where and what you want to do. I have some savings if you need some training. We will be fine but look to your future and where you want to go.'

Beth was unsure what to think. The idea she could decide her own future and embrace her own path was not something she had ever considered. Life had always been presented as work, marriage, and children, with no deviation from that route. Nellie watched her as thoughts chased themselves across her face. In turn, her eyes lit up but quickly clouded in uncertainty from fear of the unknown.

What did she want? Beth had always felt luckier than most, but her horizons had still been limited. That passivity and acceptance of her place had been disrupted by her compulsive need to speak out against conditions in the mill. Now Nellie made her pause and think. Her grandmother, more than any other, was presenting her with a gift of future choice.

Could she do something else, become someone else? Beth's approach to the union for work had come to naught. There were too many layoffs and men were always preferred first for any position available. In fact, to have a woman speak to employers and represent men was considered laughable and an insult to masculinity.

The excitement engendered by Nellie's suggestion quickly faded as Beth undertook the numbing, convent work in the morning and caring for Nora in the afternoons. Nellie welcomed the respite and took to her bed each afternoon for a few hours. Left to her own devices Beth, took Nora for walks in the park, grocery shopping or just exploring the outskirts of the town.

It was a dank, dull Monday, and only because Nellie needed some quiet, Beth headed out with Nora. Sitting by the fire with a book was more appealing but Nora would only badger Nellie if they stayed in. They had just reached the park when the heavens opened. Soaked through and totally sodden they traipsed back to the cottage. Once Nora had been changed and seated with a drink, Beth drew her curtain to shield herself as she, too, changed her clothes. The bang and screech from Nora, as she tumbled and smacked her head on the fireplace was shocking, but the silence that followed was more terrifying still. Beth, only half-dressed, cradled Nora as her eyes swooned in her head. Nellie stumbled from her bed as Nora vomited.

'She needs a doctor, Beth. Get her to the hospital and quickly,' commanded Nellie, all semblance of age disappearing as she took charge. 'Take this and get a taxi if you can find one.'

Beth grasped the money from Nellie's outstretched hand whilst shrugging on her coat. Nellie cradled the quiet and deathly pale child in a blanket before enfolding her in Beth's arms.

'Go, go, as quick as you can.'

Beth arrived at the hospital casualty department, panting and breathless, thrusting Nora into the arms of the first nurse she saw. Her words rushed in a breathless torrent as she described what happened. Nora lay quietly on the cot, eyes fluttering, more asleep than awake, and allowed a nurse and doctor to examine her. It was her passivity that disturbed Beth the most, that, and her ashen pallor. A kindly voice interrupted the worried trance that had taken possession as she sat patiently by Nora's bedside.

'Would you like a cup of tea? I am sure your baby will be fine.'

The words only served to increase her sobbing, but she muttered, 'Yes,' and was grateful for the warm drink and gentle pat on her back.

The hours passed, and Nora lay quietly on the cot anxiously watched over by Beth and checked from time to time by a member of the staff. Their efficiency and kindness but most of all their expertise as they dealt with each new emergency impressed Beth.

'Are you managing all right?' whispered a kindly voice, resonant with an Irish lilt. 'Yes, thank you, thank you,' was Beth's laconic response, and as an afterthought, 'you are from Ireland?'

'Yes, although I have been here for many a year. I trained in this hospital, oh, it must be ten years ago now. I have not been back to Ireland since.'

'How did you manage to get accepted? To train as a nurse I mean.'

'Oh, that was easy. I just replied to an advert. Are you interested in nursing yourself?'

'I think so. Maybe, I don't know to be honest.'

'Well, from all accounts there is a war looming but, regardless, there is always a need for nurses. It is tough work, mind you. I'll get some information for you before you leave. My name is Mary, by the way, Mary Kelly.'

Beth and Nora were almost six hours in the hospital before Nora was allowed home. Nora had eventually fallen into a deep sleep. When she awoke, she gazed around silently at the strange surroundings in the hospital, before screeching loudly until Beth lifted her from the cot.

'Hungry, Beth, hungry,' she gabbled and, to Beth's great relief and astonishment, ate a full bowl of sweet rice and drank her fill of milk. Once they were back in the cottage, an exhausted Beth handed a now very active Nora, to Sheila and Nellie.

'If she gets sick again, we are to return immediately to the hospital. Otherwise, she is fine. I am so tired. Goodnight, all.'

Beth lay down but sleep was elusive. Clutched in her hand was information about the hospital and the steps and requirements necessary to apply for nurse training. She read the pamphlet twice and then a third time, sure she met the necessary educational standard needed. When she broached the possibility of applying for a place in a hospital, Nellie was full of encouragement. Any misgivings were brushed aside, and Nellie dismissed any prevarication, insisting on posting the application herself.

Beth began her training in January 1939. The prospect was daunting, the reality much worse. The long hours and demanding work were not a problem. The difficulty was living in the nurses' home with an unknown group of girls, many, openly, anti-Irish. However, she was determined to stick it out. She had always read and diligently devoured the necessary textbooks. The extensive cleaning and bed-making were boring but easy. The smells, especially from soiled bedpans, took some getting used to but such a minor challenge was swiftly overcome by the appreciation of many of the patients. Beth particularly liked assisting in the theatre. She was fascinated by the skill of the surgeons. She was reminded of piano players with their long dextrous fingers, fingers, that manipulated and probed in order to heal.

It was 1940 before she encountered Dr Manning, or Peter, as he soon became known. She assisted him in theatre on quite a few occasions before he asked her to join him for a quick snack. It had been an exhausting day for them both. The stream of injured soldiers, with life-threatening and life-altering wounds, never ceased. Long hours with barely snatched sleep was a feature for all the hospital staff and although they all felt a deep satisfaction when the surgery went well, there were an equal number of occasions when all they felt was despair. Beth and Peter shared these moments of delight and despondency as they hastily swallowed tea and a sandwich in the hospital canteen. Peter was stocky, with black hair that flopped over his forehead. He ate gustily, as though his next meal was in the distant future, necessary fuel to enable him to continue his work. Aware also, perhaps, his next break was undoubtedly a moveable feast if the stream of casualties continued. Together they returned to their duties, but a companionship had been forged and continued as the war dragged on unabated.

As Beth's expertise in the theatre grew, Peter often requested her assistance. Afterwards, depending on time and weather, they would stroll in the hospital grounds or the park, often stopping for coffee and invariably discussing the procedures just completed. Beth had a fascination with Peter's work and what had drawn him to the field of surgery.

'My father was a country doctor. We grew up in a small village not far from the Lake District. My sister also qualified as a doctor, but she stayed on and married and, now that my father is retired, she runs his old practice.'

'Did you not want to take over yourself?' queried Beth.

'No, never. Once I began my training, surgery fascinated me. That meant going to work in a large teaching hospital and I still have so much more to learn. I want to specialise in cardiology, maybe travel to the States once the war is over.'

His enthusiasm infected Beth, and hours flew by with very little discussion other than medicine and surgery and their endless possibilities. Alone, Beth examined her feelings towards Peter. They definitely came from contrasting worlds, but did their social differences matter when they had so much in common? Romance was definitely missing, that heady excitement she had read so much about. He had only briefly kissed her and the spark and passion she expected to feel had not ignited. Of course, he had taken her by surprise.

Maybe that passion, that leaps off the pages of every romantic novel comes slowly, she mused, *maybe it will build to a crescendo once we are more comfortable and used to each other.*

For the moment there was no doubt common interests and friendship were very present and a good basis to forge any relationship. But Beth had to admit to herself,

He can be a little bit dismissive of my opinion sometimes.

And, if I am honest, he can be slightly offhand with those he deems unimportant. Yet, we are comfortable together, and isn't that the most important thing?

Maybe to wish for more is just greed and possibly just romantic rubbish that cannot be sustained, she further pondered. *After all, we can talk and share*

interests and that is a good foundation for any relationship. Who knows, thought Beth, *one step at a time, and who can predict where that might lead?*

Beth smiled to herself. 'Thanks, Nellie,' she murmured aloud, 'for giving me the courage to grasp my own future. You know I am very like you. The 'apple didn't fall far from the tree'.

Chapter 31

*A*nna's cheeks were strangely wet. A single drop fell unheeded and rested on the manuscript. All Anna could see was the word 'Nora', her little girl. Despite what the others thought, she had loved her, did love her still. All the nights she lay listening to her breathing, then to her gentle cries, but also to Sheila, whispering soothing words to lull her back to sleep. She wasn't the monster they thought she was. The best thing for Nora had been to let her go, or so she thought then. Now...?

Eileen was disturbed reading about Anna and how she seemed to have little or no interest in her child. Her own little boy had cemented her life, giving it meaning and purpose. A life without him did not deserve contemplation.

Eileen continued to write frequently to Mary, but she garnered from Mary's replies that there was a pall of sadness surrounding her. Her letters could not disguise the ache inside her for a child of her own. When Eileen had written about the birth of her baby boy, named Joe after her own father, Mary had sent the most beautiful, crocheted jacket. Eileen knew Mary had spent many an evening with wool and needle and was overjoyed for Eileen and Mattie, but guessed the ache inside her lingered, colouring each letter and darkening each of her days.

Mattie idolised Joe and his young world revolved around his father with the same routine duplicated each day. From the moment Joe could toddle he followed Mattie everywhere. Early in the morning, before breakfast, Joe accompanied Mattie to check on the animals. He spent the day outdoors with his mini bucket and spade and returned covered in half the muck from the fields. This routine never faltered, and when he grew a little older and started school, he dropped his bag in the yard when he returned home and, with a yelled, 'Hello, Mom,' scampered away into the fields calling for his father. After his bath and dinner, Joe snuggled between Eileen and Mattie and was asleep in minutes, ready to prepare for another day.

Eileen closed her eyes and thought of her son, her only child. Tall and strong, soft and kind, he was the image of his father but more importantly held his essence. How Mattie would have revelled in him, had he lived.

Joe was only ten when Mattie passed away.

'Joe, finish your homework and then come with me to the far meadow,' shouted Mattie as he left the farmyard. Joe put down his pen and copybook immediately and jumped to join his father.

'Joe, finish your homework first,' commanded Eileen but, as usual, Joe raced away hollering over his shoulder,

'Almost done, Ma. Won't take a minute when I return.'

Eileen had watched them as they left the farmhouse. Joe trotted quickly to catch Mattie. Once beside him, he clasped his hands behind his back and marched along in imitation of his father.

The far meadow had never been utilised and Mattie had long felt it was a waste of good land.

'I must be getting old, Joe. That walk has me breathless today.'

Mattie paused and his grey pallor was so strange that even a young lad like Joe knew something was awry.

'Daddy, I'll go get Mam. You don't look well.'

'No, no, I'll be all right in a minute.'

But even as he uttered those words Mattie slumped to the ground.

Screaming, panicked, Joe raced to the farmhouse for Eileen, but Mattie was gone before he reached the front door. The following days were a blur. Eileen was distraught but Joe needed all her attention. His pleas and his prayers for his father to return were in vain and he lashed out at his mother, knowing she loved him and understood his need to express his rage.

It was a quiet funeral, attended only by neighbours. Eileen's family were too far away to make the journey and it was too difficult for Mary to travel down in time. In many ways Eileen was relieved. Joe still demanded all her attention, but he was changed now, silent and quiet, nursing his loss, his pain visible on his face. She knew she had lost someone and something special in Mattie. Yet, Eileen was stoic, putting her own sorrow aside to attend to Joe. Over time he had to accept, as all people do, the finality of death and that fate can be cruel. Eileen remained on the farm, and Mattie, always generous with her but frugal for many years with himself, had left her reasonably well provided for. Now, an older Joe managed the farm and lived in the old farmhouse with his wife and child. Eileen had a small cottage on the edge of the land, nearest the town, and was reasonably content.

Again, Eileen placed the manuscript on the table. There was one thing she hadn't written to Mary about, one thing that perhaps needed to be told.

A year after Mattie died, she decided to extend the small farmhouse. Nothing too major but a more comfortable bathroom and a larger bedroom for Joe. She also felt it would be good for Joe to visit her childhood home and meet the few cousins still living there. Her older sister was forever urging her to visit. So, while the building work was underway, they travelled together to Kilford and, despite herself, Eileen was drawn to the convent.

Hesitantly, overcome by those old feelings of inadequacy, Eileen knocked on the imposing oak door. Sr Benedict opened it slowly, arthritic fingers fumbling with the handle.

'My goodness gracious me. Eileen, lovely Eileen,' and Eileen was smothered in a warm hug.

'Who is this lovely lad?'

'My son, Joe.'

'My heavens, you are such a big boy. Come in, come in. I remember you well, Eileen, and if your young lad is anything like you it is some tea and cake that he would love.'

Sr Benedict chatted away, and Eileen felt such warmth, a warmth that had been totally absent when she had been there before.

'Mother Superior passed away, and Sr Cornelius, do you remember her?'

Eileen nodded, biting her tongue, *How could she forget her?*

'Well, Sr Cornelius is unwell these days. She is in the nursing home up above. Mrs Walshe from the presbytery, do you remember her? She is there too.'

Eileen nodded as Sr Benedict prattled on.

'You should go and see her, Eileen.'

'Sr Cornelius?' and Eileen shuddered at the thought.

'No, no, Mrs Walshe. She would love to see you. She rarely has visitors. Her daughters live in Dublin and cannot get away too often.'

Eileen doubted Mrs Walshe would remember her, and so couldn't fathom why she would love to see her, but nodded anyway.

'Why not? We all need someone to talk to, especially when we are old and ill. I will go up now.'

'Do that,' responded Sr Benedict. 'Joe can stay here and keep me company. Do you like ice cream, Joe?'

Joe nodded enthusiastically and Eileen slipped away.

The nursing home was just a short walk up a hill at the rear of the convent. Eileen and Beth had often been there during that fateful summer, cleaning and making beds. Eileen remembered the smell and how they used to gag.

It was like a mixture of boiled cabbage and diarrhoea. She remembered and brought her handkerchief to the ready.

'I am here to see Mrs Walshe, if that is possible?' was her answer to the nurse's enquiry.

'Of course, she will be delighted to have a visitor. Follow me.'

Eileen entered a darkened room. The figure in the bed looked asleep but there was a slight movement of the head as she drew nearer the bed.

'Hello, Mrs Walshe. Do you remember me?'

'Of course, I do, of course.' Mrs Walshe patted the bed, but Eileen drew over a chair.

'A long time ago now, Mrs Walshe.'

'Call me Lily, please. We are both old enough now. Well, I am certainly old, but my memory is still good. Not so much my eyes.'

Mrs Walshe appeared to drift away, and Eileen was almost about to leave when she opened her eyes once more.

'I always hoped you would come back, that I would see you before I passed on. I was very fond of you, Anna, very fond.'

'This is Eileen, Lily, Eileen. I was in the convent.'

But Mrs Walshe seemed to have drifted away again.

'I need your forgiveness, Anna before I pass on. I am not sorry for what I did but I would like you to know and to understand.'

About to interrupt and repeat her name, Eileen was forestalled as Mrs Walshe, now quite agitated, once more began to speak.

'You see, Anna, I tried to protect you. I failed the other girls but you, you were so pretty and fiery, I knew you needed to be kept safe. I am sorry and hope things worked out all right for you. He was not a man of God.'

Intuitively, Eileen knew, Lily or Mrs Walshe, had something weighing on her mind, something that needed to be released before she died, so she didn't attempt to interrupt as she continued. Words tumbled out in her anxiety to say her piece and Eileen had to lean forward as her voice wavered in and out, sometimes barely whispering.

'Anna, that day you left, I went into the sitting room. I saw the empty box and I knew you must have taken the money. There must have been nearly £2.00 or even more in that box. Over time, I replaced that for you, so don't worry.'

Lily patted the bed, her fingers twitching, as though to confirm to herself and Anna that the church was not at a loss over the 'borrowed money.'

'The days passed, Anna, and I wondered where you were and if you were safe. One day I watched from the window as Fr Matthew walked down to the beach, pious to all who saw him as he murmured his daily prayers. I followed him; I don't know why. He walked quite briskly and, as you know, I hadn't been well, and the sand hampered me. I just couldn't keep up so, in the end, I went up onto the beach path. It leads down towards the far shore where all the rocks are. The tide comes in quite far there. Anyway, I sat down, and I could see him in the distance so he probably could see me. He must have anyway because as he got closer, he clambered up over the rocks towards me.

'Mrs Walshe,' he called, 'what are you doing here? I thought you would be preparing lunch at this

hour?'

'The nerve of him, Anna. Always thinking of himself, not a thought for you.'

'I am worried about Anna,' I said. 'I haven't heard from her.'

'Well, don't be, Mrs Walshe. Another girl with bad ways. We are better off without her.'

'Oh, Anna, he made my blood boil, but then he said, then he said,'

and Lily Walshe gabbled in her agitation and effort to relay the story. Her fingers plucked at the sheet and her colour heightened. Eileen attempted to stand so she could call a nurse, but as she made to move, Mrs Walshe's hand clasped Eileen's wrist with a firm grip, fingernails almost piercing the skin, as she pleaded,

'Don't go, Anna. I need to say this before I meet my maker. I need your forgiveness.'

Eileen settled back in the chair, unsure if she was doing the right thing, but unable to resist the plea in Mrs Walshe's eyes for understanding.

'Where was I? Yes, Anna, Fr Mathew then said,

"Sure, I will organise another girl to help you, Mrs Walshe. What have I been thinking? You have not been well, another girl, yes, another girl will be grand".'

Lily Walshe paused and closed her eyes once more, but her conscience was not yet at ease. Eileen remembered how Mrs Walshe began to softly caress her hand as she continued.

'That was when it happened. My hand, almost of its own volition, grabbed hold of a rock and I hit him. Anna, I hit the priest. I hit Fr Matthew on the head. He glared at me, stumbled, and then began to slump and just rolled off the rocks into a shallow pool. I looked down at him. He was face down in the water and blood was slowly starting to ooze from the gash on his forehead. I felt nothing, Anna. I just sat there, maybe for an hour; I can't really recall. I was in such a daze. I could hear the waves begin to splash against the rocks. The tide was coming in. Every ten minutes or so, I looked down at him. There was a small crab picking at one eye. The gulls were shrieking above as if to announce there was food below. A drizzle commenced and I still sat there. I knew he was dead now and there was no turning back the clock, but I felt nothing. After a while, I was so wet, I just had to move. I literally dragged myself back to the Presbytery. No one saw me, as there was such a downpour. I reached the house, and I went straight to the sitting room and poured myself a brandy and then another. I was shivering so much. I don't know if it was shock or if I was getting sick again. I remember making a hot water bottle and putting it in my bed. My clothes were so wet I had to struggle to remove them and I just left them on the floor. I then poured another large brandy and got into bed to drink it. I don't remember anything else until a hammering on the door the next morning. I dragged myself out of bed to answer. I looked so awful but because I had been so sick no one paid any heed. They just wanted the priest. No one had seen him since the previous day and there was always someone needing him for something. That's when the local sergeant was called. I said nothing and after a search he eventually was found.'

Mrs Walshe was breathing rapidly but her hand now clasped Eileen's wrist in a vice.

'Forgive me, Anna. You see, I don't feel guilty for killing him. He was not a man of God. But I feel such guilt for allowing him near you, for what he did, for not protecting you, for not acting sooner and allowing his evil ways to continue. That is my sin. Forgive me before I meet my Maker. I think he will understand. The God in heaven that I know will understand, but I need you to forgive me too.'

Eileen did the only thing she felt she could do,

'Lily, there is nothing to forgive. I thank you for all you did for me.'

Bending down, Eileen kissed Lily's brow.

'Be at peace, Lily. I will always remember your love and kindness.'

As she left, Mrs Walshe sighed, and her breathing eased.

A week later, on Eileen's return journey, she once more stopped at the convent.

'Lovely to see you again, Eileen. Unfortunately, Mrs Walshe passed away while you were gone.'

Eileen was unsettled as she recalled her own agitation at the time over the right course of action to take. Her week at the family home was spoiled by worry over how to handle such knowledge. It was a relief in many respects when she heard Mrs Walshe had passed away. Now her dilemma was whether she should relate her encounter with Lily, to Mary or, more especially, Anna. Anna probably had a right to know but to have such a story made public in Mary's book would be bound to hurt Lily's family to no avail. Grabbing a jacket, she marched out into the growing dusk hoping a speedy walk would settle her turmoil.

Chapter 3 2

B eth was the only one who didn't follow the dictates of the time, that of marriage and children. She went after a dream for herself, and she succeeded.

'Was she right?' mused Mary. 'Was there another life out there for me if I had had the courage to pursue it? Is there still one? A writer perhaps, if I can just manage to get this manuscript published.'

The weeks passed in a blur and Beth's fondness for Peter continued to grow especially as he was the closest to a friend since contact with Anna had all but ceased. Lately, he had taken to holding her hand on their walks. He was diffident at first, but he became more confident as the weeks passed and the ease they had always felt settled into quiet contentment with each other's company. Beth felt a mutual understanding of a shared future firmly develop. One or two other nurses had commented on how attractive a couple they made. Any invitation to an event, no matter how informal, now included both their names, a true recognition they were an 'item'. Beth felt the time was right to bring him to the cottage to meet Nellie and Sheila, probably not Anna. She dropped in occasionally to the cottage but never stayed for long, and her visits rarely coincided with Beth's own. The distance that separated Beth and Anna had grown as the years sped by. The disappointment Beth felt was only matched by her worry over the girl she had once viewed as a sister. Nellie was now getting very feeble, and Sheila had reduced her hours at the convent to both care for Nora and allow Nellie to take things easier. Anna's infrequent contributions combined with Beth's regular supplement kept the rent paid and food on the table.

For once Peter's time off coincided with Beth's and they travelled in Peter's Morris Minor to the little terraced cottage. Beth felt a little in awe as she settled into the small car. He was the only person she knew who possessed one and, as their time off was usually spent in or near the hospital, she hadn't been in it before. Sheila had been on the lookout for them and waved from the front door as they pulled into the kerb. Nora, as usual, was by her side, but when she saw Beth, she insisted on running out to hug her. The sight of Peter made her falter before she hurled herself at Beth for a cuddle. Beth was slightly nervous as she introduced Peter to Sheila and Nellie and, of course, little Nora, who gazed shyly at him from behind Sheila's legs.

It was a sunny day, and the small back terrace was redolent with the scent of flowers. Baskets overflowed and roses tumbled over the walls, all Sheila's work. Beth was proud of her family and loved their little cottage, and although aware of its shortcomings, there was nowhere else she would rather be. She radiated happiness as she settled herself at the small kitchen table that had been hauled outside so they could have tea in the sunny backyard. Sheila was attempting to engage Peter in conversation, but Beth could see from his expression that he was less than interested in what she had to say.

What is he thinking? she wondered. *Can he sense the joy and contentment in this home?*

Surprisingly, Nellie struck up a rapport with Peter, perhaps because the conversation related solely to her ailments. She agreed to allow a cursory examination at his next visit. Sheila and Beth smiled at this as Nellie had been steadfast in her refusal to see a doctor.

The next visit was some weeks away. Those weeks were a time of reflection for Peter. He did like Beth a lot. She was attractive and spoke well and together they made a handsome couple. He enjoyed having a companion he could chat with about his work and there was no doubt she was a very capable nurse. All in all, she had what he required in a companion. The downside was where she came from.

He had no wish to ever visit her Irish island home, but could it be worse than the Rochdale cottage? he mused. *He had seen too many homes like that when he was training. Granted, that smell of poverty, that mixture of damp intermingled with overcooked cabbage and sweat, and even sewage, was not apparent in the cottage. In fact, sitting outside among the few plants was reasonably pleasant but like all such places, it reeked of hardship. The living room with the curtain screening off a sleeping area made him shudder. How could anyone relax and study in such a room? The constant clatter from the neighbouring houses, children shouting, babies bawling, that overall feeling of claustrophobia. Why ever did I promise to return to check the grandmother?*

Actually, the grandmother is not too bad, he thought, *but the aunt...*

Peter shivered as he recalled Sheila. Her large frame smothered in a floral apron; a handkerchief stuffed up her sleeve. Her inane chatter about the weather and the antics of the little child, as if the whole world was interested in one little girl from this rundown neighbourhood. He moaned aloud as slight misgivings at his train of thought pricked his conscience. A little ashamed he pacified his conscience by muttering aloud,

'The grandmother is kind of feisty and has an opinion, maybe Beth takes after her.'

The next visit was some four weeks later.

'It will have to be brief, just a check on your grandmother, as agreed. I promised a colleague I would check on a patient of his who is not doing too well.'

'Peter, you are so thoughtful. You know you should take the time off that is allotted to you. You need it.'

'I know, Beth, but I have to help if I am needed,' he responded sanctimoniously.

When the car pulled up outside the cottage, Beth glanced at Peter. She tried to see it through his eyes. He had grown up in Scotland and she knew his family home was a far cry from hers. He had described it in detail one evening. It was a detached house, with large gardens, study, surgery, all the attributes of a country gentleman's home.

'*A country gentleman's house*, she corrected herself. *Who knows if it was a home? Certainly, Peter never speaks of his family with any great love and affection.*

'Old age, that is all that is wrong with me,' announced Nellie. 'I am sorry to drag you out here on your day off when you are so busy.'

'Nonsense, I promised to come and check you over. Now what is this about old age? You're only about sixty.'

'Well, that's old,' responded Nellie.

'Enough now, where can I wash my hands?'

Eyes scrutinised the room, spying the cracked and yellowed porcelain sink in a corner of the scullery, clearly visible through the open doorway. Peter visibly grimaced before Beth intervened.

'I will fetch a basin and warm water and soap. Wait a moment.'

Peter examined Nellie with his usual thoroughness.

'In general, your health is good, Nellie. Arthritis is your main problem and there is little can be done about that. Gentle exercise combined with lots of rest, and nourishing food will keep it under control. Take aspirin if it gets severe but try to limit taking pain relief as much as possible.'

Beth and Peter returned to the hospital and the pattern of their lives resumed. The opportunity for them both to visit Nellie and Sheila again never seemed to arise but Beth made the journey as often as she was able.

Out of the 'blue', Anna contacted Beth asking to meet. It was a full three weeks before Beth had a day off, and Anna would not consent to wait and see her in the cottage but insisted they met in a local café.

'I am moving to London as soon as possible, Beth,' she said.

'I thought I should let you know first, maybe prepare the ground with Sheila and Nellie.'

'What do you mean, prepare the ground? Are you taking Nora with you?' Beth's calm enquiry belied the shock lurking behind her eyes.

'Oh, good God, no. That would never do. I am leaving her in their sole care, well, Sheila's care, I suppose.'

Beth was relieved that Nora didn't feature in Anna's plans but still felt compelled to insist.

'Anna, you can't do that. You cannot move away. I know Sheila loves Nora, but you are her mother. You should at least stay nearby.'

'Not much of a mother, Beth, as you very well know. I have the chance of a job in London and well, let's say, Freddie has moved on to a younger version of me.'

'Oh, Anna, I am so sorry.'

'Don't be. I was getting tired of him anyway. There is a possibility of a job in London, but it won't be for a few weeks. In the meantime, I need somewhere to stay. Can I stay with you?'

'Anna, that's not possible. I sleep in the nurses' home near the hospital.'

'Can't I sneak in? Just for a couple of days, two weeks max?'

'No, that cannot happen. I would lose my job if you were discovered. Anyway, I share the room with four others. You must return to the cottage.'

Neither Nellie nor Sheila was pleased with the prospect of Anna's return, even for a short while. Yet, as Nora's mother, they could not deny her a bed. With great reluctance, Anna moved in but, as before, she upset the dynamic in the home. Fortunately, she had no wish to be there any longer than necessary and took to meeting Beth as often as possible during her breaks, which invariably meant meeting Peter as well. Because of the demands of Beth's work, she very often missed their agreed sojourns and now and again Peter showed up alone.

The weeks sped by and there was no sign of Anna leaving. Sheila, in particular, was anxious to see her go and questioned Beth as to when that might happen.

'What about the promised job, Beth? When will Anna leave?'

All Beth could do was pose the same questions to Anna with always a disheartening reply.

'At this point, Beth, I have no idea,' she shrugged. 'I am waiting on a letter, but it is certainly slow to arrive. I suppose it is the war delaying things and, before you ask,' continued Anna, and held up a hand to halt Beth, as she began to speak.

'I have some savings and I gave a substantial amount to Sheila the other day. Not that she thanked me. She doesn't like me much, does she?'

'Anna, she will never understand how you could leave Nora, not that she is sorry you did.'

'Well, she will have to put up with me for another while because I cannot go to London until I know I have a job and somewhere to stay.'

'Can't you get a job here in the meantime? There is lots of work with the war on. You could get a job here in the hospital. They are always looking for staff.'

'Doing what? Laundry? Cleaning floors? We are not all like you, Beth, well educated.'

There was no refrain from Beth, and they sat in pensive silence sipping tea until, finally, Beth rose to leave.

'Anna, just have a think. There might be something you could do. Anyway, I have to go back now. We are short-staffed today. Tell Peter I will see him later.'

The questions from Beth were an irritant but, overall, Anna was not really put out that the promised job had yet to materialise. As she made her way to the hospital canteen, she could see Peter in the distance. He seemed a bit staid to her, stodgy even, not really the type of man she would choose for Beth. Anna could also sense he was attracted to her, and it amused her to flirt with him a little. Irritated by her conversation with Beth, she linked Peter's arm and suggested a walk in the nearby park, and he readily agreed.

'Beth sent her apologies. They are so busy she couldn't stay long. She told me to look after you.' Anna smiled mischievously at Peter and a blush suffused his pale cheeks.

Both Beth and Peter continued, where possible, to have their breaks together and to meet at weekends for dinner or a film. Sometimes Anna was there. Other times Anna met Peter alone. Nothing was pre-arranged, but they regularly met in the nearby park after Peter's afternoon shift. A spark lit Peter's eyes whenever he spotted Anna waiting for him. An excitement rippled through him when she gently teased him, and all thoughts of Beth faded away. Anna was amused how a man so eloquent when expounding on medicine, constantly fumbled his words when addressing her, all the while, turning a vibrant shade of pink. She watched him now as he hurried towards her. The comparison to Freddie could not be more marked. Peter's dress and general appearance were much older than his years, the swagger that was such a part of Freddie, replaced by a slight stoop. She knew she excited him, and it was obvious his interest in Beth was more platonic.

Fortunately, no spark of excitement or passion in that relationship, Anna mused as she assessed Peter's crumpled and ill-fitting suit.

Clothes, that is something that needs to be sorted, Anna smiled as he puffed his way up the hill.

Awkwardly Peter leaned towards Anna and kissed her on the cheek.

'A proper kiss, Peter, please,' and Peter lost all sense of time as Anna kissed him expertly on the lips. He was also totally unaware of the couple watching him from the other side of the path.

'Good evening, Peter. Lovely time for a walk, isn't it?' from a voice Peter knew well.

'Yes, yes, it is,' he replied to two nurses he recognised from the operating theatre and from Beth's circle of friends.

'Friends of Beth's?' queried Anna.

'Yes, and I am sure they will be in a rush back to tell her they have seen you and I kiss.'

'Is that so terrible, Peter?'

'No, yes, I mean, Beth and I have a sort of understanding. She will be hurt.'

'Will she? What about me, Peter? Do we not have a 'sort' of understanding too? Otherwise,

why have we been meeting in the park?'

Peter was in a quandary, unable to frame his thoughts coherently.

'Yes, of course, Anna. I am very fond of you.' Peter's voice trailed away as he felt the heat from Anna's scathing glare.

'Please, Anna, please. Don't be annoyed. I am fond of you, more than fond. It is just I have been friends with Beth for so long that I have no wish to hurt her, and believe me, not you, either. This is just such an upsetting incident. Let me go back to the hospital now and you go home. We can both have a think and decide what is the best way forward.'

A little unsettled Anna nevertheless agreed.

Peter found it difficult to concentrate. He had been looking forward to reading a new medical journal. Instead, he found himself at the centre of two women and a maelstrom of emotions. He knew he wanted Anna, physically anyway but, in his heart, he believed Beth was a more suitable companion for him. Anna was beautiful and exciting but also a bit brash even brazen, definitely too loud at times. He had to admit Beth had more class and more conversation. She knew how to conduct herself at all those tedious conferences he had to attend, and she certainly didn't attract the attention that Anna, like a magnet, appeared to draw. Yet, it was a new sensation for Peter to be at the centre of such a drama and he allowed himself a little smug smile of satisfaction. In the end, he decided to sleep on it and let events unfold the next day.

So, Beth had written her version of events to Mary. Wow, I do seem like such a villain!

and Anna laughed out loud.

Chapter 33

Beth suppressed a slight feeling of guilt. Had she written an accurate account or was it coloured by her hurt pride? Had Anna really been so underhand, or had she allowed her own humiliation to cloud events? Purposely pushing these unwelcome thoughts into the background, Beth continued to read.

Anna stopped on the way home to procure a bottle of gin, ignoring the pointedly disapproving looks from a group of men sitting at the bar. She was disappointed at Peter's reaction to being spotted and needed to think. A gin or two would help that process. The lights in the cottage were welcoming after her walk home but she had no wish to engage in conversation with either woman. Concealing the bottle under her coat, she managed a terse nod to Nellie and Sheila and slid behind the curtain screening her sleeping area. Fortunately, Nora suddenly began to wail, and amid the mayhem, Anna uncorked the bottle and climbed into bed. She stared at the ceiling. The flakes of ceiling paint that sprinkled over the bedspread, for once, did not irritate her. The surge of exasperation that the mushroom-coloured patches of damp usually initiated, did not rush through her. Instead, Anna's focus was Beth. The more she sipped the gin, the more her thoughts meandered back and forth.

Beth, as always comes first, she moaned, *always has, always will. Will Peter rush back to her now full of apologies? Will Beth even want him back? What will she think of me? Will she believe I betrayed her?*

Peter's talk of the States after the war had intrigued Anna and she believed he was sufficiently infatuated that, with a little effort, she could persuade him to allow her to accompany him. As his wife of course. It was past time she procured a ring on her finger. She had been upfront with Peter about Nora, realising she was a subject that could not be ignored. Anna relayed how she was raped by a priest, a man she should have been able to trust. How her love for Nora was tainted by that memory and in the early days after her birth, she was unable to bond with her, and instead, to her sorrow, saw Sheila steal her child's affection.

'Peter, I truly do love her and wish to have her as my own. But I see that bond she now has with Sheila. I see the home she has. I cannot take her from that love and security. I have nothing to offer her.'

Peter nodded but was apparently less interested in Nora than in the life she described in rural Ireland. Anna wondered if he understood that Nora was actually her child as all his questions were about the priest, her reaction afterward, and if she felt affected by it now.

I suppose his interest was really medical, she surmised. *Not that it matters now if he decides to go running back to Beth.*

Vexed and more than a little queasy after her few drinks, Anna tossed and turned all night.

Beth too lay in bed and attempted to analyse her feelings. Her emotions were mixed. Embarrassment came first. The news that Anna and Peter were seen kissing in the park was speedily and breathlessly relayed back to her. Disappointment and hurt came next at the behaviour of two people she presumed were her friends. She had not been imagining Peter's affection or his intimation of a definite understanding between them. A wave of sadness washed over her. Although she and Anna had drifted apart over the years, she had foolishly thought some loyalty remained. She would never fathom how Anna could let her down in such a manner. The Anna she grew up with, the Anna, more of a sister than a friend would never have been so deceitful, but she could not deny that girl of her childhood was long gone. Beth rose the following morning with dread coursing through her.

The sooner I talk to Peter and finish things the better, and with a determined stride she walked, head held determinedly high, over towards his lodgings to intercept him before his work began. Peter's gape of surprise almost made Beth laugh as he blustered,

'But, Beth, nothing really happened. Yes, I met Anna, and we had walks together on a number of occasions. We were alone because quite often, understandably, you had to cancel our arrangement. That kiss meant nothing. You should know me better than that and Anna, too, I might add.'

It wasn't Peter's words or half-hearted apology but the way he simpered as his eyes shifted slyly, that made Beth hesitate before firmly responding.

'A kiss means something to me, Peter. Maybe you have more in common with Anna than you think. I thought we had an understanding. Obviously, I was wrong. I am glad I found out now. We will, of course, remain cordial as our paths are bound to cross, otherwise, it is definitely goodbye. So yes, goodbye, Peter.' And turning, Beth realised she meant it.

Anna no longer lived at the cottage. After the fraught confrontation with Beth, she realised she would need to leave but where to go was the question. She tramped through the streets the day after the mishap in the park. As evening drew near, she had to settle for a dingy-looking boarding house.

'Take it for two weeks or not at all. I am fully booked after that. It is only a small room mind, and you will have to share the bathroom,' pronounced a rather unkempt landlady.

Anna grimaced, but so late in the evening she had no option but to be grateful.

She scurried back to the house and packed her belongings. She said very little to Nellie and Sheila.

'Beth will explain. I am in a rush,' she retorted over her shoulder when they enquired. To Sheila's dismay, she lifted Nora into her arms and hugged her tightly before setting her down once more.

'Goodbye, little one. I will think of you often.' She walked out the door and gently closed it.

Sheila and Nellie were incensed, particularly Sheila, once they heard the full story from Beth.

'Typical behaviour from that one. One man after another. Makes me wonder if the priest was at fault at all.'

Beth attempted to intervene. Despite Anna's faults, she did not seduce Fr Matthew.

Sheila thwarted her with a wave of her hand and continued,

'That one abandoned her child and went off to live in sin. Now she deserts you. You, who did so much for her.'

And Sheila muttered further words to herself, words her Christian religion would not allow her to utter aloud. Nellie was more balanced.

'Beth, think of yourself as having a lucky escape. I liked Peter, but you know he was as dull as ditch water. He could only talk about medicine. Mark my words, Anna will leave him eventually, once she has what she needs from him. Anna is the real villain here, but she will regret losing you. In years to come, that will be her greatest sorrow.'

Peter was puzzled. Beth had left him, and his pride was severely dented.

One simple kiss, that was all. And he pacified his ego with, *A little time is all that's needed, and she will come to her senses.*

Peter conveniently forgot that he had admitted to meeting Anna, on the quiet, for some time. As the days passed and there was no sign of Beth returning, Peter's thoughts once more turned towards Anna. He recalled his anticipation before their clandestine walks and his surge of passion when they kissed. He found himself continually seeking her out and his wounded pride made him anxious to hold on to her. The more restraint Anna now displayed, the more Peter desired to possess her and the more she interfered with his dedication to his work. Thoughts of her interrupted his studies, the need to meet her, restricted his devotion to his patients. Where once he was so committed that time off was an interruption to his pursuit of academic excellence, now he was no longer the doctor always available, as Anna consumed his thoughts. He fooled himself that he was in charge and in control but, in reality, all sound judgement had disappeared.

Within ten days, Anna thankfully procured lodgings near the hospital. A little assistance from Peter had not gone astray. It was not the most comfortable room. Decorated in various shades of brown, the room was rather cold and in need of some less lumpy furniture. The rent was relatively high and so was eating into her diminished savings. Unless things changed soon Anna knew she would have to find a job. No male friends were allowed in the house, and she was restricted from visiting Peter's rooms, so meeting together presented a few obstacles. They usually strolled to the local pub which sported a secluded lounge area. Peter was abstemious in all his habits, restricting himself to one glass of wine, but generally a coffee. Anna still enjoyed a gin but didn't overindulge around Peter. More often they enjoyed a quick meal in a café followed by a stroll in the park. Peter's hot, panting breath and frantically, fumbling hands were easy to control. Anna knew though, that lying side by side on a bed in the semi-darkness, with whispered words of encouragement followed by lingering regret that things could go no further, would have made Peter easier to seduce to the point of commitment. A plan was required.

'I have tomorrow evening off, Anna. Where would you like to go?'

'If the weather is fine, Peter, let us go for a picnic. I will organise the food.'

Peter was happy to acquiesce and suggested they have a walk first up onto the nearby hills.

Anna packed carefully. Rationing was a problem, but Freddie still owed her a favour or two and she had no hesitation in requesting his help.

The evening was warm with no discernible breeze as they sauntered up into the hills. Peter carried the picnic basket and Anna laughed at all his dull jokes. After about an hour they found a secluded spot and sat down on a blanket to indulge themselves in Anna's quite extensive repast. Freddie had done her proud. Anna first poured some champagne from a small but adequate bottle before spreading chicken sandwiches and a reasonable fruit cake on the cloth. Anna settled herself elegantly and was quite conscious of Peter's eyes on her slim legs. The hint of her lacy bra peeking through the top button of her blouse, which had unfortunately become undone, sparked further attention. Anna handed him a corkscrew and a bottle of red wine.

'Anna, how did you obtain all this? Champagne and wine, never mind the food. I haven't eaten or drank so well in months.'

'Ssh, don't worry, Peter. A friend helped. Now pour us both some wine.'

'I better not, I am on call tomorrow.'

'One small glass won't hurt.'

Peter leaned towards Anna as they sipped the wine and began to gently caress her leg. Laying down his glass he placed his lips on her own. Anna returned his kiss with fervour before moving away and handing him his wine in a glass now full once more. The setting sun as dusk fell, bathed Anna in a seductive glow. The wine and the kisses, with a skirt that had risen ever-higher, inflamed an already aroused Peter to even more passion. Anna's provocative smile combined with her insistence that he stop was too much for a bewitched Peter.

'Anna, we need to be together. Come, come to America with me after the war.'

Thoughtfully, Anna responded, 'Are you asking me to marry you, Peter?'

'Well, yes, yes, I suppose I am,' was the hesitant response, and then more confidently,

'yes, yes, I am. Marry me,' and he silenced the needling finger of doubt that had suddenly pierced the haze of desire and alcohol. Anna accepted without any hesitation. A new life beckoned and if Peter was part of the package, so be it.

Once alone, Peter still found it difficult to comprehend that he was marrying Anna. In the early dawn, the morning after his proposal, his raging headache, for he was a very minimalist drinker, was exacerbated by the knowledge that he had been not just reckless, but utterly foolish and impulsive. Memories of her warm curves and soft enticing lips did a little to ease his consternation. The thought of greeting the morning with Anna next to him, her husky scent stirring his senses, incited an anticipation that calmed his panic. Nevertheless, there was no turning back as Anna had quickly announced to all and sundry that they were engaged. Peter played the part of the attentive fiancé as best he could. There had been no time to purchase an engagement ring and it didn't seem appropriate with the war still raging.

'I will buy you the biggest diamond we can afford when we get to the States,' promised Peter. 'For now, a gold band will have to do.'

The wedding had been a rushed affair as Peter was taking up a new position in London. A comfortable flat was allocated to the newlyweds but, for weeks, Anna barely saw him. He was at the hospital night and day, and when he did have time off, he slept continuously. That left little time for Anna, but she didn't mind. She was content to be respectably married and his fumbling in bed was not missed. There was money to spend but very little to be purchased. Yet, London was fascinating despite the bomb scares.

'Perhaps, you should go back to Nellie and your daughter, Anna, until the war is over,' was Peter's constant refrain. 'It's not safe in London.'

'Maybe, soon, but I will miss you,' simpered Anna. 'Anyway, I like London, the noise and bustle.'

'I worry about you, Anna. I don't want to lose you before our married life gets started.'

'I am careful, Peter. I want to be here with you,' and Anna kissed him to distract him, all the while her mind shouted, 'never, oh never, am I going back to that cottage.'

Anna couldn't sleep. Was she really that woman? Was she the person Beth had described, disloyal and thoughtless, manipulative, with no moral compass? Should she even bother to change that image?

Chapter 34

A s Anna settled down to sleep, she drifted seamlessly to the early days of her marriage. Days that would not be written about in Mary's book.

By the time the war ended, Peter had secured a placement in Boston as a cardiac surgeon. He was delighted and his newfound energy, for a while, excited Anna as well. As soon as it could be arranged, considering the continual restrictions in the aftermath of the war, they set sail for New York, and from there they would journey to Boston.

I was excited at first, recalled Anna, *until I met the 'oul biddies on the boat.*

Peter's reputation preceded him, and they were allocated a dining table adjacent to the captain for the entire journey. At first, Anna was delighted but her inadequacies soon came to the fore.

I thought I was the pinnacle of fashion until I saw what some of the 'ladies' were wearing. 'Ladies' my eye.

Anna laughed sourly as bitter humiliation swamped her.

'What a pretty dress. Did you make it yourself?'

'Where are you from? I don't think we have met before. I am sure I would remember that accent.'

Casual comments loaded with meaning.

Anna was now wide awake and reached for her latest novel in an attempt to calm the flood of memories but to no avail.

The disdain that oozed from some of her fellow passengers had shaken Anna. Her natural confidence evaporated a little more with each disparaging comment. Worse sometimes were the well-meaning kind remarks. Memories swamped Anna, a torrent impossible to stem.

I was either made to feel inferior or else like a child who knew no better. At least my claim of seasickness was also a useful barrier to avoiding Peter's advances, although they had become noticeably less frequent during our time in London.

It was on board the ship that she began to read in earnest. There was a small library situated in a comfortable lounge containing a wide selection of books for the passengers. Claiming regular bouts of seasickness, she retired early each night with a tray and her chosen novel.

The suspicion that Peter was well aware her 'seasickness' was manufactured but it suited him to have her stay in the cabin, festered, making Anna more and more disgruntled. That eased once they reached New York.

Peter had arranged for a three-night stay in the city and Anna, delighted to be off the ship, relaxed and enjoyed the sights. Even Peter seemed more at ease and kept his head out of a medical journal for most of the time. A little of their old camaraderie resurfaced but that changed the instant they arrived in Boston. Peter became totally immersed in his work. Left very much to her own devices Anna explored the city. The accommodation was provided by the hospital but there were lots of bits and pieces needed to make it comfortable. For the first time, Anna was able to indulge in her own taste and decide what she wanted in a home. Soon their spacious apartment had an elegance that even Peter had to admire. It was also armed with a selection of novels, not to mention Anna's new diet of daily newspapers. Peter paid little attention to what she bought beyond requesting she purchase a formal dinner service and napkins. He also recommended she take some cookery lessons as they would be regularly entertaining. She ignored the suggestion of lessons but, equipped with numerous recipe books, she was quick to master the skills required, yet dreaded the parties.

In the beginning, it was just one or two couples and the evenings were quite entertaining. Young doctors and their wives, all starting new lives in Boston. Peter, however, quickly moved up the ranks as his skills became known and appreciated. Consequently, the dinner parties became a weekly endurance test. At home, she could keep out of the way for much of the time as she was the chef as well as the hostess. When they went out it was a different story. The problem, she soon realised, was not the other doctors and their wives, it was Peter. He wanted her to keep quiet and not voice an opinion beyond the weather.

'Anna, you must learn to keep quiet and know your place when we go out. You are my wife and as my wife, I expect you to behave in a certain manner. Perhaps limiting your intake of alcohol might help? I find two glasses of wine sufficient. Please also lay off the harder spirits as they provide you with a false sense of confidence often resulting in less than genteel conversation. No one, least of all doctors who spend their days saving lives, wants to listen to your inane chatter.'

'I do not have inane chatter. I am well read about current affairs, and I have a right to my opinion. Anyway, they are at a dinner party not a conference.'

'Please do as I ask. Talk to the wives about children or fashion or whatever. Children, now there's a thought. Why are you not pregnant? You had a baby already so are you doing something to stop conceiving?'

'Don't be ridiculous. Maybe it is you?'

Peter flinched, eyes narrowing. Anna felt a shudder of apprehension, but he just walked out of the room.

As the winter progressed Peter spent more time at the hospital often staying overnight. The times he asked her to accompany him to the loathed dinner parties became less frequent and their own dinner parties had all but ceased. The less attention Peter paid to Anna was more than welcome, but she did miss some social interaction. For the first time, Anna recognised that she was lonely. The days meandered along until the monotony of winter eventually gave way to a beautiful spring. The sun beckoned on an April morning, and by the time May arrived, Anna was a constant visitor to the local park. After a quick circuit, she sat in a nearby café and sipped hot chocolate whilst reading the daily news. Her routine was disrupted one late May morning.

'Damn, damnit,' Anna cursed silently, 'the café is closed.'

Reluctant to go home, she wandered back into the park and found a bench opposite the lake. The squealing of kids, not to mention the quacking of the ducks, distracted her from her newspaper.

'One of them yours?' queried a kindly voice.

Anna turned in the direction of the voice and smiled into dark, brown, candid eyes that bore a question.

'Excuse me, I just wondered was one of those happy children yours? I am Alan Evans by the way.'

'Oh, hello, nice to meet you.' Anna extended her hand. 'I am Anna, how do you do and, no, not mine. Not here anyway.'

Now why did I say that? she pondered. *Why indicate to a total stranger that I have a child?*

'The café is closed today and rather than go home I decided to sit for a while.'

'Is it closed? That's unusual. Well, there is another further into the town if you are desperate for coffee.'

'I am okay. I just don't want to go home yet.'

'Well, if you don't find it too forward or too awkward, for that matter, why don't you join me? I could do with some coffee.'

Anna was slightly hesitant but as usual, thought, *What the hell.*

'Why not? You will have to tell me what to do, how to handle that,' with a nod to the wheelchair.

'Nothing, I can quite easily manage. Wheelchairs are very advanced nowadays. Walk beside me.'

So, Anna did, hesitant at first, afraid the uneven path would cause him to tumble. His blond hair flopped over his forehead as he deftly manoeuvred his wheelchair, brown eyes frowning in concentration until he caught her own, and then they sparkled in delight.

That first coffee was the introduction to many more over the following weeks. It was also the introduction to a friendship that infuriated Peter when he heard about it.

'Anna, Suzanne saw you today in the park.'

His tightened lips foretold their own story.

'Really? I never noticed her,' responded Anna, aware there was more to come from Peter.

'Yes. She took great glee in letting me know you were having lunch with a strange man. Who is he and why were you there?'

Exasperated, Anna replied in as reasoned a manner as she was able.

'He is just a friend, Peter. His name is Alan, and we meet every so often in the park for coffee or lunch.'

Peter's face reddened as he expostulated.

'You surely realise how this looks? I am a respected doctor, and my wife is openly flaunting a new man in her life.'

'Don't be ridiculous. Did your informant not also tell you he is wheelchair bound so no need to let your imagination run riot? I am and always have been totally faithful to you. Alan is just a friend, my only friend I might add. I have no other company. If you are not at the hospital, you are out with your colleagues. You are embarrassed to have me join you. I need some friends of my own.'

'You are being dramatic and foolish as per usual. I married you so how can I be ashamed of you? But you are correct in that you have little in common with my colleagues and your attempts at conversation can be slightly embarrassing.'

Anna flushed. She had presumed he thought that way but to hear it voiced aloud debased her further.

You are not to meet that man again. Have a walk if you must but do not talk to him. Take up knitting or needlework to pass the time. Maybe oblige me by having a child. That will keep you busy.'

'Having a child takes two, Peter. You haven't touched me in months.'

'Well, dear Anna, if I recall correctly you used to be quite skilled in that department so a little effort on your part might not go amiss. Although looking at you lately you appear a bit jaded, washed out in fact, so it might be wasted effort.'

Peter walked to the door but turned, pensive for a few seconds, before commenting,

'On second thoughts, maybe you are correct, and I am ashamed of you. Yes, yes indeed, you are correct in that,' and he marched out of the room.

For once, his obvious contempt infuriated rather than humiliated Anna.

Alan could sense Anna's gloom the next time they met but could find no words to penetrate the wall that enclosed her. Nervously he queried,

'What's wrong, Anna? You are very quiet today?'

'It is difficult at home, Alan. My husband, Peter, has heard about our friendship. He doesn't like it, doesn't approve.'

Alan was stoic as he replied,

'Will I see you next week, Anna?'

'I don't know, Alan. I enjoy meeting you but my husband, Peter, he is...' Anna's voice trailed away.

'I will miss you, Anna, if you decide we cannot meet again. I will respect your decision though. I would never like to come between you and your husband. However, I will be here next week if you feel you can join me.'

Anna felt her eyes well up, patted Alan on the shoulder, and walked away.

Brown eyes followed her until she was out of sight, suspiciously wet as well.

Anna vacillated for weeks over what she should do. She rarely saw Peter and when she did, they barely spoke. She walked regularly in the park and if she saw Alan sitting in the café, she waved but never joined him. He was constantly on her mind. She missed their chats and their laughter and just the comfort of sitting quietly beside someone whom she knew cared about her. When she told him about Nora, she had known there would be no judgement, just quiet acceptance of who she was.

'It took me a while to come to terms with how I felt. The priest made me feel soiled and defiled even though inside I knew he was in the wrong. I think it was the way we were reared. Women were the root of all evil, think of Eve, the great temptress. Priests were considered to be so spiritual, only girls or women could make them sin. I hated myself back then and Nora, my daughter, was so innocent and pure, I felt I was too tarnished to properly love her.'

Alan listened quietly, intently, never interrupting.

'And then there is Beth. I need to say I am sorry. I have so many regrets, Alan.'

Silence grew and lengthened between them but there was no judgment. The sun lingered for a short while bathing the sky in hues of orange, yellow, and red. Its slow descent heralded the ending of another day and hinted it was time to go home. Yet, they both remained, hands held, comfort flowing between them. Slowly, thoughtfully, Alan spoke,

'Anna, when I look at you, I see beauty but not just on the outside. This wheelchair has given me a perspective on life that misses many who have the ability to rush around. It has enabled me to study and read and understand the world as an observer. The worldview of women will alter over time, but many women, unfortunately, have internalised subordination and accept they are second class. It is time and education that will force change but it's a long road ahead.'

Winter arrived and Anna continued to dither over what to do. There was security with Peter, but his distaste was almost physical, and she knew she could not sustain a life with him. Christmas Day dawned, surprisingly, warm and sunny and Peter announced a consultant named Ray would join them for dinner.

'He is from Texas and cannot go home. Be pleasant.'

Peter's instructions were unnecessary as Ray chatted comfortably with Anna. He even helped dry dishes until Peter announced they were leaving.

'A work event. I will be home late.'

And Anna was once more alone.

There was nothing to do, and as it was only 4 o'clock, Anna went for a walk in the park. There was always the hope she might see Alan but felt it was quite a vain wish on Christmas Day. She knew he had a brother who lived reasonably close and assumed he would be with him and his family. Nevertheless, in the distance, she saw him chatting with a young couple, voluble as usual. He gave a slight wave as she caught his eye. An overwhelming urge suffused Anna, an intense yearning to be with him, someone who seemed to value and respect her, her only true friend, in fact.

As he beckoned, her despondency lifted and without further thought her pace quickened.

Anna felt a twinge of shame which she quickly suppressed.

'I did you a favour, Beth, but you probably wouldn't agree. Peter may have been a brilliant doctor, but he was impossible to live with.'

Chapter 35

Mary was once more a bundle of nerves as she made her way across the foyer of the hotel to Eileen, Beth, and Anna. She panted her apologies for being late, and breathless and flustered, awkwardly sat down.

'You seem a bit out of sorts,' muttered Anna appraisingly and pointedly pointed at her watch. 'Missed my bus and then there was a bit of a walk,' responded Mary, flushing crimson at the implied criticism.

'Sit down, Mary and catch your breath,' and Eileen patted her hand, 'there is no rush.'

There was an open wine bottle on the table, but Mary decided against a glass.

'I need a clear head,' she thought, aware there may be some criticism levelled that afternoon.

'Mary,' began Anna, 'far be it for me to criticise your book but the story is a little unfinished. Start with Eimear. She obviously went to America. How did that come about? How come you became so friendly with her anyway? She wasn't one of us.'

The implied distinction gnawed slightly but Mary responded calmly.

'You're right, Anna, she was certainly more privileged. Yet she was still bound by the rules of the day. After her baby was born, she tried to make her marriage work. Her letters veered from plans and hope for the future with Willie to despair at the way he spoke and treated her. When the baby was about a year old, I received a letter from her. She was very confused. Tommy, whom she had always loved, had once more been in contact with her but she knew, as a married woman, she would be disgraced and bring dishonour to her family if there was any inkling of impropriety. I thought her story added to ours because it showed how even privileged women were unable to exercise any choice that wasn't approved by their father or husband.'

Mary paused, hoping Anna and the others would be satisfied with her explanation. Already, from rereading her manuscript, Mary believed she had revealed too many intimate details of Eimear's story. She had no wish to elaborate further despite Eimear's insistence that there was nothing to hide. Eimear's family, and Willie, still lived in Kilford, and Mary worried about repercussions in the village and the negative impact on Eimear and Tommy should they return. The explicit details of Eimear and Tommy's first night together, unmarried, might be acceptable in New York, but 1960s Kilford was a different matter. Filled with misgivings, she now considered the three enquiring faces waiting for her to continue, intensifying her dilemma. She was prepared to divulge their secrets so was her sense of protectiveness towards Eimear justified?

Yes, yes, it is. If they asked me to keep something back, I would have no hesitation. If I thought my story would hurt the family or friends of Eileen, Beth, or Anna I would refrain from publishing that. piece.

The three women waited expectantly for Mary to continue. As the silence lengthened they began to chat amongst themselves, arguing as to the advantages of being born middle class. Mary disengaged from the discussion and recalled Eimear's story.

Tommy had been held in Cork Garda station for a number of days. The damp cell exacerbated Tommy's chronic bronchial problem and what should have been a mild attack progressed into a far more serious condition. He developed pneumonia and was admitted to hospital, and it was a full four weeks before he was released. Although he recovered well, it was slow progress, and a further month before he felt fit enough to return to Kilford to fetch Eimear. In the meantime, he wrote to Eimear. He was anxious as, despite his numerous letters, there was no response from her. As he was preparing to leave Cork for Kilford, he received a letter from Joe, Eimear's father. It was curt and to the point advising him in no uncertain terms to leave his daughter alone as she was now engaged to be married to Willie. Joe enclosed a cheque with the letter and the suggestion he utilise the funds to emigrate to America. Tommy immediately destroyed the cheque but the suggestion he emigrate lingered on, plaguing him. Despondent, instead of purchasing a train ticket to Mayo, he wandered down to Cobh, a busy town, where passengers bound for America embarked on their journey. Work was plentiful in Cobh and Tommy secured a job and lodgings. The urge to emigrate continually nagged at him, and within a year, he boarded a ship for New York, unaware Eimear had borne his son.

Of course, Tommy had no sooner landed in America when he regretted his decision. Unsettled, and unable to forget Eimear and move on, he determined to return to Ireland as soon as he had saved enough for the fare. He knew he should have spoken to her and not just accepted Joe's word. His slow recovery from illness, and anger at how he had been treated, had blunted his common sense. If she personally admitted to him that she no longer had any feelings for him and was satisfied with her marriage, he believed his yearning would be appeased. Tommy arrived back in Mayo almost two years after their fruitless journey to Cork. His first stop was his sister, still in the old family home. He persuaded her to pass a note to Eimear when she saw her at Mass the following day, urging her to meet him on the headland.

Eimear had vacillated between excitement at seeing Tommy once more and terror at being discovered. She reasoned that little Kevin should at least meet his father even if it was only the one time. She dressed their little son warmly, tucked him into his pushchair, and set off to meet his father, Tommy, a man who was still never far from her thoughts. Tommy bent over the sleeping toddler. One questioning glance and a nod from Eimear. Kevin was, without doubt, his son. Few words were required that morning. With the wind gusting around them, they would have been superfluous anyway. Instead, they held hands and spoke with their eyes. His eyes pleaded and hers acquiesced. Eimear then nodded, and leaning closer, battling the howling wind, she uttered the only words he wished to hear.

'You make all the arrangements, and we will go with you.'

Mary received a letter from Eimear shortly afterwards explaining that she needed some accommodation in Dublin for herself and Kevin. If Mary could book a room somewhere for the following weekend, she would explain all when she met her. It was an unusual request especially as she asked Mary not to mention anything about the proposed trip in her reply, just to be non-committal and confirm all was sorted. Confused and more than a little worried Mary felt she had to talk to someone. Of course, it couldn't be anyone with even the vaguest connection to Eimear. Feeling a little disloyal but needing a sounding board, Mary confided in Linda.

'I'm not sure what to think, Linda. Why is she being so secretive?'

'I think it is very strange, Mary. I don't think you should get involved. You told me she was unhappy and wanted to marry someone else. Supposing she is planning to leave her husband. You cannot help with that. You cannot interfere between husband and wife.'

Silence was Mary's only response as she considered Linda's advice. Of course, it was against God's law to meddle in another marriage, but Eimear sounded so desperate in her letter. To appease her own uneasiness and to pacify Linda, she continued,

'You are right, Linda but I am sure it is nothing as drastic as that.'

Yet, Mary couldn't soothe that sense of disquiet that permeated all through the night and next day. Somehow, she knew Linda was correct in her assumption. Nevertheless, she replied, as directed, to Eimear and sourced a genteel boarding house in Fairview, not too far from the café.

It was a three-day visit and Eimear opened her heart to Mary. She described the coldness from Willie and the contempt within which he held her. He ignored the baby and for that she was grateful, as no bond had developed that could be broken. Her eyes lit up when she spoke about her reunion with Tommy and the plans they had made. She didn't notice, or at any rate refused to acknowledge, the look of trepidation that appeared in Mary's eyes as she spoke of their plans.

'He will arrive here early Saturday morning, Mary, and organise passage to New York and our new life together.'

'Are you sure, Eimear that this is the right thing to do? Does, your father, know? What about Willie?'

'No one, but you, knows, Mary. Don't worry. Willie won't care. He will revel in the sympathy from all and sundry and I might add, in the whispers about my family! Anyway, he will retain his prize possession, the largest house in the town, compliments of my father. Don't waste any sympathy on him. I hope in time my father and mother, in fact, all my family will accept what has happened. I have written a long letter and will post it before I board the ship. And I will keep in touch, Mary. Maybe one day you will visit me. Thank you for everything. You have been a true friend.'

Mary lost in her reverie, missed the inquisitive looks flickering back and forth between the other three. Finally, her jumbled thoughts settled, and she raised her head and focused on Anna. Minimal information was all that was required.

'So, Anna, to answer your question. Eimear left Willie and she went with Kevin to live in New York with Tommy.'

'Good for her,' retorted Anna. 'I am sure there were a few raised eyebrows in Kilford though.'

And turning to Eileen, Anna continued, 'Eileen, I must say you look very well.'

'Don't sound so surprised, Anna. But, yes, I am well.'

'You know what I meant, don't take on so.'

And Anna, tactful as ever, continued, 'You were always the awkward, and eh, if I may say so, the fat one. When I read how you were married off to an old farmer, yuck,' and Anna shuddered once more. 'I just cannot imagine how awful it was.'

'Anna, did you read the story at all? I was awkward and overweight, but I was also young, naïve, and inexperienced. Yes, I was also married off to a farmer, but he was a good man. It took me some time to realise it, but he was a wonderful man. He was kind, patient and caring. He was overjoyed when we had a son and do you know what, he died many years ago now, but I still miss him every day since. I had a good life with Mattie, a better marriage than many women have.'

Anna was quiet, perhaps a little chastened but held fast to the shell that surrounded her in case it cracked.

'So, Beth, what about you?' and Anna's veneer remained in place as Beth began to speak. 'After you married and moved to London I just continued to work at the hospital. Eventually I moved back to Ireland.'

Beth's reply was precise and to the point. She did not elaborate on how the work was very satisfying. How she acquired ever more knowledge and with it, status, and fulfilment. How as war, and consequently the demands at the hospital increased, her visits to the cottage became less frequent, but her own pride at her achievement more than compensated.

Welcome peace eventually dawned but the work in the hospital was unceasing. Beth was fortunate to somehow acquire a full two weeks of leave once the Christmas season ended. Mid-January 1949, saw her ensconced in the cottage. Nora was now almost 16 and working part-time as a typist in a local newspaper while she continued to study. Sheila was still trekking almost daily to the convent and Nellie, although never in full health, was finding life easier. Beth curled contentedly by the blazing fire, lulled from the heat she dozed fitfully, her novel discarded on the floor. Wind and rain battered ill-fitting windows, so Nellie had to raise her voice to be heard.

'Beth, I have been thinking a lot of home these past few months.'

'Home, as in the islands?' muttered Beth, barely awake.

'No, not really the old farm, but just Ireland. Maybe Dublin. I think I would like to return to my home air before I die.'

As Beth attempted to expostulate, Nellie patted Beth's hand.

'Hush, now, I am not dying anytime soon. But I would like Sheila to have an easier life and Nora to know where she really comes from.'

Beth, unsure how to respond, all but shouted,

'Money, Grandma, money! That is the question. How would anyone live?'

'Ah,' replied Nellie, 'that is the thing you see. I have some money. I was always thrifty. Well, I had to be when I had a young family. But, need I remind you I had more children than just your father and Sheila. My other two emigrated to America and every so often they both send me a few dollars. I believe I have more than enough to get us a small place to live. However, I would like you to come too.'

Surprised, Beth remained quiet for some minutes before exclaiming,

'Well, that is a surprise. I have never considered in all these years that I might return to Ireland.' 'Well, consider it now,' said Nellie. 'Beth, please give it some thought. Nurses are needed in Ireland too.'

Epilogue

The table had now fallen silent as all four women became quiet and introspective recalling their lives after leaving the convent. Their contemplation was interrupted by Anna.

'Excuse me, Mary, and I hate to say this, but I found some of the story a bit boring, so I just skimmed over some chapters.'

Beth intervened, 'You were probably just interested in what was written about yourself, Anna. You haven't changed at all.'

'I don't know what you mean, Beth. You certainly paid me no compliments anyway. In fact, you did not portray me very accurately, Beth. I am not the villain you implied.'

The continual strain between Beth and Anna did not go unnoticed by Mary and Eileen. They glanced at each other from time to time, Eileen with a questioning look, and an answering shrug from Mary. It was quite evident that the fracture in the friendship that developed between Beth and Anna over Nora and Peter had never eased. Eventually, Eileen had to ask,

'Beth, what about you? How has your life panned out since you returned to Ireland?'

Beth crossed her legs, took a sip of wine, and replied calmly.

'Very well, Eileen. I never married but I do have a very good companion.

At one point I thought I would marry a doctor I met during the war but that never transpired, but you know all about that. My own work as a nurse has given me a lot of satisfaction. When I returned to Ireland, the nursing experience I gained during the war stood to my benefit and I now have quite a senior position in the Mater Hospital. I know many people, especially women, find it difficult to believe but I am glad I stayed single and devoted myself to my career. After a short while in Dublin, my grandmother Nellie eventually bought a small cottage in Wexford and settled there with my aunt Sheila and Nora. Sheila still lives there. Her daughter, Nora,' with a pointed glance at Anna, 'married a local Wexford man and lives quite near to her. She has two children of her own.'

Anna remained silent, her expression both pensive and reflective, more powerful than any question.

'So,' said Mary, 'has anyone any uncertainty about the book? Are there any details you wish removed?'

The tension at the table continued to increase as Anna switched her focus to Mary.

'Why didn't you write much about yourself, Mary? Was my life, as described by Beth, more interesting?'

'The honest answer, Anna, is yes. My life followed quite a mundane predictable path. I had some difficulty having a child but, thanks be to God, I now have two girls and a boy. Together with my husband, Gerry, they have made my life complete. Last year, however, I found I had more time on my hands because they were growing up and didn't need me so much. So, I turned, as I always did, to my pen.'

'I will probably seem like the villain,' smiled Anna, content to leave her carefully manufactured façade in place. 'Pregnant at sixteen, abandoned my child, lived with a couple of men before I married a doctor. Left him for someone else.'

Anna then caught Beth's eyes and held her gaze,

'Believe me, Beth, I never realised you had strong feelings for Peter.'

'Would it have made any difference?' was the quick retort.

'I truly cannot answer that, Beth, but I hope it would have. Anyway, we left

London after the war and travelled to America. For a while, things were fine. Peter's reputation as a cardiac surgeon was increasing all the time. I enjoyed the sunshine and the lifestyle but eventually, I became bored. Peter was not very exciting. All he spoke about was medicine and I think my lack of knowledge embarrassed him. I suppose I strayed a little and eventually we divorced. He was very generous with the settlement so, in the end, things worked out fine. Believe it or not, like Beth, I developed a few interests of my own and now live quite happily without him. So, Mary, at first, I was annoyed at how I was portrayed, especially as it was Beth's viewpoint. But now, I realise I just don't care. Put what you like in the book. I really don't mind.'

Curiosity piqued, Beth enquired, 'What do you do, Anna? Once you left Peter how did you fill your days?'

Afraid to allow even a small chink in the wall that encased her, Anna paused to think before continuing.

'Oh, I managed fine. Anyway, never you mind about me. The book will be more interesting if I remain the evil temptress.'

The harsh laugh that followed fooled no one.

Once lunch was over, they rambled out into the afternoon sunshine. Mary and Eileen strode ahead. Beth and Anna walked side-by-side. The atmosphere was cordial but neither woman had much to say. Too much water had flowed under the bridge and too much time had passed.

Turning to Anna, Beth with outstretched hand, spoke first.

'Goodbye now, Anna. I hope your life continues to work out as you wish but I doubt we will meet again.'

Anna shook Beth's hand, and her own quiet, 'Goodbye, Beth,' floated on the breeze as Beth turned swiftly away.

Beth hurried to catch up with Mary and Eileen. Anna stood and gazed after them until all three were out of sight. Her wistful expression was fleeting, and shrugging her shoulders, she turned in the opposite direction. She made for the train station to purchase a ticket to Wexford. She didn't want to be too late home. She did not live alone and did not regret keeping her privacy. There was enough about her in the book. She hurried onto the platform. Her husband, Alan, would be anxiously waiting. He would need a change first as their neighbour who had been helping out would have left some time ago. Afterwards, they would have an evening stroll. She looked forward to that quiet time together pushing his wheelchair in the September sunshine. He will have questions, she knew. He had impressed upon her to talk to Beth, to enquire about her child, but for Anna too much time had drifted by.

Despite herself, she couldn't help wondering about Nora, how they were both living in Wexford, and was she close by.

www.ingramcontent.com/pod-product-compliance
Lightning Source LLC
Chambersburg PA
CBHW031107260626
47172CB00001B/251